"Sultry days in the Big Easy get a lot stea... wrapped around the legend of a voodoo spi... darkest fantasy. All of these dovetailing stories are fun, hot and romantic." —*RT Book Reviews*

"*Possess Me* is a hot and sexy read that took me to places I didn't know I wanted to go. I love Bone Daddy. He is my favorite character in all three stories and I am so happy that the last story is his. I Joyfully Recommend that everyone read *Possess Me* so they can see the magic of these beautiful stories. R. G. Alexander is an author I love to read and *Possess Me* is no different. I am enraptured by her world and her characters and wouldn't mind seeing more of her New Orleans." —*Joyfully Reviewed*

"This erotic novel was smoking hot—a perfect summer read set in my favorite city, New Orleans . . . I honestly couldn't put this book down. It was wonderful to read something so delightfully different and deliciously magical. Sensual, seductive and filled with sexy—if you like paranormal erotica, this book's for you." —*Fangtastic Books* (4.5 fangs)

"As this was my first time reading R. G. Alexander, I am happy to report I look forward to more of her work in the future!"
—*Night Owl Reviews*

"*Possess Me* is erotic with a capital O. And so sweet and vivid! Steamy sex and true emotion? So rare. So lovely. So addictive! . . . I haven't been this enamored of a book since I began Kresley Cole's Immortals After Dark series. You can be assured I'll be stocking up with R. G. Alexander's backlist and re-reading *Possess Me* any time I need a little heat to keep me warm at night." —*Bitten by Books*

"Sinfully hot and beautifully romantic, *Three Sinful Wishes* made me laugh, made me cry, made me reach for the nearest fan—the perfect erotic romance!" —Eve Berlin, author of *Pleasure's Edge*

Three Sinful Wishes

R. G. ALEXANDER

HEAT
NEW YORK

THE BERKLEY PUBLISHING GROUP
Published by the Penguin Group
Penguin Group (USA) Inc.
375 Hudson Street, New York, New York 10014, USA
Penguin Group (Canada), 90 Eglinton Avenue East, Suite 700, Toronto, Ontario M4P 2Y3, Canada
(a division of Pearson Penguin Canada Inc.)
Penguin Books Ltd., 80 Strand, London WC2R 0RL, England
Penguin Group Ireland, 25 St. Stephen's Green, Dublin 2, Ireland (a division of Penguin Books Ltd.)
Penguin Group (Australia), 250 Camberwell Road, Camberwell, Victoria 3124, Australia
(a division of Pearson Australia Group Pty. Ltd.)
Penguin Books India Pvt. Ltd., 11 Community Centre, Panchsheel Park, New Delhi—110 017, India
Penguin Group (NZ), 67 Apollo Drive, Rosedale, Auckland 0632, New Zealand
(a division of Pearson New Zealand Ltd.)
Penguin Books (South Africa) (Pty.) Ltd., 24 Sturdee Avenue, Rosebank, Johannesburg 2196,
South Africa

Penguin Books Ltd., Registered Offices: 80 Strand, London WC2R 0RL, England

This book is an original publication of The Berkley Publishing Group.

This is a work of fiction. Names, characters, places, and incidents either are the product of the author's imagination or are used fictitiously, and any resemblance to actual persons, living or dead, business establishments, events, or locales is entirely coincidental. The publisher does not have any control over and does not assume any responsibility for author or third-party websites or their content.

PRINTING HISTORY
Heat trade paperback edition / June 2011

Library of Congress Cataloging-in-Publication Data

Alexander, R. G., (date)
    Three sinful wishes / R. G. Alexander. — Heat trade pbk. ed.
        p. cm.
    ISBN 978-0-425-24111-0 (pbk.)
    I. Title.
PS3601.L3545T47 2011
813'.6—dc22
                                        2010054381

PRINTED IN THE UNITED STATES OF AMERICA

10 9 8 7 6 5 4 3 2 1

To my own Cookie, my best friend. Thanks and love to Eve Berlin for her support and the "special" use of her book in Bailey's story, to Robin L. Rotham for her tireless effort, and to my family for everything. To Kate, for all of her hard work and support. And of course to Sedona— with all the colorful and amazing characters that have always inspired me, and the scenery that always leaves me in awe.

CONTENTS

Then we of the flowers of the earth come forth
To receive a long life of joy
We call ourselves the Butterfly Maidens.

HOPI SONG OF CREATION

Sinful Desires

One

If she's honest, every woman will admit she's had at least one moment when she realized she might have made a hasty decision regarding a man. Either she picked the wrong one because he appeared magnetic and exciting, quickly learning she'd made a dangerous mistake . . . or she became the sexless buddy of the guy she later discovered had all the makings of Mr. Right.

In her case, Dani was two for two.

Only she hadn't figured out her second miscalculation until early that morning. In the shower. With the disappearing spider.

When she first saw it she was too shocked to react. It was huge. Beautiful. Not a word she would normally associate with a spider, but this wasn't like any other she'd ever seen. The designs on its body were geometrically perfect. White and blue angled lines formed a maze, a labyrinth that was so hypnotic, so stunning, that for a moment she wished she had a camera.

The next moment she remembered why she didn't. Because she was in the shower. Unarmed. Naked. And that beautiful spider could be poisonous.

She'd like to think any other woman in her situation would have screamed as loudly as she did then, but she had her doubts.

She barely registered the sound of stomping feet up the stairs, the slam of the bathroom door as it bounced off the wall. When your life was in arachnid-induced jeopardy, everything else seemed unimportant.

Her coral-colored shower curtain was ripped open so ferociously it tore, leaving a large chunk of its vinyl body dangling from the fist of her savior.

"Spider!" Dani closed her eyes and pointed, not needing to look to know who'd come barreling in. Her roommate Liam. Her best friend. And right now her only chance of not dying a painful, ridiculous shower death that she would be embarrassed to talk about at dinner parties.

A thickly muscled arm wrapped around her waist, pulling her out of the tub and against him as he ducked his head inside the stall to face her attacker.

Dani's eyes were squeezed tight as she waited for the sounds of the inevitable battle. But there were none. A minute passed. Another. The cooler air from the open doorway made her shiver.

"Dani?"

She heard the strange note in his voice and felt like an idiot. A stereotypical female idiot. She just hadn't been expecting it. It was so . . . *large*. Hairy.

The spider. She was talking about the spider. Not the body pressed against hers.

"Is it gone? Did you kill it?"

"I don't know. Do you still see it?"

Dani's brow furrowed and she opened her eyes. The spider, the one that had been impossible to miss, that was the size of her old dog Bitsy, was gone. "What do you mean, do I still see it? Of course I don't. It's gone. Where did it go?"

She looked up at Liam and felt her breath catch. Several sensations registered at once. He smelled like heated, spicy man and coffee. She inhaled deeply. She couldn't help herself. Had he always smelled this good?

His blond waves were tousled, just-rolled-out-of-bed tousled. Heavy-lidded eyes and a jaw shadowed with stubble confirmed her theory that he hadn't been up long. It was criminally unfair that the man could look so good this early in the morning.

Her nipples hardened, with cold or awareness, poking into his side. His shirtless, warm-skinned side. He was wearing half-buttoned jeans and nothing else. And she—she bit the inside of her cheek as her body instinctively shuddered, feeling the rasp of denim against the curve of her stomach—well, she was in that nightmare where you realized you were skin to bare skin with your best friend beneath the harsh fluorescent bathroom light.

Only it didn't feel like a nightmare. More like a really good dream. One so good she didn't want to move in case she woke up.

Then he spoke and the forced playfulness in his tone brought reality crashing back in. "I had a sex dream that started out just like this."

Dani attempted to pull away, but his arm around her waist was surprisingly strong. Who knew Liam's forearm was that muscular? And since when did she think forearms were sexy?

She tried to chuckle but stopped when it came out sounding breathless. Needy. "Only instead of your roommate, you discovered Anna Paquin in my shower, hot and bothered and in need of a back scrub. Yeah, yeah, I've heard that one before."

"This time it was you *and* Anna. See? Not quite so predictable now, am I? Although, I will admit, even in my most distracting dreams I'd never fall for the spider gag."

"The spider gag?" Dani still wasn't looking at him. Instead she was subtly trying to extricate herself and get to a towel in the linen closet—or failing that, at least press a little less of her wet, naked skin against his.

All her squirming only seemed to make things worse, her breasts dragging along his side, the fabric of his jeans scraping her flesh, causing her insides to quiver. God, he felt as good as he smelled. "What spider gag?"

Liam's voice was noticeably rougher and his grip on her tightened even more, holding her still. "This gag. There was no spider, Dani. Admit it."

"Admit what? Of course there . . . was . . . a spider . . ." Her gaze leapt up to meet his at that ludicrous statement and she promptly lost her train of thought. Why on earth would she pretend to have a spider in her shower? But her voice trailed off, running away with the last of her useable brain cells at the way he was looking at her. "Why are you looking at me like that?"

His glasses were off. In three years of knowing him, she'd rarely seen him without them. This close, without those sensible wire frames to distract her, she noticed how intensely blue his eyes were. Not dark blue, like hers. Perfect sky blue. Cornflower blue. Drown inside them and never want to escape blue. And those lashes.

Who was this delicious stranger and what had he done with her best friend?

Breathe, Dani. This was the guy who saw her every day with no makeup on, wearing sweatpants and fuzzy socks. The guy who made the most elaborate, decadently fattening midnight snacks for their science fiction movie marathons. The one she shared every secret with. Who'd helped her survive her real nightmare.

This was *not* a man she was allowed to have the hots for.

That line of reasoning had always worked in the past, but for some reason, her lack of clothing and the commanding look in his darkening gaze had stolen her logic. Suddenly, and maybe for the first time since they'd become friends, she let herself really see him. As a man. A man who was looking at her like he'd eat her for breakfast.

And she wouldn't mind at all.

Liam pivoted on his bare feet and pressed her back against the cool tile wall. He leaned over to turn off the water, keeping her pinned with his piercing blue stare.

She covered her breasts. Or tried to anyway. Her tongue came out to lick her lips, and she swallowed past the lump of embarrassment in her throat, wishing she'd worn her swimsuit into the shower. Liam had seen her in her swimsuit. It concealed and slimmed and crammed every overly ample curve into a neat streamlined package. Now she was just, well, *hanging out*.

Liam stood, his six foot four frame towering over her, the fine hair on his chest a darker gold than the hair on his head, making her fingers itch to touch it. Making her regret that more of him wasn't showing.

This wasn't good. She swallowed again. "I need a towel." Or a sheet. Or a magical ring that made her invisible and wiped his memory of this whole humiliating incident.

He shook his head, making a tsking sound, which instantly riveted her to his full lower lip. "Loosen up, Shortbread. What's a little naked imaginary spider-killing between friends?"

She gritted her teeth, keeping her breathing shallow as he leaned in closer. The logical side of her brain was wondering why she wasn't whacking him on the head and making a run for it. The completely irrational hormonal side was wondering why she wasn't dragging him back to her room.

"It *wasn't* imaginary." Neither was Liam's jean-clad leg pressed between her thighs. She gasped. "It wasn't."

He bent his head, his lips a breath away from hers. Was this happening? It seemed so surreal. Was she actually considering kissing him? Longing for it?

"Is *this* imaginary?" Liam's words mirrored her own disbelief, but instead of backing away, he moved that one inch closer, brushing his lips against hers.

Holy shit. Holy shit. Holy— Dani moaned, melting into it, the warmth of his breath, the tingling sensation that spread through her limbs at the first touch of his mouth on hers.

There was no longer any thought in her head about why this was wrong. Why this would ruin everything. All her awareness, all her senses, were focused on the lips that were silently asking a question they already knew the answer to.

Yes.

At her reaction, the kiss changed. Where first it was a gentle and hesitant featherlight brushing of his lips against hers, it quickly turned carnal.

Liam changed, as well. This wasn't the embrace of a friend. It was a rough and raw seduction of her senses. An all-out assault. His thigh pressed up, high and hard against her sensitive sex, his hands prying hers from her breasts and holding them up against the wall beside her head.

God, she was close to coming already, just from this. From his masterful touch. She was melting from it. She wouldn't be surprised if the water still dripping down her body sizzled from the heat inside her.

She couldn't stop her body's reaction as it searched desperately for the release she'd denied it for so long. The contact that no fantasy could ever come close to. Her hips began to rock against his leg, her arousal dampening the denim, making Liam growl in approval.

He pressed his chest to her breasts, his big frame shuddering at the contact. Did he feel what she did? The jolt of electricity? The intensity of it?

His hands slid down her arms, lifting them above her head and then leaving them suspended as he caressed her shoulders, the sides of her breasts, down to her hips. His shaky groan against her mouth had her arching into his hands, against him, her hips rocking faster now. Imagining it was the impressive erection she could feel straining against the fly of his jeans inside her. Faster. So close. She needed this more than she needed to breathe. Needed him. She couldn't hold back anymore, and she didn't want to.

She tore her mouth from his and cried out, overwhelmed by sensation, and he was there. His grip tightened as he helped her ride out the storm of the climax that had hit her with the force of a hurricane.

Her body trembled so hard her teeth were chattering. Had she ever come like this? This quickly?

Liam.

Oh God. She'd just done that with Liam. To Liam. In front of—

"Fuck, Dani." His guttural voice was thick with need, making her realize he was still lost in it. Still hard and wanting. Still pressed up against her naked body.

She whimpered, afraid to look at him while she was still shaking from the aftershocks. She'd lost it. Just used her best friend as her own personal sex toy. Today of all days. What had she been *thinking*?

She hadn't. She hadn't been thinking at all. Her body had been the one in control. And it wanted more. Her mind, however, had returned with a vengeance. And it was screaming louder than she had when she'd seen that damn spider.

Get out. Run. Now.

"Dani? What is it?" He sensed the new tension in her muscles. The stiffness as she let herself take in the embarrassing reality.

He pulled back to look at her, his hands going to her shoulders. He must not have liked the look on her face, because he swore beneath his breath. "Don't do this."

But she was already shaking her head, pushing away from him and reaching for the pajama top she'd tossed on the floor to hold against herself. Anything to cover up so he couldn't see.

Too late.

"I'm sorry, Liam. I don't know why that— I'm sorry."

The image of him standing there, cheeks flushed and lips swollen, every muscle flexing as he forced himself to stay where he was, burned into her mind as she raced down the hall. Nothing harmless about that image.

How had she ever convinced herself Liam was harmless?

She closed the door to her bedroom and sagged against the wood weakly. Because she'd needed him to be. Needed his friendship. He was the only person she'd trusted. And until now, if asked, she would have said she loved him like the brother she'd never had.

Dani rolled her eyes. That man in there was *nothing* like a brother. Nothing like the Liam she thought she knew. But then, she hadn't recognized herself either. The sex-starved shower nymph that took over her body and gave it so willingly to her best friend.

The only reason for her strange behavior she could come up with was the dreams. The last few weeks she'd been having very graphic, sexual dreams where a shadowy figure was doing all sorts of delectably dirty things to her. And sometimes her dream lover brought a friend along to add to her pleasure.

That had to be it. This morning's aberration was a hormonal shot across the bow. Woman could not live by vibrator alone.

A year ago that hadn't been important. Back then she'd sworn off the opposite sex. Sworn off sex in general. All that had mattered was staying safe.

And that's exactly what she'd done. She'd stayed under the radar in a tourist's mecca in Arizona that boasted four million anonymous visitors a year. Sedona. The perfect place to disappear. The last place anyone from Dallas would think to look for her.

She pushed herself to her feet and walked over to the dresser, opening the top drawer and moving the underwear aside until she saw the paperwork. The information the lawyer had sent to her post office box a few days ago. Her new last name. Her new social security number. Even a new birth certificate. The old person she used to be—the foster child who'd learned to look after herself, the nurse who'd lived simply, who'd put nearly all of every paycheck into savings—that woman was gone. All that was left before she could be reborn had been done. The judge sealed her previous records and her lawyer had assured her in the attached letter that it was all over.

On paper, anyway.

Though a part of her was relieved, she didn't trust it, yet. Not entirely. Maybe that's why she hadn't instantly told Liam. She knew as soon as she did, everything would change. But the new Dani Harris, no longer the meek Danielle Craver, didn't avoid life. She faced it head-on.

And Liam deserved to know the truth. After all, he'd been with her through the whole thing. Ever since the night her psychotic ex, an online match gone horribly wrong, had nearly killed her.

Dani glanced up at the mirror above the dresser, dropped the shirt she was still clinging to and turned to stare at her side. Had Liam seen it? Felt it? She'd made sure he hadn't until now. She hadn't been able to hide the bruises back then, but this was different. There were some things no one else should have to deal with. Especially when there was nothing he could do about it.

And Liam couldn't have done anything about this. It was a ragged, S-shaped scar below her rib cage. Sal's final gift to her. His mark. Luckily, she'd gotten away before he could do any worse.

He hadn't expected her to run. Hell, neither had she. Once she started, she'd had no idea where she would go. There was no family to run to. No coworker that she trusted enough.

In a moment of weakness she'd called Liam. The one friendship that hadn't been tarnished by Sal, because she'd kept it from him. She'd been smart enough to know that the possessive Sal would have been jealous of her having a male friend, so she'd never introduced them.

Looking back, calling Liam was the best decision she'd ever made. He hadn't let her down, hadn't hesitated. When he realized she wasn't willing to go to the police since Sal had cousins on the force, he'd gotten her in touch with the right lawyer, then made a few phone calls. Before Dani knew it, they had put several states between themselves and her attacker, living rent-free in the vacation home of a wealthy man Liam used to cook for. She was so relieved at the time she hadn't questioned it. And the longer she'd known Liam, the less it surprised her.

People did things like that for him. He had a warm, confident way about him that inspired loyalty and friendship in everyone he met, men and women alike.

It was a good thing, too. Although she'd lived frugally and done every odd job for cash that came her way, her savings were running dangerously low—if she'd had to pay rent on a place like this, she'd have been broke a long time ago.

But she had some pride left, and she'd always paid her own way. Half the groceries. Half the bills. Despite that fact that he was working as a chef at one of the nicest resorts in town, despite his arguments that she should save her money, taking care of herself was instinct. There'd never been anyone else she could rely on.

That was why his decision to drop everything and come with her had been the biggest surprise of all. No question. No "I told you so," though he *had* told her that Sal sounded like he was no good on more than one occasion.

Liam had earned her trust a dozen times over. He was the best friend she'd ever had. But she'd always felt guilty for taking him away from his life. He'd had a job. A family. But at the time, he hadn't really given her a choice.

He'd said he would just stay until she got on her feet. Until she was safe.

She sighed. That time had come. The bubble they'd lived in was about to burst, giving her a chance to stand on her own again, and him the chance to get back to normal . . . a normal that might not include her. Especially if he decided to go home.

After this morning, that might be a good thing. She'd been sick in front of him, broken and fragile in front of him, but how did someone come back from this? What would she say? "Sorry about that leg hump, Liam, it's been a long dry spell"?

She sighed and grabbed jeans and a large, faded T-shirt and started to dress. She couldn't stay in her bedroom all day, hiding from the awkward situation waiting downstairs. She had a job to look for. She had to find a place to live.

Most important, she had to tell Liam the good news . . . after she apologized for leaping so far over the friend line there could be no recovery.

She walked down the stairs and into the high-ceilinged living room, looking with fresh eyes at the place that had been her home. The place she would be leaving soon. It astonished her how easily she'd gotten used to luxury. Liam had told her his friend called it a rustic getaway. *Maybe for Daddy Warbucks,* she thought with a snort.

She *had* felt like that curly-headed orphan girl Annie when she'd moved in to this Southwestern-style safe haven. Like she'd wake up to find herself back in a sterile room full of unwanted or forgotten children. Or worse, back with Sal.

This place was like nothing she'd ever imagined. Not for herself, anyway. Dani had dreamt ordinary dreams. A small house of her own, or a week's vacation on some island where drinks were served in coconuts, not a gourmet kitchen and an upstairs master suite that made her feel like royalty. She'd been spoiled. So much so that it would be hard to go back to lumpy sofas and macaroni and cheese.

He wasn't in the kitchen. She poured herself a much-needed cup of coffee and looked out the window. Had he gone?

And why was a little part of her relieved?

A rustling behind her had her turning too fast, splattering hot coffee on her hand. "Damn it."

Before she could move he was there, taking the cup away from her and putting her hand underneath a cool stream of tap water.

She tugged her wrist from his grip. "Thank you but I'm fine. It's nothing."

His touching her in any way was not part of her plan. If he did she might not say what she wanted to say.

Liam's gaze narrowed behind his glasses, watching her move away from him. His expression was closed. Hard for her to read.

It was happening already. She could feel the distance between them. The awkwardness. Her shoulders slumped and she reached for her coffee once more. She needed a clear head.

She closed her eyes, savoring her first sip, before blurting out from behind the rim of her cup, "I'm sorry."

Her lids lifted at his sigh. "Dani, there's nothing to be sorry—"

"Just—let me finish. There's something I haven't told you." She offered him a smile, though she knew he could tell it wasn't entirely genuine. "I got some great news in the mail Thursday."

Liam stilled. "I know. Terry called me last night."

Why was she surprised? Liam was the one who'd gotten her the lawyer to begin with. He didn't seem that upset about it. Had she expected him to be? This was, after all, good news for both of them. "Then you know it's over. I'm officially a new woman."

His lips quirked. "Congratulations. I hope the new you still likes sangria, because I've made a few gallons for tonight's little gathering."

Dani winced and lowered her forehead onto the granite countertop. She'd forgotten.

Until a few days ago she'd been looking forward to it. She remembered how she and Liam had laughed when they realized they'd both planned get-togethers on the same night. They'd decided, especially since her friend Kaya and his friend Jace weren't exactly, well, *friendly*, that Dani would keep her girls' night poolside, and Liam would have his poker party in the den. The kitchen would be the only neutral ground.

"Should we cancel? I mean, things are a little different now, don't you think?" That was the understatement of the century.

"Nothing's different." Liam turned away from her and reached under the cabinet for a sheet pan. "I still have to make my famous melt-in-your-mouth ribs, and you promised to be my assistant. Besides, you can't just step between Jace and his card game. The man takes it seriously. I think he was a grifter before he learned to sauté."

So that was how they were going to play it. She had to admit she'd thought there would be . . . more. More conversation, more relief, more something. Maybe now wasn't the time. Or maybe she was just selfish enough to take the reprieve he offered. To pretend for one last evening that nothing had changed between them.

Tomorrow she would have to start building her new life. No more hiding. No more shower encounters with Liam.

She couldn't cross that line again. She might be losing him as a roommate, but she couldn't imagine losing his friendship.

Some things were too important to risk.

Two

"I do love a man who can cook."

Dani smiled at Bailey's moan as her friend licked her fingertips, sending a mock leer toward Liam's backside where he stood at the grill. Dani felt a twinge of irritation, but she couldn't blame her. It was a mouthwatering sight.

Should a friend be noticing another friend's ass? Or the way his biceps flexed when he hefted the heavily laden tray of food? Just this morning she'd sworn to herself she wouldn't, that she would go back to seeing him as "Just Liam." So far it wasn't working as well as she'd like.

All afternoon she'd been secretly ogling him. Being his kitchen assistant had been torture. The large room hadn't been big enough to stop him from brushing past her a dozen times, or reaching around her to grab something.

He'd refused to talk about what happened in the shower or her news, joking and teasing as if it were any other day. Between her frustration and her, well, *frustration*—she was strung so tightly she knew it wouldn't take much to make her snap by the time their company arrived.

Her only comfort was the mantra she kept repeating in her head—that there was no harm in noticing. Friend or not. After all, she noticed Kaya was beautiful all the time, and it didn't mean anything.

Though Kaya, despite her long limbs, golden skin and lustrous dark hair, didn't make her tremble. Didn't make her thighs sweat.

Dani had also noticed the stranger that had come with Liam's friends Nick and Jace. Nick introduced him as Stax. Talk about trembling thighs. The new guy was sexy as sin.

Bailey interrupted Dani's shameful thoughts with a few of her own. "Liam? Do you think your landlord would mind if I moved in with you two? I wouldn't take up much space—I'd just curl up at the end of your bed and let you feed me."

Dani made a shushing sound, but Bailey just tilted her stubborn chin. Her green eyes sparkled, and her blonde, spiky, pink-tipped hair glistened in the candlelight. "What? I don't see why you can't share the wealth." She gestured to Liam. "Delicious chef, big house, and did I mention yummy roommate? Stop being so greedy. It's rude."

Liam set an extra plate of pork ribs, grilled corn and salt potatoes in front of them, winking at Bailey. "I would love being treated like an object as long as it was all about sex. Alas, women only want me for my skillet." He shrugged and sighed in mock regret. "There's plenty of food to go around. Just some simple Southern backyard fare, but I did make enough to feed a pack of wild dogs."

Male laughter drifted out from the kitchen and Liam smiled. "Or *that* crew of rib critics. All guys think they know how to make ribs. Ninety-nine percent of them are wrong. I plan on showing these boys the error of their ways and distracting them with meaty goodness long enough for me to take all their money."

His words evoked some wicked thoughts about *his* distracting meaty goodness that made Dani blush. "Careful, Cookie, that Texas-sized ego is showing."

Liam's gaze clashed with hers—it was the first time he'd looked directly at her all night. She'd called him Cookie. It was her response to his nickname for her. Shortbread. The relief that flashed over his expression was the first sign she'd had that he might have been as worried as she about the awkwardness between them. The tension.

His smile was cautious. "You know it. No one can resist my famous ribs."

Kaya, who'd been quietly cleaning her plate beside Dani, made a sound of agreement. "You've definitely got my vote. Your taste in male friends might be questionable, but your food is always in a class all its own." Dani watched her grin turn coy. "Maybe you should save some of this for Gillian."

A knot instantly formed between Dani's shoulder blades. Gillian. The pastry chef from the resort where Jace, Liam and Kaya all worked. The one who had taken to baking strawberry tarts for Liam twice a week.

He loved strawberry tarts.

Liam rolled his eyes. "Dani? Tell your friend that I'll sic Jace on her if she doesn't behave. Gillian is not my type."

Dani spoke before thinking. "She's *exactly* your type." An adorable, tiny-hipped redhead who made tarts. The bitch.

Bailey and Kaya looked on with interest as Liam studied Dani, an inscrutable expression on his handsome face. Finally, he shook his head. "More sangria is in the kitchen. If you ladies need anything else, let me know."

When he left, the silence was palpable, but she knew it wouldn't last long. She'd told Kaya and Bailey about her past a few months ago. Not every detail, but enough for them to get the general idea. They'd been amazing. More supportive than she'd thought she deserved.

But the admission had opened the floodgates of butt-in-itis. Especially for Bailey. If anything she seemed more determined than ever to get Dani out into the world again. Dating. Having sex.

She could literally feel Bailey restraining herself from commenting, and she took a fortifying sip of her fruity drink before waving her hand. "What? Spit it out before you explode."

Bailey placed her flattened palm against her chest with a mock look of surprise. "*What* what? I didn't say anything."

"Good." Because there was nothing to say. They didn't know she'd had her naked body pressed against Liam's just this morning. That she'd been torturing herself all day with fantasies about what would have happened if they hadn't stopped.

Kaya took her hand, her compassionate expression instantly putting Dani at ease. How did she do that?

Magic.

A part of her wondered that she believed in magic at all after what she'd been through. The life she'd had before had been all about lies and illusions, and love the biggest lie of all. It should have been a hard enough lesson to keep her feet on solid ground for good.

It must be this place. Sedona. Red rocks and runaways. Pink jeeps and possibilities. People like Bailey, with her strange fashion sense and business savvy, who'd befriended her, no questions asked. And Kaya, who, from the moment they'd met, seemed to see inside her with an ability Dani barely understood—and cared about her anyway.

Like Liam.

Kaya's grip was gentle. So was her voice. "Something happened between the two of you."

Just like that, Dani found herself telling them everything. From the spider that had conveniently disappeared to their surprise embrace. So much for keeping it a secret.

"It is about damn time." Bailey chuckled, grabbing another ear of corn with a smile.

"What do you mean?"

Bailey caught her eye and whatever she saw there made her sigh. "Oh, honey, seriously?" She tilted her head, as if weighing her words. "You know Fran, the bartender from the Laughing Coyote?" Dani nodded. "Well, she and I have had a bet since we met you. We didn't let Kaya in on the action because she's psychic and it wouldn't be sporting. But I had good, hard-earned money on the odds Liam would finally wear you down. Just you and that knight in shining chef whites in this secluded house every night? A man who obviously adores you . . . I think I've mentioned the hotness factor, right?"

Dani flinched. "That's crazy. We've never—I mean, other than today—I've never thought—" She blew out an exasperated sigh and tried to pull herself together. She had thought about it. She'd just tried really hard not to. "We're best friends. Buddies. He's not my type and I'm not his."

Gillian is his type. And he's too good for me. He knows me.

Where had those thoughts come from? She'd thought she'd outgrown those insecurities, but apparently not. At least, not when it came to Liam. He *did* know her too well. If she was honest with herself she knew that was the problem. Even if she wanted him to, how could he see her as anything more than the weak, timid woman she'd been?

"Maybe your radar is wonky, Dani." Bailey shrugged. "All I know is, if Liam looked at me the way he looks at you—which is not remotely brotherly or buddy-esque, by the way—I'd add him to my five-year plan in a heartbeat. And in that plan I would make hard, dirty love to him at least three times a day."

Dani choked on her drink, and Kaya patted her on the shoulder. "Never mind Bailey, dear. She's not really into Liam. If she was he'd be tied to her bed by now. She's nothing if not determined. Anyway, she hasn't had any in at least as long as you. The only difference is it's more about muleheadedness than anything else on her part. She wants to run the world first and thinks men are a distraction."

"What's your excuse?" Bailey grumbled. "And I don't want to run the world. Just my own inn. Then I'll invite Ewan McGregor to the opening and he'll fall madly in love with me. The end." She wrinkled her nose. "I'm a little behind schedule though. At the rate I'm going I'll have run through a lifetime supply of battery-operated boyfriends and be forced to relearn what to do with the real thing. But if it's Ewan, it'll be worth it."

Kaya made a face, but she wasn't looking at Bailey. She was looking over Dani's shoulder. "We'll discuss your five-year plan later. Dani, I really want to hear more about that spider, but first, *who* did Liam say he was playing poker with tonight?"

Dani's brow wrinkled. "Jace and his roommate, Nick . . ." She looked over at Bailey. "You've met Nick, right? He doesn't talk much. Liam says he's an unusual guy, but brilliant. Geologist or archaeologist or something like that."

"Geoarchaeologist." Kaya looked uncomfortable. "Because I love you, Dani, I like to pretend you don't let that sexist pig, Jace, or his roommate in your house. *Or* that our wonderful Liam is actually friends with them."

Bailey chortled. "Uh-huh. Just because Jace carved a naked ice sculpture of you for the resort Christmas party last year—"

"He didn't." Dani felt her eyes go wide. Liam hadn't told her. Then again, if she remembered correctly, he'd missed the party because he'd spent the whole evening taking care of her at home when she'd gotten that horrible cold.

Kaya glared at Bailey. "Don't start. It's a moot point. Even if he wasn't a Neanderthal, he and I just do not mix."

Because Jace was Navajo? Or half Navajo. And Kaya was Hopi. Dani knew Kaya would never say it, but with the stories about how traditional her family had always been, she could imagine that they wouldn't approve of her dating someone their ancestors deemed an enemy.

Secretly she agreed with Bailey. Kaya protested too much. Her friend liked the handsome chef with a chip on his shoulder. Maybe more than she wanted to.

Like Dani had any room to talk. When it came to avoiding her feelings, she took the prize. She changed the subject. "Why did you ask who was here?"

Kaya raised one perfectly arched, raven brow. "Because there is a strange man staring at you from the kitchen window. He looks rather intense."

A sharp icy fear instantly filled her veins, and Kaya jerked beside her, as though she'd felt it, too.

Had Sal found her at last? The way he promised he would? After all this time—all she'd done, all she'd put Liam through . . . Now at the end was it all for nothing? She didn't dare turn around to find out. Not even when she heard the whoosh of the patio door sliding open.

"Pardon me for intruding, ladies. Just taking a break from Jace's lesson in Texas Hold'em, and I noticed you three looked low on sangria. I have a feeling I won't be winning anything tonight, so I'm procrastinating."

Dani's shoulders slumped in relief. The voice behind her wasn't the one she was expecting. *Not Sal.* She felt like crying for joy.

The girls noticed her reaction.

"I don't know you. New in town?" Bailey's voice was low. Protective. Her question surprised Dani, since as far as she knew, the manager of one of the most picturesque little inns in Sedona knew everybody.

Dani looked over her shoulder and gasped. It was him. Nick's sexy new friend.

Her second impression of the man was even stronger than the first. He looked . . . *wild*. He had an air about him. Sensual. Predatory. All her feminine instincts went back on high alert.

He was nearly as tall as Liam, with long hair that flowed well past his shoulders, as dark as Kaya's. His sinful lips were framed by a trimmed goatee that made her wonder how a kiss from him would feel. His eyes were dark, too, and looking at her with a disconcerting awareness. A knowledge. As though he knew exactly what she wanted. And knew he could give it to her.

Her body, still sensitive from her morning interlude with Liam, responded to his silent command with a swiftness that shocked her.

Proof positive there was something seriously wrong with her. First her best friend, now a complete stranger. *Fickle body.*

Then again, reacting to this stranger was probably safer than lusting after Liam. Maybe Bailey was right. Maybe she should start her new life off with a new experience.

Or maybe she just needed a cold shower.

"I don't know you either. Who *are* you?" Kaya sounded strange. Did she sense it, too? The energy that crackled around him? Did she smell the dizzying mixture of desert rain and sandalwood?

He smiled. "You must be Kaya. Nicholas has told me all about you. Fortune-teller by day, waitress by night. You're as dazzling as he said you were."

Kaya stuttered, making the stranger laugh softly. A decidedly sexual sound, in Dani's opinion. It made her heart skip.

"My real name is too difficult to pronounce. Everyone usually calls me Stax." He set down the full pitcher of sangria and focused on Bailey. "And you may not know me, but I know you, Bailey Wagner. Most people think you could run this town if you wanted to. Though I hear your inn just got a new owner, one who bought the place sight unseen. Is he planning on making a lot of changes?"

Dani glanced away from the charismatic man and noticed Bailey's stunned expression. "He's right, but I just found out about the new ownership last week." Her gaze narrowed. "And he'd better not, at least not without my approval."

"I'm sure he'll discover that soon enough. And finally"—those dark eyes focused all their attention on Dani—"I've really been looking forward to meeting you, Dani."

"You have?"

He studied her from head to toe, as though he could see past her comfortable clothes, the ponytail she kept her thick mass of curls in. As though he saw the naked woman beneath.

He licked his lips. "I have."

"Stax, tone it down and come inside. We're starting."

Dani tore her attention away from the magnetic stranger and saw Nick appear behind him. He was stealthy for such a big bear of a man. His broad shoulders and thick arms blocked out most of the light as he stood in the doorway, but Dani could still see the gleam of mahogany red hair, the glint of brilliantly white teeth as he smiled stiltedly. "Sorry, ladies. I didn't realize he was disturbing you."

Stax sighed loudly. "Loosen the leash, Nicholas." He winked at the three women and rolled his eyes. "Do one job for this dirt digger and he starts to get bossy."

The stranger bowed, an old-world gesture as rare as it was charming. "Enjoy the rest of your evening. It's supposed to be an unusually beautiful night. And for this part of the world, that's saying something."

When the two men were gone, Dani looked at Kaya and Bailey, her eyes wide. "What was that?"

"Trouble." Kaya's words were almost too low to catch. "I wonder how Nick knows him."

She shook her head, her elegant features thoughtful. "Maybe it is the right time."

Her voice was so low Dani leaned forward. "What?"

Kaya studied Dani. "I wasn't going to mention it tonight, not with all this company, but I've been having some vivid dreams lately. And the other night—"

Bailey groaned, interrupting her. "Watch out, Dani. She has that look again. This is going to be one of those surreal moments where I feel like I'm on a hilltop in the desert with an Indian, isn't it? Like Jim Morrison."

Kaya snorted at Bailey, glancing pointedly around the large patio, the lap pool surrounded by jagged red rocks. "You *are* on a hilltop in the desert with an Indian. But I heard you sing at the last music jam at Casa Rincon. Believe me when I say you're no Jim Morrison."

"Everyone's a critic. Why can't we talk about my dream? The one where I was sandwiched between these two gorgeous men—"

"Don't make me get the switch. This is serious."

Bailey held up her hands. "I'm deadly serious. Tell me you haven't had a dream like that." She pointed at Dani. "Or you. I know, especially after what you told us, you've had fantasies. Don't leave me hanging on the kinky branch all alone, guys."

Dani covered her blushing cheeks with her hands, her mind

suddenly full of risqué images, including the fantasies she'd been having lately. Only now, instead of her shadowy dream lovers, she saw Liam . . . and Stax. "Maybe once or twice."

"See? Dani admitted it. Your turn, K."

Kaya shook her head at Bailey, but she couldn't quite keep the smile from her face. "I'm a woman, aren't I? But you are taking us way off topic here, Bailey."

"Am I?" Bailey shrugged. "I don't think so. You said your dream was about our wishes coming true. Well?" She looked up at the night sky and lifted her voice. "I wish for two Ewan McGregor look-alikes who can cook like Liam and lust after bossy women."

Dani was confused. "When did she tell you what her dream was about?"

Her friends shared a guilty look and Dani felt herself tense. She hated it when people kept things from her. She knew it was hypocritical. Her whole life here was based on a lie. Or it had been until recently. But she'd had enough of them from other people to last her a lifetime.

Kaya leaned closer to Dani, taking her hands once more. "She caught me at a weak moment. I wanted to wait to tell you until we were all together."

Her gaze softened, unfocused, as though she were remembering. "I dreamt about you, about all of us. I saw stars falling from the sky and heard a voice say, 'Wish, Butterfly Maiden.' Then I saw three paths merge into one." She blinked. "I woke up, and I knew it was more than just a dream. That it was meant for all of us. Though I didn't know we'd be invaded." She made a face in the direction of the house and the men inside.

"Butterfly Maiden?"

Kaya nodded. "It's from the creation song of my people, sung by Spider Grandmother when we first came to be. That told me, more than anything, that my dream was special. You said you saw a spider in your shower this morning, right?"

Dani sputtered. "Yes. A huge one, but what does that have to do with—" Spider Grandmother. Did Kaya think her eight-legged visitor was a sign? Like her dream?

Dani didn't doubt Kaya's sincerity. She and Bailey had both seen Kaya's abilities too many times to doubt them. Stax had been right— she worked nights at the resort with Liam and Jace, and during the day she had a room in the metaphysical bookstore as one of their resident psychics. She was good at it, too.

From some of their late-night conversations, she knew Kaya did what she did to support her two much younger siblings, Len and Yoki, as well as her very strict, very traditional aunt.

She wasn't proud of taking money for her visions, or of working in a resort that was built in a canyon sacred to her people. The fact that she hadn't gone to visit her family on the reservation for as long as Dani had known her was a testament to how much she knew they would disapprove. But she did what she had to do for those kids.

Kaya just . . . *knew* things. Things that were about to happen. Things that had happened in the past. The first time she'd shaken hands with her, Dani had seen her own pain cloud Kaya's expression before she'd smiled and said, "You and I are going to be great friends."

They'd never spoken of it. Dani hadn't been sure how much Kaya knew about her past, but she hadn't acted that surprised when she'd finally learned the truth.

"Yes," Kaya brought her back to the conversation. "I think there's a definite connection."

"Butterfly Maiden, huh?" Bailey's expression sobered. "Okay, I know how you feel about your dreams. What are we supposed to do about it?"

Kaya's expression turned rueful. "Honestly? I've been thinking about it for days and I still have no idea. Guess I'm not a very good guide." She shrugged. "But I do know we all have things in common. We've all had pain in our past that took our focus off what was truly important. To my people, the Butterfly Maiden is the feminine representation of renewal and new beginnings. Of spring. We are, each of us, looking for something new—freedom, independence, control."

She held out the hand not holding Dani's until Bailey took it. "You are more than your goals for security. You want to be seen. To be taken care of. Not to be an afterthought."

Bailey lifted her chin. "I can take care of myself." Kaya stared her down until she huffed out a shaky breath. "Okay, yes. It would be nice if I didn't have to all the time."

Dani bit her lip as tears softened Bailey's light green gaze. She thought back, unable to remember a time when her sharp-tongued friend had let her guard down. When she'd ever seemed less than superhuman. How could she have missed it? All that brash posturing, the humor and overconfidence. It was all a show. Cursing herself for being selfish, she reached out to grip Bailey's other hand in her own.

She sensed it then, the fine vibration beneath her feet. It traveled up her spine and down her arm to where their hands were joined.

They were all connected. All joined together. And the strange vibration soon became a heated tingling, an energy that seemed to arc between the three of them.

What the heck was going on?

Kaya continued. "Dani, you are one of the most beautiful souls I know. You had to remember that before you could move forward. Remember how amazing you are. You already know your true desire."

She did. "To trust again. To be able to believe that I can give my heart without it being abused or broken."

It was one wound her ex had delivered that couldn't heal. She couldn't seem to trust that the good things—her friendships, her life here, happiness—could last. That the other shoe wouldn't eventually drop. She was stronger now than she'd ever been. But it was still there. Sometimes she felt like she was walking through the world blind.

Kaya's gaze grew somber with understanding. "You trust Liam," she whispered softly. " And us. I know you do. That's a start."

"What about you, K? What's your secret desire?" Bailey tried to sound belligerent, but her voice was wavery. Fragile.

Kaya raised one softly rounded shoulder. "Simple. I want control over my own life. My happiness. I want to make my own mistakes, not spend a lifetime paying for someone else's."

The three women looked at each other, and despite their friendship and all they'd shared, Dani felt as though they were truly seeing each other for the first time.

She really did care about them. More than they knew, they'd helped to heal her, to show her the kind of woman she wanted to be. Brave like Bailey. As serene and intuitive as Kaya.

She knew, however they worded their wishes, they all really wanted the same thing. Love. They deserved to be happy. Maybe she did, too.

"So is this where we're wishing? Because don't forget—two Ewans."

The three women burst out laughing, then Kaya glanced skyward.

"Look at that."

Dani lifted her gaze to the star-studded sky above and felt her lips part in wonder. A bluish-white star was falling from the heavens. And another. And before she could blink . . . a third one fell. All just as bright and brilliant as the last.

A coyote howled in the darkness, the sound closer than she would have normally liked, but Dani didn't mind. She felt connected. A part of something big and beautiful and magical. Maybe the coyote felt it, too.

She only had one question. In the middle of one of the most magical experiences of her life . . . why couldn't she stop thinking about Liam?

Three

"And here's the River." Jace flipped over the final cards to the sound of several good-natured groans, but Liam wasn't really paying attention to their game.

He was thinking about Dani in the shower. Again.

Hell, he might start planting actual spiders in there, if that was what it took to get a glimpse of all that luscious, wet skin. To feel her in his arms.

He was pathetic, but she was adorable. And unbelievably sexy. More so because she truly had no idea of her appeal. She never had. Those dark spiraling curls that fell like rich caramel to her shoulders. Almond-shaped eyes so deeply blue he thought he might drown inside them. And her curves . . . She was only five three to his six foot four, but the lush body encased in that little package haunted his dreams.

The shower scene this morning, the way she'd reacted to him, her climax, had him on the edge. He wasn't sure why he'd tortured himself by staying so close to her all day. He just didn't want to think about the alternative.

Her leaving.

He'd known they couldn't go on like this forever. Pretending they were just roommates. Pretending there was nothing else between them. And damn it, he didn't want to. He never had.

At this point, he was close to throwing her over his shoulder and tying her to his bed until she finally saw him as more than a friend. Finally gave in to him. Hell, everything made him think of that lately. It was hard to focus on anything else. Hard being the operative word.

She was his friend, she trusted him, and he was a sick, sick man. He didn't deserve her trust, and he knew it. But that didn't stop him from wanting her. It had just slowed down his plans.

"Earth to Whipped. Come in, Whipped." Jace covered his mouth as though talking through a muffled microphone. "Gentlemen, I think he's a goner."

Nick nodded, but his friend Stax merely smiled. Another strange bird, that Stax. Apparently he'd been helping Nick decipher some cave drawings at a sensitive archaeological site, though he looked more like a hobo than a member of academia.

Liam couldn't put his finger on it but there was just something *off* about him. Something in his eyes.

Jace shook his head, drawing Liam's gaze. "Worst case I've ever seen. She has him well and truly gelded."

Liam rolled his eyes, wrapping his fingers around the neck of his beer bottle and lifting it to his lips in mock salute. "Fuck you all."

The three men toasted him in return, but Jace wasn't ready to let it go. "Liam, I love you like a brother." He smirked. "Like my ghostly pale, no rhythm, adopted brother. And I have to admit you make the best ribs I've ever eaten. But you have so completely fucked up, that, as a fellow member of the male species, I feel the need to point it out."

"Go ahead, wiseass. I'm riveted."

Jace twirled his half-empty bottle on the poker table and tapped it for emphasis. "Let the man meeting commence. We are all in agreement that you have made just about every mistake a guy can make with a woman he's interested in."

Liam frowned. "You *all* agree?"

He looked around and saw Nick, the redheaded giant, nod his head. "You don't count. You always agree with Jace."

"You'd be surprised," Nick muttered under his breath.

Stax lifted one shoulder. "I just met you. *And* Dani." Liam wanted to wipe the salacious grin off Stax's face when he mentioned Dani's name. "But if you've lived with that delicious morsel for more than twenty-four hours without claiming her, then yes, I agree, too."

"You're a guest in his house, Stax." Nick's remark was delivered offhandedly, but Liam could hear the steel beneath it. Stax just snorted.

Jace held up his hand and began to count on his callused fingers. "You became her *friend*. You became her *roommate*. You do things for her without her having to ask . . ."

Nick laughed at that last one, and Liam pinched the bridge of his nose. "Jace, have you ever *had* a girlfriend? I'm talking long-term, monogamous girlfriend, not a fuck buddy."

Nick shook his head. "I've known him for ten years. The longest he's had a woman around was April, his housekeeper. She lasted six months before he felt she was becoming too attached."

An offended expression crossed Jace's sharp features. "She was stealing my *underwear*, man. And refusing to give me my messages. Can I help it if women become easily obsessed with me?"

"Not *all* women." Nick's low words drew a glare from Jace.

Liam barked out a laugh. "Well, for future reference, people do things for people they care about. And not to get something in return. They do it because it makes *them* happy. Because they want the other person to be happy."

Or because they had a long-term plan. Never mind that Dani was screwing with his by never reacting the way he expected her to. And by telling him about the information she'd gotten from his lawyer. He'd been hoping she wouldn't want to. He knew it sounded perverse, but he was a desperate man. If she'd hesitated for one more week he could have taken it as a sign that she didn't want to leave him any more than he wanted to leave.

She'd flipped the script on him and now he wasn't sure what his next step should be. The tying her up idea sounded better all the time.

Jace shrugged. "You happy, Liam? I mean are you *really* happy with this current arrangement? With the fact that even tourists passing through town can see that you carry a torch for your roommate and she is still living in blissful ignorance? Why do you think that is?

And what do you plan to do about it?" He looked around the table. "Any ideas?"

Nick thrummed his fingers on the table. "Tell her the truth about how you feel and let the chips fall?"

Jace made a buzzing sound. "*Bzzz*. Wrong answer. You're just as bad as Liam. What about getting her blind drunk and taking advantage? That idea has promise." Jace looked surprised when Nick and Liam both grabbed a handful of mixed nuts and tossed them at his head. "What?"

"I have an opinion." Stax ignored Nick's glare.

Liam raised his eyebrows. "No one else is holding back, why should you?"

"Jace is right. You let yourself fall into the friend zone. You run the risk of losing her completely if you make the wrong move. On the other hand, if you don't do something drastic, she may never be able to see you as more than a friend."

"Drastic."

Stax studied Liam intently. Too intently. "Give her something she wants but is afraid to admit to wanting. Something she can't resist. Something you would never think of under ordinary circumstances."

Why did Liam feel like this Stax was trying to tell him something specific?

Jace huffed. "Sounds like too much work, if you ask me. I'm afraid he's screwed. We should end this man meeting and finish the game."

"Or we could just hand you all our money now and be done with it."

Jace glared at his roommate. "Where's the sport in that?"

With that the men returned to their cards, leaving Liam's head spinning.

Something she can't resist.

Somewhere between an uncomfortable, honest conversation and getting her drunk, there was an answer. He just had to find it. Soon.

"Don't be mad, sugar. She's fine. I had no idea she was such a lightweight."

Dani heard Bailey speak to Liam through a sangria-soaked haze. The part of her brain that was still working knew she should have just stopped drinking when Kaya had gotten a surprise phone call and left in a mad dash. She should have eaten more. But she'd been so thrown by what had happened, by the entire bizarre day, that Bailey's suggestion of getting blind drunk had sounded brilliant.

She never drank more than the occasional glass of wine. She hated being out of control in any way. And she'd seen what alcohol could do to people. With some of her foster parents. With Sal. How it could change them, make them violent.

Her eyes tried to focus on Liam's expression. Was it disapproving? Angry? Disgusted? "Stop moving so I can see you."

"Okay then," Liam sighed. She felt him gathering her in his arms, taking her weight from Bailey as he spoke over her shoulder. "Everyone else is gone. You all right to get home?"

"Me?" Bailey laughed. "Oh, you *are* sweet. If I thought you wanted to take advantage of me I'd pretend and say no. But we both know better." She patted Dani on the back fondly. "Aspirin and water, babycakes. That's the cure for what ails you. Hopefully we can both forget about tonight and feel better in the morning."

Dani smiled and nodded. "Mmm-hmm." She heard the door close but she didn't move. She was fine just where she was. With Liam's arms around her, the room wasn't spinning quite so much.

"You smell good, Liam. I've always thought so, but I didn't want you to think I was weird. Roommates shouldn't smell each other, should they?"

It sounded like he groaned against her hair. "And that, ladies and gentlemen, is the sound of irony."

She pulled away, pushed a stray curl out of her eyes and squinted up at him. "Huh?"

"Nothing, Shortbread." He hefted her up into his arms with an ease that surprised her and started walking. "Just remembering a conversation I had with the guys."

"The guys. Stax smelled good, too. What do you think?"

"And the hits keep coming," Liam sighed. "Come on, I need to get you to bed."

He started up the stairs and she tugged on his shirt, not ready to go to bed yet. "Kitchen. I'm hungry. I hardly got any of the ribs. Is there pie left?"

Liam swung around mid-step, causing Dani to grab her head to ensure it went with her. "Oh God. I feel awful. Why do people do this to themselves?"

"My question is, why did *you*? You know what an easy drunk you are. The first night we met you took one sip of a watered-down rum punch and started to get tipsy. How many glasses of sangria did you have tonight?"

He set her down with her bottom on the island and turned to open the refrigerator, keeping her weaving form in view.

She bit her lip. "Four."

"Four? Son of a bitch, Dani, no wonder you're soused."

She lifted her chin, stabilizing her body by placing her hands on the counter. "I. Am not. Soused. That word sounds funny. Soused." She saw what he had in his hand and forgot about balancing. "Ooh, pie!"

"I gotcha, darlin'." She was in Liam's arms again before she knew she was falling.

Dani blinked slowly, realizing how close they were. "Bailey is right. You have beautiful eyes." Sky blue. She expected to see clouds floating through at any moment.

His gaze narrowed behind his glasses, shielding the darkening sky from view. "Dani." He set her feet down on the floor, lowering her slowly against his muscular chest, his stomach, his— She shivered. If she wasn't supposed to enjoy the smell of her roommate, liking his—*that*—pressed up against her probably wasn't allowed either. But she did. She'd been thinking about it all day. And in the condition she was in, it didn't surprise her at all that she told him so.

She watched his jaw clench. "Dani, I know we need to talk, but you're in no condition. Are you sure you don't just want to go to bed?"

God that sounded good. Though she didn't think he meant what she wanted it to mean. What *did* she want? "I want pie. I need it. The spider was a Grandmother, Kaya zapped me and then Bailey wished for two Ewans on blue stars." She wrinkled her forehead. "I don't think that came out right."

Liam laughed. "God, you are so fucking cute. I have no idea what you just said, but you're cute. Two Ewans?" He hefted her back onto the counter, stepping between her legs to keep her upright, and handed her the pie tin containing the last slice of her favorite comfort food. Pumpkin pie.

She ignored the fork and scooped up the delicious filling with her finger, sliding it into her mouth. "Mmm."

He set his hands on her knees and squeezed. "I don't know why we even have utensils. You always eat with your hands."

She dipped her fingers in the soft pie center again and nodded. "Threesomes. She wished for us all to have threesomes. Bailey wants two Ewans." Her pumpkin-covered fingertips floated up to his mouth, and she grinned coaxingly. "It tastes better this way. Trust me. Here, have some."

"I made it, I don't have to taste it. I want to hear about those wishes. Is that what you asked for? Two men? Anybody I know?" He sounded grim. And Dani began to notice how stiffly he was standing, how his cheeks were looking flushed.

She chewed on her lower lip. Was he mad at her for telling him? Had she embarrassed him? And yet she couldn't keep her mouth closed. "One. Two. Do you know how long it's been since I've—"

She covered her mouth with her free hand, forcibly stopping herself from explaining how long it had been since she'd come. Apart from this morning in the shower. Oh God, his expression. She'd definitely said too much.

Liam looked down at her and growled. "Shit, Dani, don't look at me like that. I'll taste the damn pie."

He wrapped his hand around her wrist, opened his mouth over her two fingers and sucked. He swallowed every trace of the creamy pumpkin concoction, his tongue gliding across her skin, but he didn't release her hand.

The sensations sent Dani's mind into overload. She felt every swipe of his tongue against her index finger as though he were licking her thighs, her clit. Each time he sucked her fingers deeper she thought about the sizeable, jean-covered bulge currently pressed between her legs. She thought about sex.

Maybe her friends were right about her radar. How stupid she'd been not to have realized how sexy he was. How irresistible. How much she wanted to taste him again. She already knew he was better than the pie.

Almost of their own accord her legs lifted to wrap around his hips and pull him closer. Her free hand gripped the fabric of his shirt and tugged.

She saw his eyes open in surprise when she pulled her fingers out of his mouth and covered his lips with her own. He held back for a moment, mumbling her name against her lips, but she only clung tighter until he gave in with a moan.

Stars again. Falling behind her closed eyes. She had never been kissed the way he kissed her. Been consumed or felt like she would die if he took his lips from hers.

How did he know, instinctively know, she loved it when a man sucked on her lower lip, when he tangled his tongue with hers, groaning into her mouth as though her taste was all he'd ever hungered for?

He knew how to touch her, too. Before Sal she'd had one or two boyfriends, each of them either too rough or too gentle, too afraid to hurt her.

Liam wasn't afraid. He reached behind her, cupping the curving cheeks of her ass with firm hands, rocking her against his erection.

Dani couldn't stop her sounds of pleasure, couldn't stop her body from matching his rhythm. She pressed her chest to his, her hard nipples aching with the friction, wanting more.

Liam tore his mouth from hers, his chest lifting and falling rapidly, his breath coming in hard pants. "Dani, we need to ta—"

Don't stop. Don't let him stop. She reached for the hem of her T-shirt and lifted it swiftly over her head. She needed to feel his naked skin against hers again. Now.

"Damn, I love these." Liam growled, thoroughly distracted by the flesh she'd revealed. "You have no idea what I've imagined doing to them."

She didn't. But now she was dying to know.

His hands glided up her sides, stopping when he came across a strange texture on her skin.

"Dani, what's this?"

Dread like a blast of cold water ripped her out of her lust-induced daze and made her tremble as he traced her scar with his rough fingertips. What had she done? Oh God, what had she just done with her best friend? *Again.*

She pushed frantically at his hands, nearly twisting her ankle as she jumped off the counter and reached for her T-shirt. "I'm sorry. I'm so, so sorry."

"Sorry? Dani, wait."

She didn't want to see the pity in his expression. The small mark seemed huge now that he'd seen it. With anyone else she could lie, but Liam would know. At this moment that knowledge seemed insurmountable.

Liam was swearing again. "Damn it, woman. How many times are you going to walk away from me? At least let me help you before you fall down."

Dani spoke over her shoulder as she slowly and methodically climbed the stairs, one hand clutching her T-shirt. "I'm fine. I'm going to throw up, then go to bed. And don't worry. I will *never* touch sangria again."

When she finally left the bathroom, feeling empty and aching, but more clearheaded, she found a surprise. Liam had turned down her bed and left a glass of water and an aspirin on her nightstand.

She sighed. That man was bucking for sainthood. Why did he always do the perfect thing? It threw her off. It always had. Men didn't behave like that. If they didn't get what they wanted, if a woman teased them and didn't put out, men left. Or worse, stayed and refused to accept rejection.

Not Liam. He did what he'd always done. Made sure she was okay.

Dani grumbled but took the medicine and slid gratefully into her bed. She would have rather seen *Liam* waiting in her bedroom than aspirin, even though she'd pushed him away. Thankfully her night of drinking had one pleasant side effect. It immediately put her to sleep.

"You trust Liam."

"Kaya?" Dani looked around the living room, sure she'd heard her

friend's voice. Everything looked strange. Hadn't she just gone to bed? It took her a moment to realize she was dreaming.

"Shortbread, I need you."

Liam? She walked toward the kitchen, her heart pounding in her chest. She took in the scene. It was as though she'd just stepped away. He was still standing there at the counter, his face flushed, his blue eyes dark with desire. For her.

She told herself to turn around and walk away, which was what she should do. But in dreams you never did what you should do, only what you had to do. What you wanted to do. She moved closer.

When she was within arms reach he gripped her hips, lifting her back onto the counter the way he had earlier. He bent his head and closed his teeth over her nipple and she cried out in surprise.

She was naked.

Dreaming, she reminded herself. Just a dream. You can do anything in a dream.

Dani arched her neck and slid her fingers into his hair, holding him close while his tongue swirled around the hardening peak of her breast and his teeth grazed her flesh.

He leaned into her until she had no choice but to lie back against the cool wood. She looked up at him and realized he was naked, too.

She saw the Tibetan dragon tattoo on his arm. The one that had so surprised her the first time she'd seen him in the backyard without a shirt on. It looked dangerous. Sexy.

He looked down at her through those long, dark lashes, but he didn't say a word. Broad palms skimmed her thighs, higher, higher, until his thumbs met at the mouth of her sex.

She was wet, could feel her arousal pooling low in her belly, feel her body heating with need. He pressed gently on her clit, rolling it between his thumbs so lightly she thought she might scream.

"Do you want more?" His voice was guttural, his face so taut with restraint she hardly recognized him.

She thought she screamed yes, and she must have, because he gave it to her, slipping two thick fingers inside her. He thrust deep and curved them inside her, massaging that perfect spot, that magical spot that was so hard to find with a vibrator. The spot no other man had ever looked for.

Dani's body arched off the counter as though she'd been shocked with a live wire. "Please, Liam."

His laughter had a strained thread. "Do you know how long I've imagined you begging? Come on now, Shortbread. You like to eat with your fingers, don't you?"

He reached out to tug on her wrist, pulling her hand down to join his between her thighs. "Touch yourself the way I'm touching you. Fuck yourself with your fingers while I watch."

She bit her lip so hard she tasted blood, but she did what he told her to. She loved the power in his voice. The primal edge.

Her finger brushed against his inside her and she moaned. "Liam—" She was so close to having the kind of orgasm she'd had this morning. The kind that felt like dying and being reborn. Just a little bit more . . .

He pulled her hand out with his fist around her wrist, and took his own hand away. "What? No!"

"Dani." He waited until she stopped shaking her head in denial, until she looked up at him with wild, unfocused eyes. "Taste."

He brought her hand up to his mouth, and placed his own damp fingers against her lips. Her sex clenched around nothing, another flood of arousal rushing through her at his command.

Her tongue came out to lap at his fingers, tasting herself, tasting the salt of his skin mingling with her passion.

His jaw clenched and he followed suit, licking her fingers like a predatory feline, his eyes never leaving hers. "You're right, Shortbread. Finger foods are fun."

Before she could blink he was gone. Vanished as though he'd never been. But how? And why? "Isn't this my dream?" What did it say about her that even her subconscious wouldn't let her enjoy herself, wouldn't let her have him completely. "Damn it."

"Wish, Butterfly Maiden."

Dani jumped down from the counter, whirling around. "Kaya, you are so not allowed to be in my sex dream."

No one answered, but when she looked down she saw a line of cornmeal on the floor. Cornmeal? "I promise all my guardian angels, I will never drink again."

She followed the trail, her body still tingling from Liam's ministrations, every inch of her crying out for him, for her best friend.

The cornmeal path led to the kitchen door and outside, to the edge of the lap pool, the water sparkling beneath the moon.

"Liam? Kaya?"

A coyote howled in the distance at the same time a shadow stirred on the edge of her vision. Someone was there. She moved closer, hoping by the height of the figure that it would be Liam.

A glint of silver caught a beam of bright moonlight and Dani froze. The man coming out of the darkness didn't surprise her. He immobilized her. "Sal."

He came so close she could smell the stale smoke and desperation on his skin. Could see that strange spark that had always been in his eye. She'd thought it was fire, but it was insanity.

He smiled. "All paths lead to me, Dani. I'm the only destiny for you. And you know I told you no one else could have you. I promised."

He lifted the knife and she opened her mouth to scream—

It was dark in her bedroom. Dani sat straight up in bed, scrambling back until her body plastered against the headboard and turning on the light to study her surroundings. Sal wasn't here. Nothing had happened—other than her having too much to drink.

Things had been so much better lately. But she knew why he'd come back into her dreams. She was scared. Not just about Sal finding her, but about her plans to retake her life . . . and her newly awakened feelings for Liam. Feelings that were decidedly more dangerous than friendship.

She knew she couldn't let it happen. Couldn't let herself give in. She would lose him.

But it might already be too late.

Four

It was close to noon the next day when Dani lifted her fist to knock on Kaya's door, but it opened before her knuckles could make contact.

"How did you know?" Kaya gripped her wrist and dragged her inside her small cottage before Dani could say a word. Her friend looked frazzled. Exhausted. Very un-Kaya-like.

The only person who'd ever been able to breach Kaya's calm, cool serenity was Jace. Dani looked around, half expecting to find the button-pushing sous chef hovering over her shoulder.

"Know what?" she asked. Kaya tugged again, and Dani nearly lost her footing.

"What's going on, Kaya?"

Kaya stopped, looked down at the death grip she had on Dani's wrist and released her, blowing out a frustrated breath. "I'm sorry, Dani. I can't seem to get my act together this morning."

Boy, could Dani ever relate. She'd just spent a couple of hours driving around in her old Crown Victoria, the one she'd insisted on buying despite Liam's safety concerns. Instead of looking for jobs or filling out applications, she'd stopped at the scenic overlooks along the way and stared at the beautiful red rocks and cliffs without really seeing them.

What she'd seen was the end of her friendship with Liam. The awkward, uncomfortable, oh-my-god-did-I-really-get-drunk-and-make-a-pass-at-you conversation that was destined to happen, prefaced by the oh-my-god-did-I-really-make-out-with-you-in-my-bathroom apology. She could guess what would happen next. He would let her down gently, and move back to Texas. Or worse, stay to make beautiful babies with Gillian, the pastry chef, laughing with her at his old friend's pathetic attempt at seduction.

He would never do that. She knew it. She knew Liam well enough to know he would never be intentionally cruel. He would be kind. Painfully so. And that would be even worse.

Or maybe he would surprise her and kiss her again.

She inwardly shook herself. *That* wasn't an option. In fact, while she was riding around this morning, she'd laid out what she thought her choices were. Pretend nothing happened, face it and deal with the consequences, or move to Phoenix in the dead of night and avoid the whole thing. She'd come to Kaya to get her opinion, but the exotic beauty didn't look like she could help anybody at the moment.

Kaya looked over her shoulder to make sure no one was there

before turning back to Dani and lowering her voice. "The phone call I got last night? It was my aunt, who never calls me, letting me know my grandfather had gone missing. I came home to change and go out to look for him . . ." She shook her head as though she still couldn't believe it. "And he was here. He'd walked here from the reservation. Walked. It takes nearly *three* hours to drive that route, and he walked it. I can't believe anyone would let him do that in his condition."

Dani felt her jaw go lax. She got out of breath walking up the trails in Boynton Canyon. She couldn't imagine how she'd handle that kind of trek. "His condition? Is he all right?"

Kaya crossed her arms, a vulnerability in her features that Dani had never seen before. "I don't know. I've never been able to read him. But he hasn't gotten up from the couch since he woke up this morning, he's refusing to let me take him home, and the Divine Darla has the flu. Apparently there is no one to cover for her but me, and she has a zillion appointments today."

Dani pushed aside her own problems and slipped her arm through Kaya's. "Calm down, K. I'm here. I can stay with your grandfather until you get home."

Hope sparked in Kaya's doe eyes, but she shook her head. "I couldn't ask you to do that. You had plans for today. Besides, you haven't even met hi—"

"Elder Sister, is that your *Bahana* friend?" The old male voice quavered with exhaustion. Weakness.

Dani frowned at Kaya, who rolled her eyes and whispered, "My name. Kaya means elder sister. And Bahana, well, that means white."

Dani walked over and held out her hand to the elderly man who reclined on the couch, his frail body covered in a patterned blanket. "Yes, sir. My name is Danielle. Dani."

He nodded and, after an awkward moment, she let her hand drop back to her side.

His face seemed to be carved out of the red rocks themselves. Deep lines of life and laughter framed his lips and eyes. His white hair was short but wild around his head, as though he left all his grooming to the winds.

He looked up at Kaya, pulling Dani from her observation. "Go, Elder Sister. She can stay here with me."

Dani watched Kaya hesitate then walk up to her grandfather as if to kiss his darkly bronzed and weathered cheek, only to hesitate again at the last minute, stopping before she could touch him. "Be nice."

Kaya's softly muttered order made Dani smile. It was easy to see she loved him. Nearly as easy as it was to see that his impromptu arrival had severely rattled her.

Dani walked her to the door and Kaya gave her a warm hug. "Thank you, Dani. I really appreciate it. And I promise when I get home we'll talk about what happened between you and Liam."

"Wh-what happened? Why do you say that?" Was she that obvious?

Kaya smiled ruefully. "Your visit and his voice when I called a half an hour ago looking for you. Just don't make any decisions before we talk."

She didn't want to think about this now. "Get out of here before the Divine Darla's clients start a riot."

When she was gone, Dani leaned her forehead against the door. She should call Liam, let him know she was okay. It was the last thing she wanted to do. Still, she found herself reaching into her purse for her cell.

"He'll wait, young Lion Tamer. He's waited longer than this. It's good for a man's soul. Teaches us patience for when we become fathers."

Dani turned around and knew her eyes had widened in shock. The frail old man who had looked as though he was at death's door only a moment before was now standing in front of the couch, *smiling* as he folded his worn blanket.

Had he been faking?

He laughed. "What an expression you have. I *am* old, and it *was* a long journey. Not as long as the one you've taken, but long enough. Come, I feel like exploring."

He turned and walked toward the patio doors, and Dani followed him, her curiosity piqued. "Why would you want Kaya to worry?"

An old, patched-up backpack sat beside the sliding glass doors, and he bent to pick it up, digging through it as she arrived at his side. "I don't. Let me ask you a question. How do *Bahanas* make healers come?" He pulled something out, dropping the bag and revealing two dried tree roots the length of his forearm. "Pick one."

She pointed to the smaller one on the left and he grunted, nodding as though he'd expected no less. She shrugged. "I suppose they call the doctor." She bit her lip. "Do you need me to call a doctor, sir?"

His smile was so broad it made his sparkling eyes disappear. "Why would I need one, Lion Tamer? I already have a healer standing in front of me. And don't call me sir. Or Elder. I'm traveling. You have permission to call me the name my teachers gave me as a child. Will." He turned and opened the sliding glass door, stepping out into the warm desert sun.

Healer? She'd never told Kaya, never told anyone here that she used to be a nurse. In the past it would have caused too many questions. Now, well, now it was one of the things she had to figure out. Was that still who she was? What she wanted to be?

He was disappearing down the slope of Kaya's backyard. "Wait. Will, wait."

She jogged over to him just as he'd bent to look into one of Kaya's pots. "Corn in a pot?" He shook his head in dismay. "All this land and she grows her corn like this."

Dani crossed her arms, feeling defensive on her friend's behalf. "The land isn't hers. She's renting." He just shook his head and looked around, inspecting everything. He was quiet for so long it was making her nervous. She reached for a topic to end the silence. "Why did you call me Lion Tamer?"

Will looked over his shoulder, his bushy eyebrows high. "Isn't that your name? Named for Daniel of the *Bahana* god, who tamed the lions with the strength of his faith?"

Dani grimaced. "According to all sources, I was named after a tropical storm that flooded my town a few months before I was born. I'm more of a trouble magnet than a lion tamer."

Kaya's grandfather lifted one shoulder. "Or the gift of sunlight after a time of darkness. I suppose it depends on your point of view. Ah, I found it."

Dani came closer. "Found what?"

He sat down on a stump in the shade of a juniper tree, his expression content. "The perfect sitting spot." He reached into the pocket of his frayed jeans and pulled out a small, gleaming carving knife. "Sit down and tell me about what's troubling your heart."

She sat on the ground like an obedient child, drawn to the charisma, the aura around this man. "How did you know I was a . . . well, a healer?"

The old man turned the root in his hand, studying it carefully. "The same way I know this is a root from a strong cottonwood. The same way I can see the shape it is, and the shape it wants to be. It simply is." He pierced her with his sharp gaze. "You are as much a healer now as you were yesterday. You care about people. More than you do about yourself. You stayed with a rude old man because you care. You hold back what you truly feel from others because you care."

He was right. A part of the reason she'd never returned Liam's teasing flirtations earlier in their relationship was not that she hadn't seen them, but because she cared about him too much to let him make a mistake with her. Now though, she was beginning to realize her feelings for him had grown, changed. She didn't want him to feel obligated.

She looked up and noticed the old man Will still watching her, studying her as he had the root, as though he could see inside her to what she truly was.

No wonder Kaya seemed so magical. She must have gotten it from him. "Are you going to stay for a while?" She grimaced at the yearning she couldn't quite hide.

"As long as I'm needed. At least until *Nimon*, when the *katsinam*, the *kachinas*, return home." Her confused expression had him smiling again. "I think I must like you, Lion Tamer. I almost forgot you were *Bahana*."

He leaned back against the tree, his knife whittling a form with a skill Dani could only marvel at. "Get comfortable, and I will tell you about the last ceremony of the season."

She glanced at the door behind her, thinking once more about calling Liam.

"I'm older than your young man. Trust me, he can wait."

"I can't wait, man. I need to talk to you now." Liam hung up after leaving his message, pacing the perimeter of the large lap pool in the backyard like a caged animal. He wanted to break something. He wanted to shout.

Most of all he wanted Dani to stop avoiding him. If Kaya hadn't called him back from her work phone to tell him where Dani was, he would have been tearing Sedona apart by now. It wasn't like her not to call and check in. Wasn't like her to leave before saying good-bye.

He knew why. The reason he was climbing the walls to see her was the same reason she was avoiding him. He'd kissed her, touched her. And she'd kissed him back. More than that. Twice in one day he'd come close to exploding, his cock so hard it could chisel stone, only to have her run away.

It was enough to drive a man to drink.

She'd been drunk, a truth that had repeated like a drumbeat in his head from the moment he'd lifted her into his arms. A drunken siren. Without her inhibitions she'd looked at him, said things that gave him hope that their earlier embrace wasn't a one-shot deal for her.

And then he'd seen the scar. The jagged S-shaped scar that looked like it had been sewn together in a rough and careless manner. Painful. How had he not seen that before? She'd told Liam Sal had threatened to kill her, that he'd hit her, not that he'd cut into her.

His desire to take her then was momentarily overruled by his need to protect her. To find the bastard who'd done this and make him suffer.

He'd hired his brother-in-law, the private investigator who'd worked for his family for years before marrying his sister. He'd promised to keep an eye on Dani's ex. To make sure the bastard wasn't coming for her. Asking questions. According to his information, Sal had been a boy scout for the last six months. No women, no suspicious activities. But that didn't make Liam feel any better. Not after last night.

Liam hadn't told Dani. But then, there were a lot of things he hadn't told her.

He hadn't told her that he'd wanted her from the moment he'd seen her. The timing had always been off. He'd had a date that first night he met her at a charity event being held in a new wing of the hospital where she worked.

He'd seen her laughing with a group of wheelchair-bound patients and ignoring the wealthy donors completely. There was no artifice, no pretense—and the boring, obligatory evening he'd been resigned to suddenly changed. He'd "accidentally" bumped into her and started a conversation. She was perfect. Real. Easy to talk to, smart and funny; so much so that Liam had forgotten he wasn't alone until it was pointed out to him.

But he'd discovered they had friends in common, and he'd made it his mission to run into her again, this time without another woman on his arm. Only once he did, Dani had told him that she'd met someone on an online dating site. Someone she had so much in common with. That someone was Sal.

But Liam was nothing if not patient. He'd learned that if he wanted something, really wanted it, he could get it. He just had to have a plan. His father had taught him that, and the success of his family business had proven that lesson again and again.

That was the other thing he hadn't told her. Liam ran a frustrated hand through his hair and looked up at the outside of the two-story adobe house that had been his home for over a year. Their home.

There was no wealthy friend. This place belonged to Liam. He'd purchased it, sight unseen, on the phone on the way to Arizona. He'd come to Sedona with his father several times as a child to camp and fish. It was the first place that came to mind when she'd said she needed to get away from Dallas.

He loved it here. And he enjoyed his work at the resort, enjoyed being a part of a kitchen again, though he didn't have to work. Ever.

All things Dani didn't know.

He was selfish. He liked being just plain Liam. Not the wealthy co-owner of one of the most successful chains of restaurants in Texas. Not the heir to the proverbial throne. Just Liam.

He'd wanted to tell Dani so many times. When he'd met her, he hadn't mentioned it, thinking she would know, that she would ask around about him and find out like everyone else did. He'd been so blown away when he realized she thought he was simply a cook, struggling like her, that he kept his mouth shut. He just wanted to get to know her first, without the money getting in the way. Like it always had before.

Every time he'd gotten close to a woman in the past, it was the same. His last serious relationship had been the biggest sham of all. She'd insinuated herself into his family, befriended his sister, charmed his father. Slept with his cousin.

All because of the damn money.

Dani had seemed different. Special. But his doubts had made him hesitate. It never seemed to be the right time. And the longer he'd waited, the harder it had gotten to slip into conversation.

When he saw her all bruised up and shaken in her car that fateful night, he'd been about to tell her. He could use his influence, get her the best lawyers, the best protection money could buy. Keep her safe.

"You may be the only human being I can trust right now. The only one I know won't lie."

That was what she'd said. And that had sealed his fate. Created the one wrinkle in his foolproof plan that he wasn't sure how to fix.

He loved her. And now, if he told her that he was more than he'd led her to believe, that he'd lied about who he was, he'd lose her forever. Especially now that there was no reason for her to stay.

"That is some dark thundercloud hanging over your head, my friend. Want to talk about it?"

Liam spun around to find Stax wandering toward him casually. What the hell? "Forget something, *friend*?"

Stax smiled, reaching for an object leaning against the wall of the house. Where had that come from?

"Yeah. My stick."

He held it up for Liam to see. It was a thick, twisted length of wood, the carvings on it so detailed that Liam couldn't believe he hadn't seen it earlier.

He looked closer. "Some stick. Did you make this?"

Stax shrugged. "Keeps my hands busy."

"You should sell them."

Stax twirled the staff in his hands and shook his head. "I don't need money. That's something you and I have in common, in a way, isn't it?"

Liam stilled, his smile tightening. "Not sure what you're talking about, Stax."

The long-haired man chuckled. "I'm not shaking you down, friend. Just making conversation. Nick thinks I don't understand the subtleties of civilized communication, but I'd rather say what I think than bite my own tongue. My fangs are far too sharp."

Liam snorted, sitting down in the nearest lounge chair and scrubbing his face with his hands. He was in really bad shape if he was willing to talk to a trespassing stranger instead of thinking about his current situation. "Sit down, Stax."

The lean man sat on the concrete beside the pool, looking up at the sky thoughtfully. "Not that it's any of my business, but you've made a home here. Friends. You respect this land. She isn't the only reason you stay."

He was right. Liam loved his family, but anytime he thought about going back to the crowded, towering buildings, the busy freeways—his old life—his stomach knotted. As far as the business, he'd read all the status reports from his sister, given his advice. But she didn't seem to need his presence. Kristi was a natural.

He'd made a life here. The only way it could be better was if Dani was in his bed. If she loved him back.

"I've been considering your situation, thinking of a way you can throw her off kilter, change the landscape of your relationship."

"So have I." Liam sighed. Telling her the truth about who he was would throw her off. But he didn't think that's what Stax had in mind. "Any ideas? I'm willing to try anything at this point."

"The planner throwing his plans away is the first step. Love doesn't follow timetables. Passion doesn't appear on schedule."

Stax's words threw Liam for a loop. How did he know about his plan? And what was with all the clichés? "What are you, a fortune cookie?"

"I have good instincts. And I know more than you think. Between the two of you and your long list of rules and fears, you may lose what you have and what you could be. You don't want that." He leaned forward, watching Liam through his curtain of hair. "I know she wants you, too. But she won't give in. Not unless her inhibitions are lowered." He bared his teeth in a wicked semblance of a smile. "Which is where I come in."

Liam snarled. "What, exactly, do *you* have to do with this plan? She doesn't know you, wouldn't lower anything around you."

Stax caressed the carved image of a coyote on the walking stick in his lap, drawing Liam's gaze. "She wouldn't be able to help herself. I have that effect on people. A magical gift, you could say."

This was the strangest conversation Liam had ever had. And he'd lived in Sedona for a year now, so that was saying something. People around here were always laying claim to magical powers or connecting with their spirit guides.

Dani wanted to believe in all that hokum, but he didn't. He only dealt with what he could see. With what was real.

Yet, there was something about this Stax. He'd noticed it the other night. A look in his eyes. An otherworldly air that was convincing. Or maybe he was just so desperate to have her he was willing to believe the sky was green if it meant she'd be his. "I don't want to trick her."

Stax stretched, coming to a standing position slowly, obviously enjoying himself. "No tricks. That's not my way, despite what people think. Besides, none are necessary. I suggest, but people will only do what they want to do, what they truly desire. Think of me as a clear reflection in the lake. Or a—" He looked around as though searching for a word in the ether. "A truth serum." He pinned Liam with his gaze. "If the gardener doesn't change, the same flowers will grow, and the butterfly may seek out a different garden. How's that for a fortune cookie?"

Strange as the platitude was, Liam actually understood it. They'd both been a little rattled out of their complacency the other day, when she'd kissed him, when he'd made her come. But it had only pushed her further away, leaving him pounding his head against a brick wall, desperate to tear it down.

The last thing he wanted was to lose her friendship. It meant too much to him. He just wanted more.

He needed to know. "What will you do? What's in it for you?"

"One night."

A simple two word answer that made Liam want to pounce and

shout out an instant denial. He wanted her for himself. Why would he share her with anyone?

Dani's conversation about threesomes last night immediately sprang to mind. Had it been the sangria talking? More important, was that something Liam could actually offer? Could he share her, when all he wanted was to claim her for his own?

Stax turned and began to walk away, before Liam could come up with a response. "Think about it. Take a few days. Nick will know how to find me."

Just like that he was gone, and Liam was more lost than ever. Yes, he knew Dani. Better than he'd known anyone in his life.

Her most forbidden fantasies.

His cock hardened. Jesus, was he really that desperate?

It was a rhetorical question. He already knew the answer.

Five

"I'm not saying you need an intervention. I'm saying if you've started dating Kaya's grandfather, Thanksgiving could be awkward."

Dani chuckled as she walked through the crowd of tourists along the Tlaquepaque sidewalk and recalled her lunchtime conversation with Bailey and Kaya. She'd been going on and on about her visit with Will, Kaya's grandfather, and Bailey had made her laugh so hard she may have strained something. She'd definitely scared the poor waiter.

Not that she *wasn't* a little in love with the old man. How could she not be? He'd helped her, more than either of her friends could ever know.

It was because of him that she'd called the lawyer this morning and asked him to set the final phase in motion, the one she hadn't been sure she wanted to do before: transferring her nursing license to her new name without leaving a paper trail.

Will was right, she was a healer. She'd always loved helping people. She'd just needed to be reminded that not all the things from her old life were bad. And for that, she would always be grateful.

It was a good feeling, having a direction again. A powerful sensation.

She stopped at a shop window, noticing the beautiful carving of a howling coyote on display. It made her think of watching Will carving on that root again. And about the coyote that had come up to the tree line beside them.

Dani had frozen, ready to run screaming back into the cottage, but Will had just chuckled and shaken his head.

"The land watches over you, Lion Tamer. Its guardians will protect you from any who would seek to do you harm. Trust me, it's a good sign."

He'd made a motion with his hand and just like that, the coyote had turned and loped away.

She studied the carving again. Maybe she should buy it as a reminder. She usually avoided this little art village, full of craft shops and restaurants and people. But today she couldn't stop smiling as the crowd pushed by.

The only thing left for her to figure out was how to tell Liam that she wanted him to be happy, that she just plain wanted him . . . and that she was moving out.

She bit her lip regretfully as she walked away from the statue and toward the parking lot. She'd come back for it with her first paycheck. Hopefully it would still be there by then.

Her car keys were in the lock when she saw him. He was smiling at her from over the roof of her car. And he looked just as sinfully attractive in the daylight.

"Stax. What are you doing here?"

He laid his hands on the white roof and smiled. "This is a small town. I was bound to run into you sooner or later."

"Were you looking for me?"

"Hoping. That's all." He tapped out a hypnotic rhythm, and Dani felt her heartbeat change to match it. "Actually, I was just leaving. Too many people for my taste. I think I understand now why Nicholas prefers rocks and ruins to shopping malls. Do you suppose you could give me a ride?"

She nodded without thinking and opened her car door, mumbling to herself as she leaned over to unlock the passenger's side. What was she doing? She barely knew this man.

There was just something about him.

He slid in beside her, putting a long, intricately designed walking stick in the backseat before closing the door. She was instantly surrounded by his scent.

"Where do you need to go?"

"Just a few miles down. It's on your way home. You are going home now, aren't you?"

She nodded again, trying to focus on the winding road in front of her. He shifted in his seat and she knew without looking that he was staring at her. Her grip on the steering wheel tightened. "So, you work with Nick, right?"

His chuckle was low. Intimate. "You don't want to know that."

"I don't?"

"No," he assured her. "There are many things you'd love to ask me that are far more interesting. And there are things I want to know about you as well. Why pretend otherwise?"

She swallowed, no thought in her mind of denying it. She *was* curious about him. About the strange affect he had on people. On her. Where he came from. Why he smelled that good, and why Nick seemed so wary of him. But now her overriding question was, "What do you want to know about *me*?"

Stax lifted his hand and touched one stray curl that had escaped her ponytail. "The same things Liam wants to know."

The car swerved slightly as she turned to look at him, completely taken aback by his response. "Liam? What does he have to do with it?"

Stax shrugged, then directed her gaze back to the road with his chin. "For you? He has everything to do with it. Pull over here."

They'd passed the center of town. There was nothing on either side of the road but desert and brush. He wanted to stop here?

She pulled over, leaving her car idling as she looked at him. How did he know? He'd only met her for a few minutes the night before last. Was she that obvious about her feelings for Liam? How could she be when she was only just discovering herself how strong they were?

Stax looked down at her lips. "You are a beautiful armful, aren't you? No wonder he wants you so much."

Liam? "I think you've got the wrong idea about us. Liam and I are, well, we're just friends."

That statement was feeling less and less complete. They were just friends who had lived together like an old married couple sans the sex for over a year. They were just friends who'd had a few wet or drunken encounters that, she at least, found herself wanting to repeat.

They were more than just friends. A lot more. But what that more was, she still wasn't quite sure.

The mysterious man leaned in closer. There went her fickle body again, reacting. How could she trust her feelings for Liam, bet their relationship on telling him the truth about them, when she could still be aroused by Stax?

He caressed her face. "You think too much. Liam does as well. It's a human failing." His fingers traced her lower lip. "Think about this instead. I talked to him yesterday, did he tell you? We have a lot in common, he and I. We both wonder about you. What you taste like. What it would feel like to be inside you when you come. How sweet you'd look, lost in passion between us."

Dani moaned, hardly aware of the car door opening until he was gone, leaving behind those mouthwatering images and his scent. Sandalwood and desert rain. How could he do that? Leave her like this? She wasn't even sure she could drive in the state she was in.

She needed to get home. Needed release.

Needed Liam.

Liam unbuttoned his chef coat slowly as he walked through the dimly lit living room, feeling the emptiness like a physical ache. There was a time when, no matter how late it was, she was waiting for him with coffee and a smile, ready to find out about his night.

He'd seen her car in the driveway, so he knew she was here. He'd also seen Stax's damn walking stick in her backseat.

He moved into the kitchen, not bothering to turn on the lights as he opened the refrigerator to grab a beer. It took all his restraint not to tear the house apart looking for the long-haired heathen. Not to break down her bedroom door to demand she tell him what she'd been doing with Nick's strange friend. The man who just yesterday had been trying to convince Liam to share her.

Had it been a ruse? Was Stax trying to steal her before Liam had a chance to make her his? Was Stax playing some kind of a mind game with him?

If he was it had been working. Liam hadn't been able to stop imagining the scenario Stax had laid out since yesterday. Hell, since Dani had mentioned her not-so-sweet-and-innocent wish.

He wanted her to belong to him. And only him. Yet the idea of giving her that kind of passion, of being the one to make her most erotic fantasies come true, was seductive.

But only if she was his to pleasure.

He heard a splash and looked out the kitchen window into the well-lit pool and his anger disappeared. Shit.

The beer bottle nearly slipped from his hands but he caught it before it could shatter on the floor, alerting her to his presence.

She was a river nymph. A goddess. The moon shone down on her like a spotlight as she stood at the water's edge, gazing up at the stars.

Wet and naked.

He was going to hell. Because he knew he should turn around, walk away and give her privacy. The same way he knew there was no way on heaven or earth that was going to happen.

Beautiful was too tame for what she was. Dani always complained about being heavy, but her hourglass figure was full everywhere it should be. Large breasts, round ass, hips he could hang on to and a waist he could span with his hands. She was every fantasy he'd ever had rolled up into one tiny, luscious package.

He would do anything to have her.

Anything.

She dove into the water again, her body skimming the surface as she headed toward the shallow end. She sat down on the stairs, unknowingly giving Liam a groan-inducing view as she leaned back on her elbow, her nipples peaked and dripping with water.

"Mercy," Liam muttered under his breath.

Her expression was strained, her cheeks flushed. He knew that face. She'd worn it when she was pressed against him, reaching for her climax.

Liam glanced down at her hand beneath the clear water. The ripples above her wrist matched the swaying of her body. Fuck, was she . . . ? Yes. She was touching herself. Out beneath the night sky like a wild thing, unaware of her surroundings, lost to sensation.

Her neck arched and he heard her soft cry floating toward him through the glass that separated them.

He walked toward the sliding glass doors, still watching her. Willing her to step out of the water and come to him.

But Dani wasn't done. She whimpered and bit her lip, reaching for something on the rim of the pool and lowering it into the water.

A dildo? Shit, he supposed it was stupid of him, but he hadn't even known she'd had one of those in the house. If he had, he would have gotten a lot less sleep at night imagining what she was doing with it.

He watched her mouth open, her hips lift off the stairs and tilt as she took it in. Water splashed against her body with the power of her thrusts.

God, she was sexy. And she was doing it again. Fucking herself while he watched. Torturing him. How much could a man take?

Whatever the limit was, Liam had reached it.

No more Mr. Nice Guy. It was time to change the landscape. With or without Stax.

He took off his clothes, wincing as the rough fabric of his pants scraped his sensitive erection. There was a silent whoosh as he slid open the patio door, but Dani didn't look up. She was too aroused.

He could imagine. His blood was pounding so loudly in his ears he was amazed she couldn't hear it. He licked his palm and lowered his hand to grip his cock, his jaw tightening to hold back his moan.

He walked closer to the pool, his gaze never leaving her as he caught her rhythm, stroking himself with a tightly fingered fist, wishing it was her soaked sex wrapped around him instead.

Look at me, baby. See me.

No sooner had he thought the words than she opened up her eyes. The deep blue was dark with more need than he'd ever seen. And not as much surprise as he'd been expecting. But enough.

Her thrusts stopped.

"No." He lowered his voice, trying to soften the rough tone, but he knew he was close to begging. "Not again, Dani. Don't run away

from me again. Don't stop. I want to watch you. I want to look into your eyes as I come."

She'd been alone in the house, so restless she couldn't relax, and the pool had called to her. It felt bold and sexy and dangerous, skinny-dipping for the first time. But it wasn't enough to ease the ache that Stax had started.

That she'd wanted Liam to finish.

She'd learned something about the new her. She was greedy. She'd come against her hand half a dozen times since she got home, and it wasn't enough.

She'd thought the jelly-like sex toy would satisfy her craving to have someone inside her. Liam. But the more she rocked her hips against it, the more she knew it, too, wouldn't satisfy her.

What was happening to her?

When she'd opened her eyes to find Liam, standing over her in all his bare, beautiful glory, her first instinct was to stop. They had too much still between them to sort out. They needed to talk.

Then she looked into his eyes as he asked her not to stop. In their depths she saw a greed that matched her own. A desire—for her—that sent shudders through her body.

Without a word she lifted her hips until she was above the top step, the cool concrete against her cheeks. She spread her legs wide, shameless, and began to thrust the toy inside her again. Waiting for Liam's reaction.

He stepped into the pool beside her and dropped to his knees, his gaze drawn to her stretched sex.

"Jesus, Dani."

She licked her lips and looked at his erection and his white-knuckled grip. She'd never seen him completely naked before, and her fantasies hadn't held a candle to the real thing.

Just imagining his thick width inside her sent a rush of hot sensation through her body, the dildo slipping easily through her arousal.

Liam groaned again. "You're so wet. So damn sexy, Shortbread. You like that little toy of yours, don't you? Or is it that I'm watching you?"

"Yes. But it's not enough." Had she just said that out loud? She couldn't help herself. She wanted him to touch her.

He must have read her need in her expression. He smiled. "You need more? I can help with that."

She watched his free hand slide up her thigh, her movements faltering at the feel of his callused fingers on her skin.

"Don't stop, Dani. If you do, I won't do this." Liam had reached the top of her inner thigh, and his thumb pressed hard on her clit, making her cry out.

She wouldn't stop. Not as long as he kept touching her. She pushed the cock-shaped toy as deep as she could, until her fingers brushed against the lips of her sex, brushed against his.

He leaned in close, so close she could feel his breath on her breasts. "That's right. Now tell me what you were imagining before I came outside. Were you thinking about me? Someone else? Or were you fantasizing about two men taking you?"

God, why were his words turning her on? Was this a trap? She shook her head. No man wanted to hear that the woman whose body he was caressing had imagined another set of hands along

THREE SINFUL WISHES

with his own. Besides, since he'd shown up, he was the only one in her mind.

Liam. She wanted him. More than she'd ever imagined wanting anyone.

His lips pressed against the curve of her breast and she could feel his smile. "You can't lie to me, Shortbread. You've already told me about that wish of yours."

His fingers circled around the toy inside her and below, covering himself in her juices before slipping between the cheeks of her ass.

"Oh God." That felt good. Too good. "Liam, please."

"I love hearing that. Fuck, I want to be inside you."

"Yes." Her body was on fire. Every cell alive with sensation. Her spine arched when he pushed one thick finger against that forbidden place. The idea of it. Of being surrounded. Claimed.

Her climax crashed over her and she quaked against him. At Liam's growl she forced her eyes open, watching through her own orgasm as his overtook him.

His hips thrust his cock through his fist, faster and faster. His teeth closed over the flesh of her breast and he shouted, his body jerking as the pearly liquid splashed against her stomach.

She lay back against the concrete, looking up at the clear night sky. So many stars, but not one of them glimmering with the blue light she'd seen the other night. Was this the answer to the wish she'd made? Had it been Liam all along?

The cool desert night sent a shiver through her as Liam pulled away from her body, gently removing the dildo from her sex.

Her fists clenched in frustration. Seconds after her climax and she was already feeling the need swell again.

She couldn't seem to control it. Couldn't sate it. She sat up, pulling her knees up to her chest and wrapping her arms around her legs.

After a few long moments of silence, she worked up the courage to look at her best friend. What would she see in his eyes?

"No more pulling away, Danielle. Not from me. Not tonight."

Her friend was there, but so was a different Liam. One she didn't know as well. There was a predatory look in his gaze. A steely determination that she'd rarely seen. And something else. Something that gave her hope.

He dipped his body beneath the surface of the pool, then stood, water dripping off his gleaming muscles. His slim hips. His . . . oh, she was in trouble.

"Stay right there, Shortbread. I mean it. No moving. And no regrets."

She nodded, watching the flex of his ass cheeks as he strode back toward the house. It was strange, since she was usually riddled with them, but she had no regrets.

If this was all they got, if he ended up deciding to return to Texas after she moved into her own place, she wouldn't regret finally giving in to what was between them.

When had it happened? When had she become so willing to take this kind of risk?

Sometime over the past few days . . . when she realized she was in love with him.

She shivered again, and decided she could bend the not moving rule long enough to get a towel from the chaise lounge.

She'd just begun to dry off when she saw them. A pair of unblinking eyes watching her through the open gate of the fence.

Hadn't it been closed?

That wasn't the most important thing to worry about when facing a wild animal. "Hey, pretty coyote. Are you the one that's been following me? Protecting me like Will said?" She stepped closer to the sliding doors and he growled. "Maybe not. Just let me get inside where you can't bite something important off and I'll get Liam to give you a nice juicy side of beef that isn't me."

Fear turned to disbelief as the air shimmered around the animal. After a moment Dani decided she was going crazy. That was the only explanation for what she was seeing. Or maybe one of their neighbors was smoking peyote and the fumes had reached her backyard. It had to be a hallucination. A coyote *did not* just morph into Nick's friend Stax.

Stuff like that didn't actually happen.

He took a step forward and she stumbled back, holding on to her towel for dear life. She believed Sedona was a magical place, especially over these last few days. You couldn't throw a rock in this town without hitting someone who claimed to have gone to Cathedral Rock, Boynton Canyon or Bell Rock, who'd seen the Joshua trees that twisted with what the tour guides called the power of the vortex, and been healed or strangely affected by some unseen force. She'd felt it, too. And she'd heard all the theories about dimensional portals, aliens and the power of the ancestors.

But she couldn't remember anything about coyotes turning into hot men in other people's backyards. That just slipped too far into cuckoo land, even for her.

"You're not crazy, sweet Dani."

There it was again. Desert rain and sandalwood. Fantasyinducing charisma. It was him. *He* was the reason she hadn't been able to stem the tide of her arousal all day. The reason she and Liam had . . . Had he planted a suggestion when she'd given him a ride? Maybe he was a hypnotist as well as an illusionist. Hell, they had everything else in this town, why not magicians?

"I'm no magician. And it was more a gentle push in a direction you already wanted to go." Stax glanced toward the patio door and raised his finger to his lips as it opened.

Dani knew her eyes were wild when they met Liam's gaze. "Thank goodness. Liam, Stax is—"

"Just who I wanted to see. I was about to call Nick to find you." Liam had thrown on a pair of shorts. When had he done that? And why had he wanted to see Stax?

The coyote man smiled at her friend as Dani looked on in shock. He lifted his walking stick. "I came back for this and I just had a feeling. I see you've already made one decision. How far are you willing to go?"

Liam nodded tersely, but she could hear the restrained excitement in his voice. "Pretty damn far, apparently. I'll talk about that staff of yours later, but you're right. I've made my decision. As long as you know there are rules. You'll only do what I say. Nothing more."

"Of course." The grinning Stax nodded. "But I warn you now, I will do my best to find a loophole. It's instinct."

What were they talking about? She had to tell Liam what she'd just seen. "Stax is—I saw him come in and then he—"

He cut her off. Again. "I invited him. Well, I was planning to. He's going to help me give you something you've wanted for a long time now."

Wait, *what?* Curiosity and a little trepidation replaced her need to inform Liam about Stax's transformation. "What I've wanted?"

Liam's eyes darkened as he studied her. "Your fantasy. Two men. One night. You and Stax . . . and me."

Dani's knees almost buckled. Maybe it *was* peyote. Or she was having another sex dream. All the elements to prove it were there. Naked? Check. Coyote man-*cum*-sexy stranger? Check. Her best friend turning into a hot, commanding lover willing to fulfill her every dark and naughty daydream? Check, check and check.

Only this felt real. Maybe she should pinch something.

"I think she's speechless, my friend."

Liam ignored Stax and stepped closer to Dani, cupping her bare shoulders with his hands. "She needs to say yes." He tried to smile, but she could see the tension in his body, see something tightly reined in fighting to be set free. "Come on, Shortbread. Say yes. One night, give me one night."

"Yes." And she wouldn't regret it. Dream or not, Liam wanted her. As badly as she'd wanted him. Enough to give her everything. Anything.

If she was dreaming, she didn't want to wake up until she'd taken it.

"She's shivering, Liam. Nights in the desert can turn cold. Why don't we take her inside?"

Stax's words set Liam in motion. He bent his knees and lifted her up into his arms, clinging towel and all.

Dani glanced at Stax over Liam's shoulder. He was following behind, smiling in that secret, knowing way he had before. Like he'd always known this was going to happen.

He must be magical. She felt as though she were under some sort of spell.

Liam didn't stop until they were in his bedroom. She buried her face in his neck, inhaling deeply. She did love the way he smelled. Different from Stax, more familiar. More beloved. And it was stronger now, darker. Delicious.

He set her down gently in the center of the bed, pulling back with an expression of masculine satisfaction.

There it was again. The feeling that she didn't know this Liam. Not like she knew her friend. The thought of what her sexy stranger and his accomplice might do to her had Dani trembling with nerves. With desire.

Liam didn't move, though she could see the fine tremor of his muscles, the sheen on his skin from holding back.

Stax's charming voice whispered in her ear, and she realized he'd joined her on the bed, his fingers tracing the edge of her cotton towel. "You saw it earlier, by the pool, how strong his need is. He won't tell you how often he's fantasized about having you here, how hard it was to hold this part of himself away from you for years. So I will. Imagine it, beauty. All that passion bottled up. All for you."

His words wove a seductive cocoon around them, arousing Dani despite her doubts. Surely Liam would have told her. But Stax wasn't done.

"Tell her, Liam."

He didn't pretend to misunderstand. "That I've always wanted her? That I've dreamt about taking her in every room of this house, in every way possible? That letting her go that morning because she was scared, that night in the kitchen because she'd had too much to drink, were the hardest things I can remember doing in my life?"

His smile was self-deprecating. "It's all true." He looked down at her breasts swelling over the towel and his nostrils flared, his cheeks darkly flushed. "Fuck, Dani, you're perfect."

She squeaked when the cool air of the room washed over her, looking down in time to see her towel in Stax's fist, his mouth on her bare thigh.

Liam growled. "My permission. Remember?"

"She smelled so good, I couldn't resist a taste."

Dani's heart caught in her throat at Liam's response.

"Me first."

Stax lifted himself away from her, but refused to return her towel. "Tell me, Dani . . . who is the man you desire?"

She blushed. "Liam."

Liam jerked in surprise. How could he doubt it? Even Stax had seen right through her.

Liam's voice shook. "Say it again."

There was no hesitation inside her as she looked into his eyes. This was true. Let that other shoe go ahead and drop. She wouldn't let fear of losing his friendship stop her anymore. "Liam. You're the one I want."

Stax lifted a hand to caress her shoulder, watching Liam for any sign of discomfort. When he didn't find it, he touched her. "Tell me what you want from him. What you need."

She hesitated at that, and Liam leaned closer, cupping her bare knees with his palms. She shivered. "Tell me, Dani. Tell me what you want me to do."

Dani took a breath and it rushed out along with her words. "I want you not to treat me as though I'm fragile. I was, but I'm not anymore. I want to be taken. By you. Really taken." She stopped for a moment, studying his hands on her skin, feeling his touch to her core. "I want you inside me."

Liam jerked and she saw him turning to look questioningly at Stax, who shook his head. "Truth serum, remember? No tricks. This is all coming from her. I suggest you give her what she wants, since you want it, too."

Dani felt the importance of the moment. Knew they were about to cross a line they couldn't walk away from. And oddly, she was totally okay with that.

His. She was his. No matter what came tomorrow, tonight she would give herself completely to this fantasy. To Liam.

He slipped off his shorts and stood, shoulders back, in silence. What was he waiting for? Stax was whispering in her ear again. "He wants you to see him. Finally see him."

Restraint was etched in every muscle as Liam waited for her reaction.

Once she looked, she couldn't turn away. Couldn't even blink. She was staring, her eyes level with his hips, her chest rising rapidly. She knew it was rude, but she couldn't seem to stop.

"I had no idea it was so . . . I mean, I knew you were . . . at the pool I saw but . . ."

He put his hands on his hips. "What, Dani?"

"Wow."

He couldn't stop his lips from quirking. "Wow?"

She nodded, swallowing hard and he chuckled. "I'm glad you approve."

Six

Approve? She must. She was ogling Liam's body and wondering how, after all this time, she could have missed the fact that her roommate was sex incarnate.

She swallowed again. His erection was without question the largest, most beautiful body part she'd ever seen up close. She wondered again at her own oblivious naiveté in thinking him safe. Non-threatening. How had he escaped a year of living here without a hundred Gillians pounding on the door, demanding entrance?

A hand caressed her shoulder again, making her jump. She'd forgotten Stax was there. A miracle in itself. How could it have slipped from her mind that there was a sexy shape-shifter in her bed?

He was the mischievous troublemaker type. It rolled off him in waves of playful heat. A week ago, or even an hour ago, she'd have beaten a bad boy like him off with a broom, but with Liam here, Stax was no threat. He was a gift sent to bring her pleasure. Bring them all pleasure.

The idea of both men watching her, of Liam naked and wanting, was overwhelming. A rush.

She knew Liam better than she'd known any man in her life. Trusted him enough to give in to this fantasy, to give herself completely. To both of them.

She smiled and opened her arms, and it was like watching a dam burst. Liam's expression was almost one of pain. He fell to his knees beside her on the bed, eating at her mouth with a hunger that shook her.

No holding back. No careful restraint. He devoured her lips, his tongue exploring her mouth, gliding against hers.

She'd already become addicted to this. To his kiss. So intimate. Passionate and wild, yet tender. She melted into it, until her world was his breath mingling with hers, his heart pounding hard against her chest.

His warm hand was caressing her face and she reached up to cover it with hers, dragging it down her body until he was cupping her heavy breast.

Liam lifted his mouth and pressed his forehead against hers. "You're trying to drive me crazy, aren't you? I've already come once but I'm too close. I want to make this last. Make it special." His full lips twitched. "Not for you, you understand. It's a pride thing. Stax is holding it together and I don't want him outlasting me."

A sound of pure joy and surprise escaped her throat. Leave it to Liam to touch her heart, turn her on and make her laugh at the same time.

She slid off his glasses and set them on the bedside table. "That's the only help I can give you. You're just going to have to work harder, Cookie. Touch me and think of England."

His sky blue eyes sparkled. "Smartass." Her giggle turned into a moan when he pinched one nipple between his thumb and forefinger, gently biting down on the other. She gasped and he soothed it instantly with a lick of his tongue, only to scrape his teeth against the underside of her breast.

He touched the scar on her side and she stilled, wondering if he would mention the ugly mark. She didn't want to ruin the moment again. To remind him of her past.

Liam stared at her in silence for a long, tender moment, then bent his head to her side, running his tongue along the raised flesh.

"You're perfect, Dani. Beautiful."

She could feel his sincerity. Feel his desire. And she smiled. Her back arched, loving everything he was doing. Wanting more. Her thighs squeezed together, her whole body on fire, needing his touch.

Liam sensed the movement and his fingers left her nipple to circle her quivering belly and lower, tugging playfully on the curls of her sex until she spread her legs for him.

"*Damn.* You feel like heaven. I knew you'd be like this. You're soaking my fingers, baby. I have to—"

He didn't finish his sentence and Dani groaned in denial when he left her breasts to climb on the bed between her thighs. He gripped them in his hands and spread them wider, opening her up to his gaze.

"If I could paint, I would paint this. You are a goddess, Dani. Isn't she, Stax?"

She turned her head to see his response and her throat went dry. Stax was naked. When had he taken off his clothes?

His lips pressed against her shoulder and he smiled. "The Creator broke the mold," he agreed. "I'll admit, I'm more drawn to her with every passing moment."

"Dani." Liam waited for her to turn back to him. "I'm going to let him kiss you—your neck, your breasts—while I taste you."

Her mouth opened and closed at the sensual authority of his tone. Stax lifted up onto his elbow beside her. "May we pleasure you?"

May they . . . ? "Uh, s-sure." She closed her eyes for a moment, trying to get her bearings. She wasn't the girl this sort of thing happened to. Wasn't anyone's inspiration for a letter to *Penthouse*. She was ordinary. At least, the old her was. But they didn't seem to agree. And they were extremely convincing.

Stax's long, silken hair fell across her belly and he blew on one hard, sensitive nipple just as Liam placed his lips over her clit.

Dani squirmed breathlessly. "Oh my God."

Stax bit the side of her breast, a little harder than Liam had, his teeth sharper. But the sensation was more thrilling than painful.

Liam's growl rumbled against her sex and she whimpered at the vibration. He held her legs high and wide, burying his face between them and sampling her with the flat of his tongue. Again and again he licked her, moaning in approval as he thrust inside her.

Dani couldn't lay still, the scent of desert rain and Liam filled the heating room, and her body was under sexual siege. Stax was sucking each breast in turn, and she felt the pull all the way to her toes. Liam's tongue drove deeper inside her, the greedy noises he made making her greedy, too.

She was climbing, yearning for something just out of reach. Her hand reached down and gripped his soft, short, blond waves, holding him to her as she pumped her hips against his mouth.

Close now. She was close. Stax lifted his head from her breast and snarled. "Let go, little beauty. Come for us."

She screamed. Falling like a burning star through the sky, hot and bright and breathtaking. Addictive. Her hand covered her face and she struggled to catch her breath. Her whole body was shaking.

Dani heard them talking as if through a tunnel. "Stax, top drawer. Now."

"You're taking this in-charge thing seriously. A closed box." Stax made a disappointed sound at the sealed container of unused condoms. "The spirits would cry at the waste."

She peered through her fingers in time to watch Liam, now kneeling between her thighs, unrolling a condom on his—heaven help her—intimidatingly thick erection.

Her body started to heat again with the promise of more pleasure. Of Liam joining his body with hers. He caught her staring and licked his wet lips. "I have never tasted anything as sweet as you, darlin'. I'm not sure I'll ever get enough."

She licked her own lips unconsciously, and he swallowed. He climbed up her body, hands on the mattress on either side of her head before he stopped. "I know that look. That's your can-I-have-some look. Do you want a taste?"

Dani barely had the chance to nod before he was kissing her again. She could taste herself on his lips, his tongue, mingled with that taste that was uniquely Liam.

He pulled back and she opened her eyes. He was looking at her with an expression she wasn't prepared for. Her brow furrowed and his lashes fell, shielding the look from her view.

"Not that I don't love profound silence fraught with meaning, but I'm a little impatient for the main event."

Dani's eyes widened and Liam smirked at Stax's comment. "Remind you of anyone?"

She nodded and they looked over at Stax. He and Bailey had a lot in common. Both bossy, both sassy. She should fix them up.

Stax seemed to read her expression. "Don't get any ideas for me, little one. I'm only here for this. For you. You're special." His smile was wicked. "I want to watch your face when Liam fucks you. I want to see the ecstasy in his expression when he feels the grip of your tight, wet—"

"Enough." Liam's voice was rough, raspy. "I think you've made your point."

Stax raised an eyebrow. "And yet none of us is moving."

Dani covered her mouth to hold in her laugh and wrapped her legs around Liam's waist, tugging him closer. "We don't want to let him down, now do we?"

Liam's gaze heated, narrowed. All traces of laughter disappeared and she became aware of his hard shaft burning against her stomach. Suddenly she couldn't wait anymore. She wanted him inside her. Now.

She used her thighs to push, throwing him off guard and onto his back. Liam shouted in surprise, his eyebrows rising. "Impatient?"

No more games. She didn't smile, didn't look away or blush. "For you."

He gripped her hips and lifted her until she could feel the head of his cock and then let her sink slowly—achingly slowly—onto his shaft.

"*Damn*."

"Oh my *God*."

His fingers dug into her hips, while hers curled into his chest as she took him an inch at a time. "Dani, you feel good. So tight, baby."

She bit her lip. "Maybe too tight." She blew out, trying to take more of him, her body stretching almost painfully to accept him.

Liam's laugh was breathless. "No such thing, Shortbread. You can take me. That's right. Oh fuck, *yes*, rock like that."

She'd swirled her hips experimentally, and a jolt of pleasure, as well as his response, had her doing it again.

A few more swivels and Liam was gritting his teeth. "Take all of me, Dani. Please." He tensed and his hips pumped upward until he was completely inside her.

Her neck arched and she cried out, seeing stars. So full. Incredible.

Complete.

She started to rock against him, reveling in the sensations she felt in this position. She controlled *his* pleasure. The pace. She drove him wild.

She noticed Stax from the corner of her eye, watching them, stroking his own impressive erection in time to her movements.

A thrill raced through her, making her feel powerful. She was drunk with it. Heady. She looked at his cock, wondering how it would taste.

"Whatever you want, Dani." She looked down at Liam to find him watching the exchange. He was smiling, lust and a hint of vulnerability in his beautiful blue eyes.

"I want you."

He groaned, but she saw by his smile that he'd understood. "Damned if I don't love hearing you say that, Dani. And I want you. I want you to experience every kinky, erotic thing this night can bring us. Stax, aren't her lips the sexiest fucking lips you've ever seen?"

Dani parted her lips on a panting breath as Stax rose to his knees beside them and sighed. "I can't think of anything hotter."

Liam thrust up inside her, reminding her, as if she could forget, of his presence. "Remember, no secrets tonight. Take what you want."

Dani took. She leaned over Liam, her breasts brushing against his face, her lips a heartbeat away from Stax's now condom-covered erection.

For a moment she was disappointed; she wanted to taste him. Stax caressed her chin with his fingers. "I'm a wild man, little beauty. Don't worry, I will enjoy whatever you do."

He rubbed his cock against her lips. "Kiss me, Dani. And show poor Liam some mercy."

She opened her mouth and wrapped her lips around his shaft, her hips following the rhythm Liam was setting.

Her eyes closed and she heard two male groans of pleasure, two hissing breaths as she took both of them.

The earthy, rain-soaked scent of Stax surrounded her, making her dizzy, heightening her arousal. Liam dragged her down against him over and over again, harder and faster.

Dani's body felt as though it had been hooked up to a live wire; shocks of pure ecstasy jolted through her limbs, up her spine.

She wasn't sure how much time had passed lost in pleasure until Stax made a haunting sound of release, almost like a howl. His hand curled in her hair, hips jerking as he came.

The moment he pulled himself out of her mouth, Liam flipped her over onto her back, his strokes deep and hard as he kissed the memory of any other man away from her mind.

They came together, lips separating long enough to look into each other's eyes before the conflagration consumed them.

He called her name, burying his face in her neck, his body shaking. Dani wrapped her arms around him, so tightly she hoped he could breathe, but she couldn't let go. She didn't want this feeling to end.

Satisfaction. She felt it. This was what she'd needed. What she'd craved. Liam.

As the shock waves settled into ripples and they came back to earth, they heard Stax humming happily beside the bed.

Dani looked away from Liam and caught the pleased sparkle in Stax's dark eyes. He was getting dressed.

He was leaving? Already?

Liam spoke, his voice rich with satisfaction. "You don't have to leave, Stax."

Stax grinned and shook his head. "Yes, I do. I know when I'm not needed anymore." He bowed his head toward Dani. "I have thoroughly enjoyed myself, but I have a feeling your man doesn't want to share you beyond this. And that," he shrugged, unconcerned, "is how it should be between you. At least for tonight."

He walked toward the bedroom door, looking back at them one last time. "But don't worry. I'll be around. Should you ever have need." He winked. "I'll be watching."

They heard the front door open and close, neither of them moving for long, silent moments.

Liam looked down at her and Dani grinned, bemused. "Did that really just happen?"

"Yes." Liam chuckled as he dragged himself off her, leaping off the bed before lifting her into his arms again. "And it is a story we will never tell our grandchildren."

Dani tilted her head. "Where are you taking me?"

"To my shower. I've had plans for you and that shower for a while now."

She nodded somberly. "You know you're carrying me again. I think I'm getting spoiled."

Liam bit her chin and kept walking. "Get used to it, Shortbread. It looks good on you."

A moment before Liam turned on the water, Dani heard a coyote howl. A deeper-timbred howl joined in, making her eyes widen. Another one?

Not that she blamed either one of them. She felt like howling, too.

Who knew an all-night marathon of kinky sex could be such a workout? Dani couldn't help but smile as she thought about what happened last night.

She was a sexual Olympian. She'd done things and been in positions she had never even heard of. It was still a little disconcerting, the way the night had started. She had a million questions. About Stax. About whether or not she'd actually seen what she thought she'd seen. And why she and Liam had both felt so comfortable with him that they'd shared their first sexual encounter.

Maybe it was the stranger aspect. One night, no questions or repercussions. He was a buffer. An anomaly. The reason they'd behaved so out of character.

But that didn't explain the rest of the night. The shower, the stairs, the kitchen counter where they'd re-created her sexual fantasy near dawn. This time with the perfect ending.

"You must be having one hell of a dream to be smiling like that."

Speaking of sexual athletes. She opened her eyes to see Liam leaning on his hand above her. "Just thinking that I had no idea how little I knew about you."

"What?" He looked startled.

She hummed and snuggled closer. "I mean, I know about all the limbs you've broken as a child, the name of the first girl you kissed and your not-so-secret obsession with science fiction. But I had no idea you'd been hiding such a . . . big light under that bushel."

He laughed and pulled her closer. "Oh. That."

"Yes, that," she snorted. "Although I admit it would have been harder being your roommate if I'd known the truth about you."

"Dani . . . I need to tell you something."

"That sounds serious." She rolled onto her stomach and raised herself up to study him. "More secret talents I should be worried about?"

Her smile disappeared at his expression. What had made him suddenly somber? Her confidence wobbled. Was this it, then? When he told her he was leaving now that she wasn't in danger? Now when she knew with absolute certainty that she didn't want her new life if it didn't include him.

"Dani, I have to tell you the—"

There was a God and he loved her. She was so thankful for the ringing of the phone that she practically leapt from the bed to reach it. "Hello?"

"Have you forgotten our shopping trip? Kaya and I have been waiting for you for twenty long minutes."

Bailey's voice sounded far away. It might have been all the blood rushing to her head. Her racing heart. "What?"

"The last big hurrah before Casa Rincon closes? The birthday party? Ringing any bells yet?"

"Shit. I'll be there in ten minutes."

She hung up before Bailey could respond and reached for the pool towel lying at the foot of the bed. She covered herself and looked back toward Liam.

"I have to go. I have to get a present for the party tonight. I promised Bailey and Kaya . . ."

"I forgot that was tonight. Dani, maybe we could stay here and ta—"

"We can't miss it." She couldn't look at him. Where had her newfound courage gone? "We can talk later. Oh and I forgot to tell you, one of Kaya's work friends told me the little apartment near the New Age shop is opening up. It's cheap, too. Maybe you can come and walk through it with me, make sure there isn't anything wrong with it."

"Son of a bitch."

He sounded mad. She needed to get out of here long enough to think clearly. "I'm gonna throw on some clothes and scoot, but I'll see you tonight."

Maybe by then she'd be ready to hear what he had to say.

Seven

"What have you done with Dani, and can we please fool around until she gets back?"

She started at the words and turned to find Jace staring at her scantily clad body with an admiring grin.

She'd been so busy pretending not to watch the door for signs of Liam that she hadn't seen him come up. She'd barely noticed anyone—a feat in itself. Casa Rincon was packed, and so loud it should have been hard to think, but Dani hadn't noticed. She'd been lost in her own world all day.

Her reaction to Liam this morning had been childish. She knew it. She should have stayed and let him tell her whatever it was he'd wanted to. Instead she'd run away, and cowardly given him an out by telling him about that apartment.

Last night had been a revelation for her. A dream that had come true. Magical, in so many ways. But there was a part of her that still didn't believe.

This morning after she'd left she finally realized. She'd made the wrong wish. It wasn't other people she had a problem trusting. It was herself. Her judgment. Her decisions.

Her heart.

"Apparently my powers of seduction are a little off. Or that dress is cutting off your circulation. If it's the latter, I'd be more than happy to help you out of it."

She looked at Jace's puppy dog expression and tried to smile, tugging absently on the short hem. She'd let Bailey pick out her dress for her. She'd wanted to feel confident and sexy, but maybe she'd gone a bit overboard.

She wasn't sure how she'd been talked into buying this thing. At least there wasn't a neon pink zebra stripe in sight. What the sedately dark blue dress lacked in eccentricity, however, it made up for in slink. Her bathing suit hid more of her body than this. But then, Liam had seen her in much less.

Jace slid his arm around her and she whacked his shoulder. "My circulation is just fine, and I'm far too smart to fall for that sorry line." She looked around. "Did you come alone? Are Nick and Stax here?"

She wasn't sure how she'd face Stax without blushing after last night, but she was curious. She wanted to ask him about what she'd seen. And heard. Did he have a friend? Was Sedona full of coyote men? Did he know how to use his "truth serum" on Liam, so she could find out how he really felt about her?

Jace's open expression shuttered. "Tired of me already? You know Nick never comes to these things. Not a big fan of crowds, he says." He smiled. "Besides, it's a full moon. He's probably out in the desert howling."

Dani paled, studying Jace carefully. Why did he say that? Did they know about Stax? "I was just wondering. Uncle Marc is a legend around here. I thought his birthday party was mandatory."

"Nick never does anything he doesn't want to do. Why? Thinking of hooking him up with one of your friends?" Jace grimaced. "Don't. My roommate is a moody bastard, not like yours. And not at all like me, the life of the party."

He leaned his elbow on the bar beside her and attempted a casual stance as he scanned the room. "Speaking of friends, where's Kaya?"

Despite her mood, Dani couldn't quite contain her mirth. He wasn't fooling anyone. At least, anyone with eyes. Like a little boy who tugged the braids of the girl he liked and ran away, Jace teased and tormented Kaya because he liked her.

He didn't notice the female tourists who salivated over his dark good looks, sharp cheekbones and lean, muscular physique. He could have any of them, and from what she'd heard he rarely deprived himself. But it was Kaya he was chasing.

Maybe because she was the only one running away.

"Feel like getting into a fight tonight, Tonto?"

Dani saw the glimmer of excitement flash in his eyes before he turned to face Kaya, who'd come up behind him with a grinning Bailey in tow.

He held up his hand. "How 'bout we make love not war? I'll be Tonto if you play Pocahontas, beautiful."

Kaya pursed her lips. "How about you disappear and I won't tell Liam that you were staring down Dani's dress?"

Dani's hand popped up to cover her revealing cleavage and Jace sighed dramatically. "You ruin all my fun. Fine. I'll go, but not too far. I want to be in earshot when Liam sees how you've dressed his woman."

His slow, low-slung stride had all three women watching him walk away. He knew it, too.

Dani huffed. "I'm not Liam's woman." Bailey and Kaya both turned back to her and gave her a blank look. "Well, I'm not."

At least, she wasn't entirely sure she was. Especially after her graceless escape this morning. But at least she wasn't lying to herself anymore. She wanted to be.

Bailey tossed a friendly arm over Dani's shoulder. "So you keep saying, babycakes."

A loud cheer went up in the restaurant and Dani and the others looked toward the stage. Uncle Marc, the tall, bald, barrel-chested man, was grinning from ear to ear behind his bushy mustache. "Welcome to my party! Thanks to Dmitri for the food, to the chefs from the resort for making me edible." He pointed at Jace and a few of his fellow chefs, who waved at the crowd from beside their masterpiece—a milk chocolate trumpet player that looked incredibly like the man currently on stage. "And thanks to all of you. Sedona loves you, I love you and I know we're all sorry to see the Casa close. So, if you'll indulge me, I would like to invite a few of my friends up here for a final birthday jam."

The roar of approval was deafening. The three women watched as Uncle Marc pulled out his trumpet and a chaotic stream of people took to the stage.

Dani shook her head at the variety of performers. A long-haired rocker in a leather jacket and biker boots stood in front of the microphone, a man with a Civil War–era beard and a long hemp caftan played the bongos, a small, awkward-looking youth wailed on the didgeridoo and Joan Jett's older sister jammed on bass.

As much as the Red Rocks and spires and vortexes were Sedona, so were these people. All so seemingly different, but blending together seamlessly doing what they loved to do in front of an appreciative crowd.

This place was more home to her than any she'd ever known. She'd never fit in anywhere, but here that was a compliment. Here, she fit. No one questioned why she came, why she stayed, why she lived platonically with Liam . . . until last night. Okay, Bailey questioned that all the time, but not with anything more than pure curiosity.

She wouldn't be moving to Phoenix. Just as she'd finally come to understand her feelings for Liam, she knew she wanted to stay. No matter what the future brought her way, she was home. This was home. She saw Liam's broad-shouldered body coming toward her through the crowd and crossed her fingers that he wanted to stay with her. Not out of loyalty or some twisted gentleman's chivalry. But because he loved her.

Where were those falling stars when she needed them?

Liam saw her and she smiled. She couldn't help herself. She wanted to leap into his arms, apologize for this morning and demand he take her home for another slippery shower. Wanted to remind him there were still places in his friend's house that they hadn't thoroughly debauched.

It was at that moment that a movement in the doorway caught her attention. A second later, her new world came crashing down.

Sal had found her. Just like he'd promised he would.

"Dani, what is it? I can feel your panic." Kaya sounded distraught, but Dani couldn't help her. Her survival instincts had kicked in, and adrenaline was pumping so furiously she could barely make out her friend's voice.

Don't panic. Breathe.

"Don't talk to me. He might notice. Get Jace and tell him to bring a friend and go around back. I may need reinforcements."

She edged her way along the bar, slipping off her heels in case she needed to run.

She'd had nightmares like this. Ones where he waited until she was happy, until she finally felt safe, and then came for her. That was just what monsters did. But monsters could be defeated. She just had to get him away from all these people.

Liam. Oh God, Liam was between her and the door, saying hello to his friends. Panic rose up in her again. Sal still might not know about him, and maybe it would be smarter if she handled this on her own . . . but she needed him. How could she get his attention without letting Sal see?

Just then she noticed Gillian making a beeline for Liam, knocking aside tourists like a linebacker. Great.

Dani headed toward the exit, one eye on Sal circling the room, the other on Gillian, who was wrapping her arms around a surprised Liam's neck. Her heart broke a little when the redhead pressed her lips to his. Not because of jealousy. Not anymore. Because there was no more time.

She made it out the door without being seen and walked to her car, pulling the keys out of her small clutch purse, as if she were leaving. A year ago, hell a few months ago, that might have been true. The only thoughts in her head would have been *flee. Run. Escape.*

But she'd changed. And she wasn't alone anymore. She did trust Liam. And she had to trust her friends, trust *herself* to get her out of this.

The small rocks in the parking lot dug into her heels, but she didn't mind. It was nothing compared to the pain she'd already suffered through. She let it fuel her. She had more to lose than her freedom now. She wouldn't let him take it away.

She couldn't help the morbid thought that entered her mind. If everything was connected, as Kaya's grandfather claimed, if everything meant something—what was this? Sal arriving as soon as she'd made her decision to stay. As soon as she realized she loved Liam. Was this punishment for having a night of passion? For being happy for a few glorious hours?

Or her chance to face her demons?

She heard him scuffling behind her and whirled, scraping his face with the sharp edge of her keys.

Sal shrieked and grabbed his cheek. Then his face contorted in an ugly smile and he seized a handful of her hair and threw her down to the ground.

She felt the sharp tearing of skin along her thigh, and for a moment she wondered if this was what Liam would find—her body in the parking lot, her blood on the ground.

No. She wasn't going to let that happen.

"Miss me, baby?" Sal's sneering voice made her wince. More than that, it made her angry. If she could channel Stax right now, she'd change into a coyote and rip his evil throat out.

"Let me go, Sal. Now."

He tried to kick her, but she rolled away, up onto her knees, every muscle alert as he took out his knife. That same knife he'd used on her before.

Sal's laugh was a vile sound. "So brave now that you have a sugar daddy. Think I wouldn't find out about him? How you had little rich boy waiting in the wings to take you away from me with his army of lawyers and private detectives?" He sneered. "As if I wouldn't know that I was being followed, that your prince was trying to keep us apart. No one can, Danielle. I thought I'd proven that by now. But it looks like you need another reminder."

He waved the knife threateningly, making an S shape in the air. "Maybe I can give you a little present on your face to match the last one. He won't want you then."

Dani laughed at him. Knowing the danger but not caring. He was a small man compared to Liam. The smallest she'd ever known, as well as delusional. He'd built a fantasy in his head about why she'd left him, but she couldn't let him think Liam was the reason. If he was hurt because of her . . .

She saw Jace, Kaya and Bailey coming around the back of the building and knew she had to keep Sal distracted. The cavalry was coming. "Believe what you want. I didn't leave you for anybody but myself. You are a liar and a bastard, and I deserve better than you. I'm not afraid of you, Sal. You're nothing."

The rage that burned into his expression was one she knew well. One she used to fear. She was still hearing that call to run, but it had faded. She was so sick of running. It wasn't who she was anymore. She had to try and get that knife out of his hand.

"She told you to leave her *alone*."

There was a dull metallic *thwonk* and Dani gasped as Sal fell to his knees in shock, still staring at her, blood gushing out of his nose and mouth.

Liam? Oh, thank God. She hadn't seen him come outside.

He dropped the small pan he'd used as a bat on the side of Sal's face and kicked away the knife that had fallen to the ground. "You're lucky I didn't grab the cast iron, you son of a bitch."

He knocked her bleeding ex onto his back and straddled him, then punched him once. Twice. He raised his fist to hit the unconscious man again but Dani pulled herself out of her frozen state and grabbed his arm, shaking him.

"Liam, stop. You're killing him."

"That's the plan."

"He's not worth it. Please."

He must have heard the concern in her voice, because he stopped, standing up and taking her into his arms in one swift move that had her crying out in relief.

"That. Was. *Awesome!*" Bailey lowered her voice. "'You're lucky I didn't grab the cast iron.' *Awe. Some.*"

Dani chuckled a little hysterically, calming when she felt Kaya's hand on her back. She buried her face in Liam's chest and sighed. She'd slain her dragon. Okay, Liam had, but she hadn't run. She didn't have to anymore. She heard a groan from the ground and refused to shiver. Whether Sal kept coming or not, she wasn't going to let him ruin her life.

"You didn't need us after all." Kaya's tone was gentle. "Liam was in more danger from Gillian."

Jace grunted beside her. "Too bad he wasn't in more danger. I'd love to have gotten a crack at that asshole. What did you hit him with anyway?"

Liam's voice was muffled against her neck. "A fondue pot from the buffet table."

Jace laughed. "The chef's weapon of choice."

Liam shuddered and pulled back to look at Dani. He was feeling pretty shaken up. And it was more than just the run-in with Sal. It was what he'd heard.

Liar and a bastard.

She lifted her head and looked up at him. Her worried gaze tearing a hole in his heart. "What is it, Liam?"

"I'm a liar and a bastard, too."

He watched her step away from him, instantly missing the feel of her safe in his arms.

"What do you mean?"

"I was trying to tell you earlier. I've been trying to tell you for a year, but I was too afraid of losing you. Of losing this." The words came pouring out, surprising him as much as they surprised her. "Sal was right, I *am* rich. The restaurant that catered the charity when you met me was one of mine. You didn't know and I had never . . . Well, there's no excuse. What you said to him was right. You deserve better. You deserve the truth."

Dani stumbled a little, and he reached out instinctively but dropped his hands when he saw Kaya wrap a protective arm around her.

Bailey whistled. "Okay, dude, your timing is way off. It's not exactly the perfect moment for this type of revelation."

He knew it. But he couldn't lie. Not anymore. After seeing Sal hold a knife to her. After seeing it all happening in front of him. He wanted to kill Sal with his bare hands.

When she left his bed this morning, obviously not wanting to hear what he'd been trying to say, it had thrown him. He didn't want anything to sully what they'd shared. He had to tell her. No more secrets.

But she hadn't come home between shopping and the party. The only reason he'd come tonight was to finally pin her down. And now it felt like too little, too late.

"Why?" Dani sounded strangely calm. Too calm. "You know every horrible, ugly thing about me. Why would you lie about that? To me? Not just for one year but all this time. *Three years, Liam.* Why?"

Because I was afraid you'd run away from me. Afraid you'd stay for the wrong reasons. Nothing that was going through his mind would sound right, and he knew it. There was no damn excuse for what he'd done.

He must have hesitated too long. Kaya sighed. "I've been in your corner until now, Liam, and I know you meant well, but I really think this might be too much for Dani to take tonight. You can explain it to her tomorrow."

Dani pulled away from Kaya. "I don't need protecting anymore." She smiled gently to soften the blow. "But I appreciate the effort."

Jace laid a hand on Liam's shoulder. "This may not be the best time, but we should probably call the cops now. Wouldn't want this guy getting away."

Kaya made a strange sound of surprise. "I don't think we have to worry about that."

Liam turned along with the others, bracing himself to see a corpse instead of a passed out psychopath, and froze.

"What the hell?"

A coyote was stalking Sal's body, followed closely by a large, mean-looking gray timber wolf. They barely glanced at the five people standing next to the prone man, but the wolf ducked his head as though embarrassed at being seen.

"Stax."

Dani's confusing whisper wasn't enough to drag Liam's attention away from the strange sight. He looked on in disbelief as the animals moved in unison to either shoulder, closing their jaws around Sal's flesh and slowly dragging him backward.

He'd never seen anything like this. Animals this wild behaving so fearlessly in front of humans. He couldn't let this happen. No matter how he felt about Sal.

"We have to stop them. Make a loud noise and scare them away. Shoo!" Liam moved to intercept the two canines, but Jace and Kaya both held him back.

Jace's tone was sober. "I may be only half Navajo, buddy, but this is one of those moments where you just need to trust me. I don't think we want to mess around with the spirits."

"What? Those aren't spirits, Jace. They are *wild animals*. They'll eat him for dinner. It's murder if we let him die like that."

"I can't believe I'm saying this, but I agree with Jace. I don't think interfering would be the best idea, for any of us. But I have a feeling he'll only get what he deserves. No more. No less."

Liam turned to look down at Dani, stunned when she didn't say a word in disagreement. "Why has everyone suddenly gone crazy?" He turned to Kaya. "I respect your beliefs but there is a limit to—"

"Look." Dani was adamant, so Liam reluctantly obeyed.

The wolf was dragging the unconscious Sal into the brush that framed the restaurant. Into the desert. The coyote, however, had paused at the edge of the parking lot.

It was staring at Liam. The air around it started to shimmer.

"Oh my God." Liam dropped onto the graveled parking lot hard, feeling the jar of it from his tailbone to his teeth, but he couldn't react. He could barely blink.

Stax was standing there. At the edge of the parking lot, where the coyote had been only seconds before.

The dark-haired man bowed to Liam and the others respectfully, and he heard a voice in his head.

My gift for you and Dani. I told her I'd be watching if she needed me. Stax smiled. *Don't worry, we won't eat him.*

Liam grabbed his head, looking around to see if anyone else was hearing Stax talk without moving his lips.

Dani did. He could tell by her expression.

You are the only ones, my friends. This man is a spirit thief. He steals lives. He killed before he met her. He would again. When we are through with him, he will understand his crimes. It may take a hundred years. But I am Istaqa. I have all the time in the world.

With that, Stax winked at Kaya, then disappeared around the corner.

He couldn't wrap his mind around it. This same man who'd come into his house. Advised him. Who'd shared Dani's pleasure. Dani's body. Who—*what* was he?

Dani beat him to it. "Istaqa? What does that mean?"

Kaya's voice was shaken. Liam noticed Jace take a step closer to her in response. "Istaqa. The coyote spirit. He brings messages and knowledge. And occasionally . . . he delivers the guilty for judgment. I *knew* there was something about him." She turned to Jace. "Does Nick know about him? What he is?"

Jace held up his hands. "I know nothing." Kaya glared but he held firm. "What? You tell me that all the time."

Liam ran a hand through his hair. "Istaqa?" Wasn't that what Stax had said? Istaqa has all the time in the world? He'd also implied that Sal had killed someone before. If he'd killed Dani . . . Liam shuddered. A hundred years of torture was nothing compared to what *he* would have done to the bastard.

"Well, I need to get drunk. How about all of you?" Bailey sounded thoroughly shaken. Liam didn't blame her at all.

"I think that's a good plan." Jace bent down and patted Liam on the back in commiseration. "Don't try to understand this one, buddy. Believe me, it's a bitch."

Eight

Dani sat by the pool, watching the sunrise. Jace, Bailey and Kaya were all passed out inside the house, and Liam was making breakfast.

They'd talked all night long. About what they'd seen. About what Kaya knew about Istaqa. About Bailey's theories pertaining to hallucinogens in the water. About Stax and the wolf that had joined him in carrying Sal away, and why they'd all felt helpless to do anything about it.

Stax wasn't a magician, he was something far more unbelievable. He was a Native American legend that shouldn't exist. One that she'd shared a night of passion with. One who'd taken Sal somewhere he could never reach her again.

She still wasn't sure how she felt about that. But she kept hearing

Kaya's grandfather tell her the coyote spirit would protect her. And it had. It had done what judges and lawyers and all the sealed records in the world couldn't.

But it hadn't protected her completely.

Liam had lied. He had money. Family money as well as his own. Enough that he didn't have to lift a finger ever again.

She thought back over the last few years.

When she'd first met Liam, he'd been different, more guarded. But as soon as he introduced himself, they'd clicked. They talked for hours about favorite movies and food, nothing too deep. A noisy party wasn't the best place to bare your soul.

If he'd told her then, she might have been intimidated. Dani had struggled her whole life. Bussed around from one poor, distant relative or foster family to another; working to pay her way by the time she was fourteen. She would have assumed they'd have nothing in common.

And she would have been wrong.

Sal, on the other hand, had looked so good on paper. Online he'd been her perfect match. He'd told her he had a master's degree, a job as an engineer, a loving family that couldn't wait to meet her. He'd told her he loved her and wanted to treat her like a queen. But he'd lied about everything.

He was still lying the night he'd begun carving his name into her flesh, sewing it himself instead of taking her to a hospital when he'd gone too deep. "I'd do anything for you. You're mine and you always will be. My queen."

She hadn't realized until it was too late, until she was scared. His lies had almost destroyed her. And now, she was trying to come to terms with Liam's. The one person she trusted the most.

But she was still here.

A shuffling noise brought her gaze up to find Kaya's grandfather standing by the fence gate.

"Will?"

He shushed her and gestured her over, speaking in low tones when she finally stood beside him. "It's time for me to give you your gift. Have you been crying?"

Her hand came up to touch her cheek. "A little. But I'm okay."

Kaya's grandfather sighed. "I know it must have been hard for you, living most of your life surrounded by two-hearts. But you've done well, *Bahana*."

"Two-hearts?"

"Two-hearts think with their head *instead* of their heart. They analyze and plan and live life for themselves. Two-hearts never do for others without expectation, never give up comfort to give it to another . . . never hear the coyote's howl and recognize its song."

Dani peered at him. Coyote? "That reminds me—have you ever met a guy named Stax, Will?"

He smiled, his eyes disappearing again. "I'm an old man. I don't get out much. Besides, I've been too busy finishing your *tihu*." He reached into the hide pouch and pulled out the wooden figurine she had watched him create.

"It's beautiful." He was a true artisan. She'd seen so many of these in the shops around town, but the fact that it had been created for her made it special. "Which kachina is this?"

His voice held a reverent tone. "The White Bear Kachina. He is a powerful warrior and gives us strength, but he is also a healer, drawn to other healers, like you."

Dani bit her lip, suddenly feeling like she might cry again. "Thank you. But I still don't think I'm that much of a warrior."

He made a noise of impatience. "There you go, thinking with your head instead of your heart. Trying to define bravery and strength. Truth and lies. Feel the truth in your warrior heart. Let Hon, the bear, guide you."

She looked down at the doll and she could have sworn it heated in her hands. Think with her heart? Was that what she'd been doing? Why she hadn't taken Kaya's way out last night? Hadn't run away when the other shoe dropped with a giant thud?

It was different. She was different. Sal lied to get what he wanted. Liam did what he did to keep her safe, to keep her from being alone. Still a lie, but after their talk she could see some of the reasoning behind it.

Images filled her mind as she held the kachina. Liam taking care of her when she was sick, making her laugh when she took things too seriously . . . fixing her car . . . protecting her from a spider in her shower. Invisible or not.

His actions weren't that of a man who was playing an angle. They were just kind. Good. Loving. Liam.

He loved her. Even if he hadn't told her she knew it with a certainty that had her rocking back on her heels. She'd seen it in his eyes last night, felt it in every kiss, every touch.

And she loved him, too. Had she always? He'd fallen off that pedestal she'd placed him on, but maybe that was a good thing. No one could live up to that kind of standard. Set up that high, eventually you have to fall.

She'd found her path. Was this her wish being granted? Maybe it was. She trusted herself. Her heart wasn't wrong; it knew what it wanted.

Liam walked out into the backyard, his heart jumping into his throat when he didn't see Dani where he'd left her.

Hell, he knew he was lucky she'd stayed at all after what he'd put her through. But he wasn't taking it for granted. He'd been fighting for her. For them. Telling her everything. She deserved that from him.

The idea of going back to the life he'd known before, the life that didn't include her, tied him up in knots. He didn't want that life.

Bastard that he was, he didn't want to be noble this time. To be the man who stepped aside. Regardless of what he'd done, he would earn her trust back. What they'd shared this past year, what he felt for her, was too strong not to fight for.

"Looking for me?"

Liam narrowed his gaze as she appeared beside him, holding something in her hand. She was smiling. Why was she smiling?

"I wasn't sure where you'd gone." God, she was beautiful when she smiled. He hadn't been sure he'd see that again anytime soon.

The relief made it impossible not to tell her how he felt. "I love you, Dani."

The smile on her full lips widened. "I know."

"You know?"

She walked past him to the table. "Breakfast. I'm starving." She set the strange doll in the center of the patio table and sat.

He joined her. "I also brought some sunscreen." He pulled out a green bottle, squeezed out a dollop of gel and gently slathered it on her nose. "You're supposed to wear sunscreen. We live in the desert, you know."

She started to laugh. A deep, carefree laugh so full of joy it staggered him. Had he driven her insane? "Dani?"

She wiped happy tears from her eyes. "Yes, Cookie?"

"Care to let me in on the joke? What happened between me going in to cook breakfast and now?"

"Don't worry, I'm still mad at you." Her eyes were sparkling. "And you're going to promise me that you will never lie to me again, not even for a surprise party. *And* that you will tell the truth from now on . . . to everyone."

"I promise. Dani. And if you still want to move into that apartment—"

"I love you, too."

"What?"

She placed her hand on his chest, over his heart. "I love you. Not because of what you have, but because of who you are. My best friend. My lover. My heart."

He was shaken. "Are you sure?" For an instant he was terrified she was stringing him along, paying him back for all his half truths and omissions. But this was Dani. He knew her. She wouldn't lie.

She didn't answer him, taking the bottle out of his hand and standing up.

"Where are you going?"

Her smile was mischievous. Sensual. "I'm not hungry anymore. I think I want to take a nap. Unfortunately, Bailey is in my bed." She took his hand and he found himself walking with her toward the house. "This is a lot to take in. You look like you need to lie down, too. You're always taking care of me, I think it's time I took care of you."

If he was dreaming, he never wanted to wake up. "I am a little achy."

She pursed her lips and made a cooing sound, pulling him through the kitchen and down the hall to his bedroom. "Oh, poor Cookie. Let me kiss it and make it better."

"I had a fantasy that started just like this."

She laughed and pulled him into the bedroom, shutting the door behind them. "If you say Anna Paquin was in it I might bop you."

He wrapped his arms around her and fell back with her onto the bed. "Only you, Dani. Only you."

He kissed her, so overwhelmed that he almost didn't hear the coyote's howl in the distance.

He lifted his lips from hers. "Dani, do you think Stax—"

She shook her head, a knowing sparkle in her dark blue eyes. "Stax has eternity. He can wait. I can't."

Liam let her tug his head down, more than happy to oblige. It could wait. *This* was well overdue.

Sinful Sensations

One

Envy was not an attractive emotion. Bailey had gone through most of her life without feeling it. But there were times, like today for example, when she really wished she could trade places with some-body else. Madonna, for example. The Material Girl would never put up with this kind of bull. Never start her day at five thirty laboring under a clogged bathroom sink or helping an old man find his teeth so he could partake in the complimentary muffins she had brought to the inn each morning from the local bakery.

She'd also never end up dangling from the attic door at ten o'clock at night, in nothing but her nightshirt and Superman undies, with no one to save her when the ladder broke off and dropped to the floor.

Bailey wasn't a screamer. It wasn't her style to cry for help and wait to be saved. Besides, who would come? She only had three guests currently residing at the inn: one couple in their late seventies and one very unusual woman from Minnesota, who'd informed Bailey that aliens from Sirius had told her to come to Sedona and await further instructions.

Then again, after the last few weeks, who was she to say aliens were unusual? She'd participated in a bizarre girls' night recently. What started as a few simple wishes had ended up including a psycho with a switchblade and a coyote that turned into a man.

After that aliens were a piece of cake.

Now if only she could work up the nerve to drop from this attic. It was just, well, really *friggin* high.

"This wasn't exactly the welcome I was expecting."

Great. Bailey banged her forehead on the edge of the attic door, feeling the rough wood scrape her head as she tried to see who stood beneath her. It wasn't the voice of a seventy-year-old man.

With her luck it would be Ewan McGregor. After all, *Dani's* wish had come true with a vengeance. Why shouldn't hers? Though she'd wanted to be dressed better for the momentous occasion. "Excuse my manners. Welcome to the Enchanted Inn, would you mind helping me down?"

She heard a shout of surprised male laughter and wiggled her feet expectantly. But he didn't come closer.

"Hello?"

"I don't know. You have to admit this isn't an everyday situation."

Bailey muttered beneath her breath. "For you maybe."

"What was that?"

She raised her voice. "A gentleman wouldn't hesitate like this."

There was a smile of satisfaction in his voice. "Then you already know something about me. A gentleman also wouldn't comment on your choice of underwear. Are superheroes a fetish of yours? Did you get yourself in this position because you thought you could fly? Are you hoarding any kryptonite I should know about?"

She wanted to make a smart-mouthed rejoinder, but she was busy staring something down. It had eight legs and pincers. It was the size of a small dog.

There was something familiar about this spider. The designs on its back, like a maze, its size . . . *No.* No it couldn't be. There was no way this could be Dani's disappearing spider, the one Kaya said was a sign. "I don't think so, buddy."

"Did you say something?"

The man may not have heard her, but the spider certainly did. It turned in her direction. She really didn't like the look in its eyes. And then, without any warning, it charged.

She didn't know spiders did that.

Now Bailey wasn't one of those silly, helpless girls. She didn't squeal or giggle. Sure she liked to shop and pink was her favorite color, but she also liked horror flicks, the more gore the better.

But what woman, or man for that matter, could stay calm and collected when a giant spider was making a kamikaze-like run at their face?

"Ack!"

Bailey lifted her hands to protect herself and fell. She braced herself for the hard floor, but strong arms caught her before she hit, knocking the breath out of her lungs.

"*Oomph.* I gotcha."

She looked up into quite possibly the handsomest face she'd ever seen in her life—*sorry, Ewan*—and frowned. "Damn spider."

If that was Kaya's Spider Grandmother, she wanted to have a private word. Now? Now with bits of dust and possibly insulation in her hair? *This* is when last month's cover of *GQ* shows up to play white knight?

"Does management always hang around half naked at this inn? If so, I think you're missing a key marketing demographic by not advertising it as a perk."

"Then the white knight opened his mouth, forcing the princess to beat him senseless, and she lived happily ever after without him. The end." Bailey sighed in mock disappointment, trying to wriggle out of his arms with a tiny amount of grace intact.

GQ just grinned, as if enjoying her irritation. "Aren't you at least going to thank me for saving you before you insult me?"

She raised one eyebrow. "Oh, I think you've been thanked enough. Or is that someone *else's* hand squeezing my ass?"

He lowered her slowly to the ground, that ridiculously irresistible smile still in place, his gray eyes sparkling. "Point taken."

Man oh man was he attractive. In a clean-cut, dimpled-chin outdoor-living kind of way. Rugged chic. His white buttoned-down shirt felt expensive. Hell, everything about him, from the perfect chestnut waves on his head to his obviously well loved cowboy boots screamed, "If I'm fishing, I'll be fishing on a yacht." A guy like this usually made a beeline to the fancy resort up the hill for a conference. A guy like this didn't come to her broken down, if centrally located, little inn.

And that, of course, made her suspicious.

She backed out of his arms and tugged her extra large T-shirt down over her underwear. Despite her attire, she made sure her expression was all business. "Thank you for catching me. May I help you, sir?"

His lips lost their curve. "Ah, that. Back to business. Okay then, Ms. Wagner. I'm here to talk to you about the recent acquisition of this property. Why don't I wait for you in your office while you change?"

She knew it. One of Cameron Locke's henchmen assistants no doubt. Too bad. She'd really wanted to lick his dimple. "My office?"

Like she actually had an office. Bailey shook her head and crooked her finger. "Come with me."

Bailey reached her bedroom door, still ajar from her mad dash to the attic. She'd gotten two phone calls from her guests, and she'd heard the ominous scraping sounds herself, so she'd gone to investigate. The weird thing was, it had stopped at the same moment the ladder fell out from beneath her.

Grabbing a pair of jeans from the top of her dresser, she started to put them on.

"Shouldn't you close the door?"

Bailey snorted. "You've seen me in my underwear, but watching me put my jeans *on* is upsetting you?" She pulled up her zipper then placed her hands on her hips, lifting her chin defensively. "Since these aren't the usual hours for a business meeting, and I'm not usually hanging from the attic in my unmentionables, I say we embrace the humor of the situation, and hope that you and your boss forgive me my lack of late-night decorum."

"You mean *our* boss." He'd narrowed his gaze on her in a way that made her nervous.

She shrugged inwardly. In for a penny . . . "For the moment. No disrespect intended, but from what I've heard Mr. Locke has a tendency to lose interest in a property not long after he acquires it. But I'm happy for Mr. Pikeson at least. He's had this place on the market for a few years now."

GQ definitely wasn't smiling anymore. "No disrespect taken. And I know. I also know a B. Wagner was trying to come up with the funding to purchase the Enchanted Inn herself but couldn't raise enough capital."

Bailey winced. She should have known they'd do their homework. That's what she got for trying to push her five-year plan ahead of schedule. Mr. Pikeson liked her well enough but not enough to go down on his asking price. Maybe Cameron Locke would. When he got tired of the inn, that is. Lord knew he had enough money to be generous. She'd read all of Pikeson's paperwork on the sale.

He was staring at her in a way that made her antsy. Studying her. She crossed her arms. "Why *are* you here so late, Mr. . . . ?"

He smirked. "Mr. Locke believes the best way to get a feel for a property is to check in on it when it's least expected. *Mr. Locke* thinks it's the only way to make a truly honest appraisal and begin to form a plan of action as to how to improve the property's value."

Oh shit. Bailey closed her eyes for one long breath. She should have known. She was so going to be fired. "Does Mr. Locke also like to talk about himself in the third person?"

She glanced at him through her lashes and saw him lean against her door frame with a confident expression. "They told me you were smart." He reached down into his briefcase and pulled out a file.

"And efficient. I hear my accommodations are ready and all the arrangements I requested for my associates have been made."

"Yes, sir." She tried. Hard. But she couldn't keep all the sarcasm out of her tone.

He noticed, and his storm-colored gaze darkened. "But they didn't tell me everything." He unbent and moved in closer, into her small bedroom. Crowding her. "They didn't tell me that B. Wagner was so young." He looked at her hair with a slightly bemused expression. "That she was so . . . colorful." He snared her gaze again. "That she had an independent streak and a total lack of respect for authority."

Her heart was pounding. He smelled edible. It was making it hard to concentrate. She had spent too long with her battery-operated boyfriends. If only the pickings in this town didn't consist of irritating tourists and dirty road dogs—the name the natives gave to the dreadlocked, barefoot young men and women who descended on the town like a flock of singing, hippie birds every summer—maybe she wouldn't be so susceptible.

If she was reacting like this to a man like Cameron Locke, as he was preparing to let her go, maybe she should just give one of the others a chance. After they showered, of course. She'd certainly have the time for it now, since she was out of a job.

"I understand. I'll have my things out by morning."

He leaned back with a stunned expression. "You're not fired."

Now it was her turn to look surprised. "I'm not?"

"Of course not." Poor GQ. He looked so frustrated that Bailey almost wanted to smile. Almost.

"You were certainly acting like you were going to fire me." Why couldn't she stop? Why was the little devil in her subconscious demanding she egg him on?

It was that dimple.

"I was not."

She counted on her fingers. "You criticized my behavior, my clothing, you insinuated that you weren't info—"

His hand shot out, fingers wrapping around hers to stop her. "Are you *trying* to get fired? If I dismissed you for wearing Underoos to bed you could sue me for harassment. As to your spirit, well, I'm not the kind of boss who is easily intimidated. I like being challenged. In fact, a little fire is a prerequisite." His eyes went dark again. "Boring and safe don't interest me. Honesty does."

"Okay then."

"All right."

She licked her lower lip. "Can I have my fingers back, Mr. Locke?"

He dropped them like they were poisonous. "Damn. Of course. But don't call me Mr. Locke. My grandfather is Mr. Locke, I'm Cam. And I hope you'll allow me to call you Bailey."

He'd put on that charming expression again, and Bailey had a sneaking suspicion that she was going to have trouble with him. More than new owner/old manager trouble.

More like hot man/sex-starved woman trouble.

She nodded and he rubbed his hands together.

"I should be getting up the hill, I need to welcome all the new arrivals. But I've seen enough for tonight to know I've made the right purchase. This place is a definite challenge. Ragged around the edges, but it has potential."

He turned, grabbing his briefcase and heading down the hall before she could lambaste him for calling her inn ragged. Of course it was; no owner had been willing to shell out the money for improvements. But Bailey had kept it up as well as she could.

She stepped into the hall and heard it. A loud grating sound, like someone dragging a metal pipe along the attic floor. Or the roof tearing off.

Cameron Locke turned and looked up at the ceiling. "So that's why you were up there."

She made a face. It kind of took the wind out of your ego sails when the place you'd been keeping up was falling apart in front of the owner. "That's why."

"Call the roofer in the morning. I'll take care of it."

He closed the door and Bailey slumped her shoulders in relief. She wasn't fired, and unlike old man Pikeson, he was actually going to pay to have something fixed.

Too bad he wouldn't do it himself. Shirtless.

"I take it from your expression that you're happy with your latest purchase?"

Cam studied the nighttime view from his window. The limousine was more flamboyant than he liked, but they'd arrived too late to pick up the jeep from the salesman in Cottonwood. Purchasing a car from a local dealership was one of his traditions. His own way of welcoming himself to the neighborhood, helping the community.

Not driving gave him more time to think about Bailey Wagner. Not at all what he'd thought she'd be. Pikeson had done her a real injustice. "Stout, sturdy and stubborn as a bulldog" weren't the words Cam would use to describe her.

Stubborn, yes. Decidedly stubborn. But if she was built like anything, it was a sexy, old-world tavern wench. Just imagining her in that costume had him shifting in his seat uncomfortably. Enough breast to fill his hands, and an ass . . . He could write an epic poem about her ass.

And all the ways he wanted to defile it.

Davide tapped on the glass with his fingers. "Now I'm curious. Before you left this car you wouldn't stop talking. What happened in there?"

Cam shifted again, a little restlessly against the leather. "A slight deviation from our original plans."

"Since when is that a new thing?" Davide sighed, relaxing back into his seat across from Cam. "What are we doing now? Are we still going to fix it up before we turn it over? Did you want to take Aaron's idea of a nightclub out for another spin? Or do we pick door number three, chuck the plan entirely and get an earlier plane to Switzerland?"

This was what working with friends got you. Backtalk. But that's why he'd hired Davide. He kept Cameron honest. Not to mention, he shared enough of his unusual proclivities to understand Cameron's need for privacy.

It was the backtalk that drew him to Ms. Wagner. Along with her ass. She hadn't been the tiniest bit intimidated by him. Not even when she thought he was about to fire her.

"I need more research on Bailey Wagner."

Davide chuckled. "Oh. That kind of deviation. I see."

Cam frowned. "What is that supposed to mean? I'm merely taking an active interest in my new employee. It's not a crime, is it?"

"Not yet. Not until we have to pay an enormous sum of money to keep them quiet when you lose interest."

Davide's words made him grit his teeth. "You say that like it's a regular occurrence."

His friend shrugged. "Once should have been enough for you to stick to the rules. Far be it for me to tell you what to do, Cam. But you do pay me to watch your back."

Cam was fuming, staring his friend down in stony silence until Davide held up his hands. "I'm sorry. It had to be said. Now that I have . . . what's she like? She must have made a hell of an impression to get you in this state."

Cam looked down at his cupped hands, still tingling from touching her, and gave his head a subtle shake. He told Davide all about her, from her spiky pink-tipped blonde hair to her sassy, kissable mouth.

By the time they arrived at the rambling house Bailey had rented for them, Davide was laughing so hard tears were pouring down his cheeks.

"*Superman?* Oh, that settles it. I have *got* to see this woman for myself."

Cameron smiled. As long as Davide remembered who saw her first.

Two

"Have I gotten any missives?"

Bailey sat back on her heels in the garden, squinting up at the frail-looking woman in her fifties who stood in the open door. "Missives? Ms. Littleton, I don't think anyone has gotten a *missive* since the Brontë sisters were alive. If you get any *messages*, I promise I'll tell you right away." She gestured toward the bright, blue-skied day. "You should go for a walk, or go on a vortex tour. If those alien guys are anywhere, it'd be somewhere around those things."

Ms. Littleton's eyes sparkled. "Do you think?"

Bailey nodded. "Absolutely. In any case, you can't come all this way and not enjoy the sunshine. Or that view."

The woman clutched her purse closer to her body and started down the steps. "You're probably right. I'll be back soon though."

Bailey smiled. Hopefully she'd accidentally have a little fun while she was gone. The woman hadn't left the inn in days.

And it *was* beautiful here. Growing up twenty-five minutes away from Sedona, in Cottonwood, Bailey had thought she would have gotten her fill of the desert long ago.

Before her mother decided to move on to greener pastures, she used to argue that this wasn't a dead land. Northern Arizona was an explosion of life, vibrant and flowering all around them. That if Mother Earth herself could choose a place to call home, this would be it.

Bailey would just sigh, tell her mother to go back to the sixties and slip her headphones back on, though she secretly agreed with the sentiment.

Sedona gave Bailey the best of both worlds. Raw and harsh, majestic and stunning nature—and some of the best people-watching on the planet. What else could you expect from a town of runaways? Or running-tos. From New Age mystics to millionaire tourists, all of them looking for their own piece of the magic.

Her friend Dani had been a runaway. Bailey had known it from the moment she saw her. When Dani had first moved into town, she'd been anxious, overly shy. Jumpy.

And now Bailey knew why.

But she and Kaya had been running, too, each in their own way, from their pasts for years. Maybe that's why they were all drawn to each other.

Enough of that! She gave herself a little mental smack. Maudlin was not the word for today. People-watching on the other hand . . .

Bailey tipped back her hat and glanced up at the roof, where the men had been productively pounding all morning long.

There were three of them, all shirtless, but she was only interested in one particular— Wait, where was he? Mr. Buffly Studhammer. It was the nickname she'd secretly given to the roofer with the fabulously chiseled abs and exotic features.

Where had he gone?

"This water for us?"

The subtly accented voice behind her made her more than aware of her kneeling position, and what she was wearing.

She'd been feeling particularly feisty this morning, probably because she'd faced down the intimidating Cameron Locke the night before. So she decided to wear her saucy gardening gear.

She had her pink boots on, a thin white tank top and her cowboy hat. She looked over her shoulder to confirm the direction of his stare.

Yep. They were glued to her bedazzled Daisy Duke jean shorts.

"Yes."

He swallowed, his eyes blinking furiously as he struggled to meet her gaze. "Huh?"

"Yes, the water is for you. For the men. For anyone really." Smooth.

Buffly Studhammer grinned endearingly. *"Grazie."*

Oh heaven help her, he was Italian.

He bent down to open the cooler and Bailey sighed. Brown skin shimmering with sweat, the sun reflecting off his flexing muscles. Midnight hair curling damply along his neck, framing his perfect Roman nose and cheekbones sharp enough to carve a T-bone. It was enough to give a girl the vapors.

She bit her cheek. Vapors? She'd been talking to Ms. Littleton too much. The point was, he was a feast of eye candy and she was definitely feasting.

He took several deep gulps of water, allowing a little to escape and splash along his corded neck and chest.

Bailey moaned, then covered it up with a ragged chuckle. "That's enough of that. The owner isn't paying you to do an Evian commercial." The poor roofer started choking, nearly dropping the water in the process. And Bailey could breathe again. Mission accomplished. "Have you been able to find out where that noise was coming from?"

He shook his head, looking at her sideways, as though he wasn't quite sure what to make of her. "There's enough wrong with the roof to keep us busy for days. But we didn't see anything that could have made the sounds in the attic you were describing. You said you looked around up there the other night?"

As much as she could, until the ladder calamity. She pushed herself to her feet and wiped off her knees. "Yes. But I'll go check again. I wouldn't want the guests suffering another sleepless night if it's something I can fix."

She knew there was another ladder in the small storage shed. She'd just use that. Bailey began to walk around the corner of the inn, surprised when Buffly followed.

"Where are you going?"

His grin was disarming. "With you. I can help. I'm Davide."

Who was she to argue with a helpful man? Especially when he looked like that. But she was going to have to stop calling him Buffly now. Too bad. It was one of her better nicknames. "Thanks. I'm Bailey."

"I know."

She opened the shed and he walked inside before she could, his back muscles flexing as he reached for the ladder. Bailey's jaw dropped. Man, he was pretty.

He turned and caught her in the act, a knowing twinkle in his dark gaze. "See anything you like?"

"Are you kidding?" Lord, she had a big mouth. But really, what were the odds? Two men in two days who were absolutely doable. Maybe it was more than coincidence. It was enough to make a girl start wishing on every star in sight.

He set the ladder down and walked over to her. The way he was looking at her had her reaching behind her for the solid weight of the door, anything to keep herself from reaching out to touch those biceps. "What about the attic?"

Davide placed one hand against the door over her shoulder, caging her in. Was he going to kiss her?

He studied her lips. "What attic?"

"The one you're going to check while I talk to Bailey. Unless you've decided you're not working today."

The sexy roofer sent her a regretful glance and stepped away, turning to face Cameron Locke. Well, hell.

"Sure thing, Cam."

Bailey's spine straightened. Cam? They knew each other? Worked with each other?

Of course they did.

When Davide disappeared, ladder over his shoulder, Bailey began methodically removing her zebra-striped gardening gloves, the ones she'd forgotten to take off. Anything not to look at the handsome Mr. Locke. "So I should just assume any attractive men who show up on my doorstep work for you, I suppose."

Cameron, who'd been studying her outfit with sparkling eyes, frowned. "I guess you *would* think he was attractive." He crossed his arms impatiently, glancing toward the door Davide had disappeared through and mumbled, "In an obvious, obnoxious sort of way."

Bailey smiled. "What can I do for you, Mr. Locke?"

He didn't answer her question; instead he strode closer and gripped her hands in his. The gloves were well worn, and they weren't much of a deterrent from calluses and blisters.

He studied the red marks at the base of her thumbs. "Couldn't you wait for the gardener?"

She snorted. It just came out. "First I have my own office, now a gardener. You're not used to this small an operation are you?"

His frown deepened, drawing her attention to that darn dimple again. "I know you don't do everything yourself. You've hired out several times in this past year alone."

Bailey tugged until he released her hands, and turned to head in out of the sun. "Can we have this conversation inside?"

She felt him following her, felt him watching her like it was a physical caress. The spying roofer was perfection, a Roman godling that she probably would have enjoyed kissing, but there was something about Cameron Locke that really made her . . . restless.

She slid behind the front counter before she turned to face him again. "I have hired out. Anna Morningstar started a maid service, and when I have particularly obnoxious guests, I hire her to help me clean up after them. Otherwise a six-bedroom inn doesn't need a full-time cleaning staff. Oh, and there's Cyndy, the woman who watches over the front desk on my days off."

Bailey's fingers were tapping out a rhythm on the counter. A nervous habit, she knew, but she couldn't stop. He would want to know about the strange notations in the ledger, where money disappeared without proper billing. She might as well get it out in the open.

"I've also paid a few people under the table. A musician who needed the money to fix his truck worked on the shed when a storm knocked down a wall. A woman in a difficult situation painted two of the bedrooms for some extra pocket change." An image of Dani flashed in her mind, and she bit her lip. After Dani had confided in her a few months ago about the need to hide from her ex-boyfriend, Bailey had given her friend the job.

She wondered if someone like him would understand. "It's a small town, Mr. Locke. And an unusual one. People up the hill where you're staying are millionaires. Comfortable. People who live in town or in the communities around Sedona depend on the tourist trade and sometimes each other to get by." She shrugged. "For the most part I do everything myself, and other than room and board, I don't get anything extra for that. It all comes out even at the end of the year."

Why was she telling him all this? He was the enemy. The owner. Her big mouth was the bane of her existence. She needed to learn serenity. The kind Kaya had. She needed to learn when to shut up.

Cameron had his elbow on the desk, chin in his hand while he listened to her. His expression was hard to describe. Was he angry? Would he fire her *now*?

She heard a crash down the hall and they both took off at a run.

The muscular roofer was on his ass, with one of her older male guests, Mr. Olyphant, looking down at him. "Quite a fall you took, boy. Guess you heard it, too, huh?"

Cameron and Bailey both spoke at once.

"Davide, what the hell?"

"Mr. Olyphant, I thought your wife told me you were going shopping today."

The old man's face wrinkled as he made a sour expression. "*Mrs.* Olyphant goes shopping. Her husband takes naps. I was lying in my bed, and I meant to thank you, Miss Bailey, for the comfortable neck pillow you got me, when I heard it. I'd just gotten to the door when this man fell. Is there a hole in the roof?"

Bailey shook her head and patted the older gentleman's arm. "Not yet." She watched Cameron helping a rattled-looking Davide to his feet. "You okay, guy?"

Davide shook his head as though clearing it. "I'm not sure. I pulled myself up to take a look around, didn't find anything up there but some old trunks, knickknacks, things you'd find in any attic. But then I could have sworn I heard—"

"Children's laughter. I know cause I heard it, too. Eerie sound, all tinny and off-putting." Mr. Olyphant raised his bushy eyebrows. "Course that could just be my hearing aid acting up again."

Bailey held her tongue as she eyed the old man. Eerie children's laughter? "Mr. Olyphant, I'm sure there's a logical explanation."

"No." Davide stretched, rubbing his tailbone, distracting her with that flexing muscle trick again. "He's right, Cam. I heard it, too, like it was right behind me. I turned and fell and then, well, that's it."

Bailey came over to inspect him, turning him around to look at his back. She ran her hands down his arms methodically, checking for broken bones. "Any numbness? Any sharp pains?"

Davide groaned and her hands froze. Had she hurt him? She looked over his shoulder at Cameron, who was glaring at Davide warningly.

"He's fine, Bailey. All those muscles broke his fall."

They all stood in the hall for a long, uncomfortable moment of silence, before Mr. Olyphant coughed. "I don't hear it anymore. Think I'll go back to my nap before the missus decides where we're going to dinner tonight. That woman is a dynamo."

Davide stepped away from Bailey and nodded gratefully. "*Grazie* again, Bailey Wagner. I think the best thing for me right now is a hot shower." He glanced at Cameron. "With your permission . . . *boss.*"

Bailey smirked at the emphasis and Cameron's irritated reaction.

After he left, Cameron bent his head until their gazes were even. "I need to talk to you. In *your office.*" He gripped her elbow and walked her to her bedroom.

Bailey's heart was pounding, but she had no idea why. This man was totally throwing her off. She had no equilibrium in his presence. She was never sure what to expect from him. Less than twenty-four hours since she'd met him and he was already driving her crazy.

He opened her door and guided her inside, closing it with a decisive click behind him.

Bailey swallowed. "I'm sorry Buffly, um, I mean Davide, fell from the attic. I'll check it out myse—"

"No."

"No?"

Cameron lowered his lashes, shielding his eyes. "No, you will not check it out yourself. Not without me anyway. But that's not what I wanted to talk to you about. I want you to make a list of everything you need to have done. And I want it in my hands tonight. We'll talk about your Buffly comment later." He stepped away from the door and lifted his hand to take off her cowboy hat, revealing her mussed multicolored hair.

"I'm having a party this evening for associates, friends and a few locals. A private party, where people who enjoy *indulging* feel comfortable enough to do so. You'll bring the list and stay to enjoy yourself if you like. That Cyndy person you were telling me about can watch the inn."

"Indulging?"

He smiled, his eyes going dark and smoky, making her shiver. He noticed her body's reaction. "I don't think I have to spell it out. Not for someone as smart as you. And I don't think I'm wrong that this sort of get-together might interest you. Am I?"

"No comment."

Bailey reached for the hat but he tossed it on the bed. Spoiled jerk. That's what he was. There were so many ways that invitation was inappropriate and wrong she didn't know where to start. But still . . . she had to admit it had a certain appeal. The party, not the company.

All sorts of decadent images raced through her mind, and Bailey's body heated. Unfair. This was so unfair. She'd gone without for so long and here he was, throwing sex parties his second night in town. And that was what he was doing. There was no mistaking the implication in his words.

She had to resist. "I don't have to go to the party to tell you what I need, Mr. Locke. I need to fix the ladder for the attic, the heater, obviously the roof needs more repair and—"

He shook his head, his smile sensual, knowing. "What you need, Ms. Wagner, is a night off. And a spanking. You definitely need one of those."

She felt her mouth open in shock. "Did you actually just say that?"

He laughed softly. "You'll come tonight. It's not in either of us to resist a challenge." He studied her outfit. "You don't even have to change. You'll fit right in."

She'd show him who needed a spanking. Before she could find a sharp enough reply, he was gone.

What just happened? One minute they were dealing with roofs and ghosts, the next this playboy, this . . . this stranger—because really, what did she actually know about him?—dared her to come to an orgy. Or whatever the heck he had planned.

A spanking. Her bra-burning mother would have a heart attack, especially if she knew how the idea fascinated Bailey. That alone made it more tempting. Of course there was no man with big enough *cojones* to actually try it. Intimidation through mockery and derision was Bailey's special gift. One that usually made the thickest-skinned man back down. But still, the idea was titillating.

Not a good sign.

Bailey set her plate of food down and leaned back on the couch, waiting patiently for her friends to stop laughing.

Dani was clutching her stomach, curled into a ball and leaning against Kaya. Obviously infectious, Dani's hysterics had affected Kaya in a strange way. The usually quiet Hopi beauty was laughing, too. Loudly. Unrestrained.

Sure they were laughing at her, but it was all a part of her plan. "Yuk it up, ladies. At least Liam still respects me."

Bailey looked up at Liam to find him biting his lips, cheeks flushed and blue eyes filling with laughter as he handed her a slice of chocolate cheesecake. Her favorite.

She sighed. "You, too, huh? Well, at least you give me food."

"We're sorry, Bailey." Kaya took a few deep breaths, trying to regain control. "Just the way you tell the story . . . it's obviously been a busy few days for you."

They didn't know the half of it. She'd left out a few minor details. The glistening, bare-chested Davide. The fact that she had almost decided to go to Cameron Locke's smutty soiree, and changed her mind a dozen times in the last few hours.

She'd come to have dinner with her friends, hoping they would be a calming influence. Hoping they would remind her of all the reasons she shouldn't do something she would regret later. That Kaya would know something was up and talk her out of it.

She didn't have to wait long.

"So, this Locke fellow." Kaya tapped her fork against her chin. "Is he good-looking?"

Bailey swallowed the small bite of rich dessert in her mouth. "Ridiculously."

"Rich?" Liam interjected.

"Makes your family look like paupers."

Dani's dark blue eyes widened. "Really? So rich *and* good-looking. Is he single?"

"Decidedly." At least, she thought so. With her luck she'd arrive ready to end her drought, only to find out Cameron and Davide were together. As in a couple. It wouldn't be the first time she'd been in *that* situation.

Liam was sitting in the comfortable leather recliner near Dani, his hand absently sifting through her hair. "Is he a jackass? Because you know that I have mad skills with cooking utensils." He made a swiping motion that reminded her of the culinary Kung Fu he'd displayed the night he'd protected Dani from her attacker.

Dani leaned her head on Liam's knee at his words and Bailey smiled. This was how it should be. She'd been watching Liam watch Dani for so long now, it was strange seeing them together. Strange but right. She still wasn't sure how he'd gotten up the nerve to tell her how he felt. How Dani had figured out that she was best friends with the best catch in town. But now, seeing the two of them so happy, it didn't matter.

"Someone's getting misty-eyed."

The smile in Kaya's voice had Bailey rolling her eyes. "As if. I was just thinking about our wishes. Maybe we should tell Liam about the two Ewans clause."

Dani quickly glanced up at Liam, then focused on Bailey, a dark, embarrassed blush painting her cheeks. "Were we not supposed to tell Liam?"

Liam, his own cheeks slightly ruddy, ducked his head. "I already know about that, and believe me, it came true."

Kaya was the only one confused. "What are you talking about?"

Bailey was in shock. He was talking about a threesome? With Dani? "Who? Who was it?"

She didn't think Dani's face could get any redder. "Stax."

"Coyote boy?" Bailey was the one laughing now. "This is priceless. Our innocent Dani is the first to get the entirety of her wish granted. And with a mythical figure no less. Talk about overachieving. I really should have wished for a winning lottery ticket."

Kaya's shocked expression told Bailey she'd finally joined the party. "You had a . . ." She lowered her voice as she turned to Dani and Liam. "A threesome with an Istaqa? The coyote spirit?"

Liam nodded soberly. "It happened the night before we saw him . . . you know . . . change. I didn't know at the time he could do that."

"I did."

Bailey knew her jaw had dropped at Dani's words. She'd known? And she'd done it anyway? Holy shit. Bailey had to admit Stax was magnetic, but she hadn't thought Dani had it in her. She knew her friend was strong, but she had no idea she would be so bold. That she would take such a kinky leap.

It helped clarify her own dilemma. If Dani, of all people, could do it, why not her? Why *couldn't* she go to an orgy? Be spanked? Maybe rock that handsome Italian's world or show Cameron Locke that she was not the easily intimidated, small-town innkeeper he thought she was.

Bailey stood and fluffed her little black dress. Or her version of a little black dress. The pink taffeta underskirt and crisscross back made it unique.

No one had asked why she'd dressed up to come over to Dani and

Liam's for dinner. Maybe her shocking fashion style was growing on them. If so, she might have to revisit her wardrobe. But right now, she had more important fish to fry. "I'm off."

Kaya stood with her. "What? Wait. I thought you were going to tell us about the rich, handsome, single Mr. Locke."

Bailey let her smile widen. "I've been inspired. I may not be able to have exactly what I asked for . . . but two hotties in the hand is worth a Ewan in the bush, right?"

She turned and left before she could be grilled for more information or talked out of her new plan.

New plan: ditch the battery-operated boyfriend for the night and try the real thing. Make it as dirty and memorable as she could, because who knew the next time an offer like this would come around?

It was either that or let Mr. Locke think she'd chickened out. He certainly knew how to push her buttons. Bailey never could resist a challenge.

Three

"Do you want to join us?"

Cam looked down at the couple on the couch in the den, forcing himself to smile politely despite his impatience. "I appreciate the offer, but I'm going to have to decline."

The slim blonde pouted, but her male counterpart pulled her back down on top of him, abruptly ending the discussion.

Cam turned on his heel and headed outside to the balcony. He'd done this more times than he could recall, been the host of a hedonistic gathering of like-minded others. People who shared his desires. Voyeurism, exhibitionism, experimental BDSM. The desire to see and be seen. He knew enough of them to recognize the signs.

He saw them in Bailey. That's why he'd told her to come. There was no other deep-seated reason. It wasn't because he had to see her again. That he couldn't stop thinking about her. That he wanted to see her in his world. Or so he kept assuring himself.

"It's beautiful here. I had no idea."

Cam smiled at Davide absently, his eyes scanning the twisting road below. "I know. I've never seen such brilliant sunsets. And this house." It was perfect. Three levels, an indoor swimming pool and sauna, a gourmet kitchen. "I'm going to call the Realtor in the morning and make it official. Once I buy it we can come back whenever we want."

"How long have we known each other, Cam?"

They'd met in boarding school. Until five years ago, Davide's family had nearly as much money as the Locke's, and even more prestige. Now cash poor and title wealthy, the younger generation had been forced into marriages or, Cam acknowledged with a self-mocking grin, working for their high-maintenance friends. "A long time, my friend."

Davide nodded. "She is unique, that Ms. Wagner. But I have to wonder if that's enough."

Cam sighed heavily. "Why are you always the voice of doom? You're at a party with several dozen stunning and scantily clad women, all willing to do whatever you require."

"So are you." Davide patted Cam on the back. "And as long as I've known you, you have never stood alone and melancholy on a balcony while the fun went on around you. You're waiting for her."

Cam met his friend's knowing gaze. "So are you."

He didn't deny it. Cam wasn't sure how he felt about that. He and Davide had shared women before. Often, in fact. There was nothing more satisfying than bringing a woman to that ultimate threshold, taking her so completely, so utterly, that she was devastated by her own forbidden bliss.

But he had always been about the forbidden. Maybe he *was* spoiled. He recalled what Bailey had said about "Mr. Locke's" swiftly fading interest. She had a point. Places, property, cars, women. Anything he wanted, he got. Was it any wonder that he sought out new challenges, new mountains to scale?

Passion was an equalizer. In passion, rich or poor didn't matter, only pleasure. That raw, open, vulnerable place that shredded all your illusions of control, that made a mockery of mastery and skill.

He *was* melancholy. All this philosophical hooey would not bring Bailey to his door any quicker.

But she would come. He knew it. And for a reason he refused to contemplate, he needed her to.

"I can't believe I'm doing this. I should turn around right now. Seriously, Bailey, turn around."

She was walking around the expensive cars parked in the lot, heading toward the door and talking to herself. This was what Cameron Locke had driven her to. Maybe she'd surprise him; hand him the list and turn right back around.

Then she could turn her phone back on and talk to Kaya. Her friend must have speed-dialed her ten times in the eight miles between Dani and Liam's house and Locke's rental. Bailey knew what she wanted. To find out where she was going. Maybe even to talk her out of it.

Which is why she hadn't answered the phone.

She shivered in the night air. It smelled like rain. The lonesome howl of a coyote momentarily rose above the rhythmic beat coming from the house and Bailey wrapped her arms around herself, chuckling a bit hysterically. "Oh no, you don't, Stax. I have someone else in mind. Besides, I have two rules. No sloppy seconds. And no dogs. No offense."

She sincerely hoped she wouldn't get struck by lightning and dragged away because he took offense. After what she'd seen, she wouldn't put it past him.

And now she needed a drink.

She lifted her hand to knock on the door, but hesitated. They wouldn't hear her. It was too loud. It might be better if she just lef—

The door opened and the noise swelled through the opening and out into the night.

"Bailey?"

"Hey, um, Alwin. Didn't know you knew my boss."

Great. Alwin was another line chef at the resort, a friend of both Jace and Liam. Now the whole world would know she'd come here.

The large German laughed out loud, holding two giggling women hostage at his ample sides. "Your boss lives in this paradise? Lucky man, eh? The sights I have seen tonight. And it's just begun, ladies. It's just begun."

Awkward. This was the actual definition of that word. "Hey, before you leave. Did you recognize anybody else in there? Did Jace come with you?" Because if he did, she would have to leave immediately and tell Kaya. There. She had an official out.

The rotund chef chuckled again. "None of my friends are here.

Americans are so boring. Food is boring, music is boring, sex is . . . well, sex is always good, right? Life is to be *lived*."

She realized that she'd never actually heard him talk this much since she'd met him. He must have had a *lot* of fun.

Alwin's wobbly wink proved her case. "Speaking of living and sex, would you like to join us? We're going back to this one's place." He squeezed the grinning brunette. "She says she has a *trampoline*."

"I appreciate the imagery, but I have some paperwork to give my boss, then I'm going home."

The trio moved past her and down the slanted driveway. "Paperwork? Hah, that's a good one."

"I should go before this gets any weirder." Surely imagining Alwin's sexual bouncing antics was enough excitement for one night. In fact, it was making her rethink the whole ever needing sex again issue.

"Bailey Wagner. I almost didn't recognize you without your . . . cowboy hat. You look stunning. And Cam was right. Pink suits you."

Davide. His voice alone was enough to melt a woman's panties at thirty paces. Dirty pool, having the sexy Italian Buffly meet her at the door. He almost made up for Alwin.

Almost.

"Mr. Locke wanted me to make a list and bring it to him. For the inn. A list for the inn. Don't let me interrupt the revelry."

Davide's smile was full of sensual promise. "Bailey, we were waiting for you. Now the real revelry begins."

He was like a hypnotist. No wonder Cameron kept him around.

Bailey felt his fingers twine with hers and he tugged her gently across the threshold. And into another world.

She'd seen movies like this. They were usually movies about vampires or crime lords of the underworld, during a scene when an innocent human ingénue was tempted by the dark, sexy immortal/gangster.

Normal people didn't go to these kinds of parties. They went to play cards, bringing their Tupperware containing Aunt Mildred's secret casserole recipe, always a crowd-pleaser. They didn't dress in strips of leather and latex, or—she noticed the beautiful dark-skinned woman watching her from across the room—a bikini made of chains.

Not everyone was wearing the latest in dungeon fashions. In fact, most people were only partially clothed. She noticed a drummer from the regular local music jams and ducked her head on the off chance he would recognize her, distracted as he was by his . . . bongos. She walked swiftly behind Davide, determined to see this through. To hand her boss his list, and get out of here before she lost her head.

"She looks delicious."

Bailey jumped a little when Davide stopped, and she looked up to see that the chain bikini woman had crossed the room with a surprising swiftness to intercept them.

Davide squeezed her hand. "Bailey, this is Bunny. Bunny Joy."

Bailey raised both eyebrows but smiled and held out her hand. "Was your mother at Woodstock, too?"

The crowd immediately around them seemed to hold its collective breath and Bailey's smile wavered. Damn her big mouth.

Bunny threw back her long, shimmering braids and laughed, taking her hand and pulling her closer. Or as close as she could, since Davide didn't seem to want to let go.

"I was right," Bunny crowed. "Delicious. And yes, the story goes I was conceived there."

Bailey chuckled. "I came a little later, but apparently that's when my mother decided her first child would be named Baby Love. I changed it, of course, so let's just keep that between the two of us."

"Oh it's far too late for that."

Bailey growled when she heard Cameron's voice behind her. "Why is it you're always sneaking up behind me?"

His hand slid across her back, touching her skin between the strips of fabric, making her shiver. He whispered in her ear. "Because I really like the view, Baby Love."

Good answer. But he wasn't done. "Bunny is an old friend of mine. We share many of the same tastes. In food, in women. I shouldn't be surprised at her reaction to you."

Bailey's breathing grew shallow. Cameron's voice in her ear, Davide's hand in hers and the majestic Bunny looking down at her like she was an ice cream cone were all combining to throw her hormones into a tailspin.

She had always admired beautiful women. Kaya was the perfect example. She'd often joked with the elegant Hopi that if she didn't like men so much, she would definitely be all over her.

But actual arousal? That was unusual. She'd forgotten what Cameron had said. "Hmmm?"

Bunny's full red lips softened. "I'd like to kiss her. Be the first to welcome her to the party."

Bailey shivered, and they all felt it. Cameron's touch on her back grew firmer. "What do you think, *Baby Love*? Brave enough to give her what she wants? What we all want to see?"

She gritted her teeth. "Tell you what, Locke. If I let you watch, you stop calling me that for the rest of . . . *ever.*"

Davide and Cameron both chuckled beside her. Cameron's hand guided her closer to Bunny's scantily-clad body. "I promise I'll stop. For tonight. But only if you make it good."

Bailey sensed the eyes on her. So many. All watching her. Seeing her. Wanting her to kiss the confident Bunny. Holding their collective breath as they waited. It was a heady sensation. Powerful.

She met Bunny's gaze and grinned. They shared a look that was rich with knowledge and awareness. Awareness of their femininity, of how to use it to drive a man wild. Awareness of each other.

When the statuesque beauty released her hand to cup her cheek, Bailey slid hers around her waist, allowing herself to enjoy the silken texture of the soft skin beneath her fingers. Feeling the pulse of a dozen hearts racing with hers, watching her.

Yes.

She could still sense Cameron behind her, and Davide's fingers caressed her palm restlessly. It only added to the moment. She wanted them to see. Wanted to be fearless.

Bailey met Bunny's lips without hesitation. Her adrenaline was raging through her veins, electric sparks of excitement arcing up her spine.

Soft lips. Sweet lips. Tasting of cherry gloss and secrets. They weren't aggressive, they were accepting. Bailey was the aggressor. Bailey sought entrance with her tongue riding the seam of the other woman's mouth. Bailey lifted up on her toes and curled her fingers into the flesh of the tiny waist until Bunny moaned in delight.

Davide groaned and pressed her hand between the both of his, kneading her fingers in time to the kiss. She knew instinctively that he was imagining her kissing him, imagining her hands on his skin.

Was Cameron?

Her hand left Bunny's waist and reached behind her. She wasn't sure why but she needed to know. Did he like this? Was he behind her, ready if she needed him?

And she did need him.

He took her hand and came to stand directly behind her, guiding her until her palm was cupping his long, hard erection. The erection that was blazingly hot through the linen of his pants. Hot and hard. Because of her.

It suddenly hit her that this was more than a power trip for her. More than a dare. She was no shrinking violet, had never been afraid of her own sexuality. She'd just been too busy to explore it.

She wanted to explore it now. She wanted Cameron. Despite herself, maybe. But she wanted him.

She curled her fingers around his shaft at the same time she opened her mouth wider, allowing Bunny to take the lead, reveling in the woman's gracefully slender fingers lowering from her cheeks to her neck, circling her breasts.

Noises of pleasure started to filter into her awareness. The sounds of sex. She could still feel all the attention on her, and the idea that people were so aroused they couldn't hold back—that they were touching each other, touching themselves as they watched, made her thighs tremble.

Her sex was so wet that she was sure he knew. Cameron. Knew how this was affecting her. Her fingers tightened around him and he gripped her wrist hard. He bent his head, his teeth opening over her bare shoulder. "Enough."

Bunny released her reluctantly, a smile of appreciation and regret on her shiny, lovely lips. "Not planning on sharing her with the rest of us, then?"

Bailey watched Bunny stare at Cameron over her shoulder. He didn't answer, but his expression seemed to suffice.

Her smile warmed when she glanced at Bailey once more. "Thank you for that. You did taste as good as I imagined. If Cam treats you badly, you can always come to me. I know exactly how to make him squirm." She winked and turned into the crowd, instantly surrounded by three men and a woman, all wearing the same expressions of lust for her.

Who could blame them?

But why had she felt a little ping of jealousy when Bunny implied that she'd been with Cam? She wouldn't be surprised if everyone in this room had.

Coming back to herself with a solid thud, she tried to move her hand away, but Cameron didn't seem inclined to let her go.

"Oh no you don't. Davide, clear out the library. *Now.*"

Davide released her other hand and disappeared into the crowd, while Cameron whirled her around to face him.

Bailey tried to free her mind from the sexually induced haze that had descended. Her body was still tingling, her nipples sharp and aching for a firmer caress than the one Bunny had given. She wanted. And she was mad as hell with herself for wanting.

"I should leave. I'll mail you the list."

Cameron spoke through his teeth, his gray eyes dark as a thunderstorm. The vein in his temple was throbbing. "What list, Bailey? Are you hiding it in the pocket of that kinky little dress of yours? You didn't bring it, did you? Say it."

She hadn't. Shit, why hadn't she?

"You didn't and I know why." Cameron seemed to hear her thoughts. A wholly disturbing idea. "You just can't wait for that spanking, can you? You didn't have to give me a reason, baby." He released her hand so both of his could cup her behind, pulling her tight against him. "From the second I saw this luscious fucking ass, all I could think about was what I wanted to do to it."

"Clear." Davide's gruff voice sounded deeper, more thickly accented. Aroused.

Cameron focused on her. "All that's left is for you to say yes, Bailey. Davide and I want you. Want to fulfill your every fantasy. All you have to do is say yes."

Davide and I? Oh, Mama. "This doesn't mean I like you." She had to try and save face, even though she was melting inside.

He smiled. "I can live with that. Just one word, Bailey. No rules, no repercussions, no regrets. You don't work for me here. Tonight. Just say it."

"Yes."

Cameron nodded, twirling her around until she was walking between him and Davide through the writhing throng and down the hall.

This house was huge. You could fit two Enchanted Inns in it. Maybe three. Bailey had picked it because it was the most expensive rental on the list. But it was obviously worth the money.

As they walked down the narrow corridor, she could hear splashing and laughter coming from the floor below. The indoor swimming pool. She could just imagine what was going on down there. She loved the feel of water on her naked skin. She'd love it even more if her wet body was pressed against Cameron's . . .

Cameron took her shoulders and turned her toward an open door, into the library.

"Holy shit."

Davide laughed. "I know. This is my favorite room in the house."

She could see why. It was a tower room. A fairy-tale room. Row upon row of books over a story high, several rolling brass ladders stationed against the shelves in case a book exceeded your reach. Though some of them were obviously for show, with only a few, widely spaced rungs.

Every wall was covered floor to ceiling in beautiful books of every shape and size. Except one. The far wall and part of the floor appeared to be made of one-way glass. It had to be one-way; she'd never seen this room from the outside. But she could see out. The distinctive shapes of the red rock formations beneath a sky full of stars.

"Beautiful."

Cameron spun her around again. "You are. And I can't wait another minute for this."

He kissed her. So different from Bunny. His lips took, conquered, demanded everything. His tongue mated with hers, owned hers. His teeth bit down and then he licked the pain away.

Saying he was a good kisser would be the understatement of the century.

Bailey wrapped her arms around his neck, giving herself up to his mastery. He'd won this round and she was ready to give him his spoils. As long as it involved more kissing.

Shouldn't she be thinking how wrong this was? How he was her boss and what would he do after their night of wickedness was over, regardless of his promises?

Cameron lifted his lips with a groan. "I can hear you thinking, Bailey. There is no thinking allowed while I'm kissing you. It's a rule."

Davide's laughter was raspy, and startling to her. How had she forgotten they weren't alone in the room? "You've done it now, Bailey. Broken rules come with consequences."

A delicious shiver raced up her spine. She tilted her chin defiantly. "I can take whatever you dish out."

Cameron closed his eyes for several heartbeats. When he opened them again they were nearly black. "We'll find out, won't we?"

He lifted her up, his hands beneath her arms and walked her toward the closest wall of books. "Davide, your belt if you please."

Belt? "Wait a second. If you think you're going to swat me with a—"

"I won't do anything you don't want, Bailey. All you have to do is tell me to stop."

He turned her so she was facing one of the decorative ladders, lifting her arms to a higher rung, one she had to stretch to reach. Davide was on the other side of the ladder, his back against the shelves, his belt in hand. He wrapped it around her wrists and the bar, tightening the strap until it was snug.

"Oh." Oh, there was something wrong with her. Looking into Davide's beautiful features as he secured her, feeling Cameron behind her, impatient and commanding, was . . . electrifyingly potent.

Cameron nipped her shoulder again. "Yes, *oh*. I wouldn't use that. Not this first time, anyway."

Not this first time. The implication was clear. Arousing.

"What now, guys?"

She was trying to be her usual jocular self, but it was getting harder to maintain. She was so turned on her arousal was dampening her thighs. The position she'd been put in had her breasts pressing together, spilling out over the top of her dress. Sensitive. Needy. She hated how needy she was.

Davide looked down and swore in Italian. "Usually I look forward to this part," he whispered raggedly. "I love to watch women give themselves up to it, to learn to equate the sting with desire, the precious pain with pleasure."

He pulled his shirt off impatiently, tearing a hole in the left shoulder in his haste. "Right now all I can think about, all Cameron can think about, is fucking you."

Oh my God, it was really going to happen. Bailey let herself feel it for the first time. Both of them. They wanted her. They were going to take her, together. Her arms started to shake.

Cameron stroked her back in between undoing her laces. "Shh, baby. That's right. Think about everything we're going to do to you. Shall I tell you?" He didn't wait for her response. "I'm going to spank your ass until it's red, until you're begging me to let you come. But you can't. Not until Davide and I are both inside you, filling you. Then, I promise, you'll have the most intense release you've ever imagined. And then we'll start all over again."

"Fuck." Bailey leaned against the ladder, feeling the lower rung pressing right above her pubic bone.

The cool air of the library blew across her nipples and she realized that Cameron had pushed down the top of her dress to her waist, leaving her breasts bare to Davide's avid stare.

"Slip off your shoes, Bailey."

She did as Cameron asked, sliding them out of the way, feeling the tug against her arms, the tightening of the belt as she did it. Why did that feel so good?

"You can let go." Davide licked his lips, his fingers coming up to trace her collarbone, lingering over the small butterfly tattoo beneath it. Over her heart. "You don't have to be in control here. Give it to us. Just feel. Let us make you feel."

Temptation. The wicked snake. The delicious apple. She hadn't known it, but those words were her "Open Sesame." They were magical words that sent a flood of emotion through her. Overwhelming her with its intensity.

"She's ready."

Cameron grunted at Davide. "I can see that." He pushed the dress down over her hips until it landed, a black and pink cloud at her feet.

A pained growl rumbled in his chest. "Bad girl. You bad, beautiful girl."

Bailey managed a shaky smile. No Superman Underoos this time. No anything. "Surprise."

Four

Cameron leaned against her back, his shirt open, his jaw tightening at the lightning jolt of pleasure he got from the contact of her skin against his. That was all. Just the scrape of his nipples against her creamy flesh. Just holding her. He could only imagine what she'd do to him once he got inside.

He needed to maintain long enough to deliver on his promise, but she was making it damned difficult. She'd managed to get under his skin better than anyone he'd ever met.

He barely knew her.

Yet he felt he knew her like the back of his hand.

And with an intensity that floored him, he wanted her.

He reached past her and over Davide's shoulder, grabbing the first soft-covered book he saw.

"What is *that* for?"

Bailey's voice was quavering, wanting. *Good*. He wanted her to wonder. Wanted to surprise her. To throw her off the way she did every time she opened her mouth. Every time she *breathed*.

He kissed her temple. "Guess."

She made a choking sound. A strange noise that sounded shockingly similar to . . .

"Laughing? Are you laughing?" The adrenaline spike, the excitement, must explain her reaction. Some women cried, he knew. Though usually not *before* the actual act. "Why?"

"Did you look at it? What you picked up?"

Cam glanced down at the cover for a long moment. A naked couple embraced on the cover, their faces hidden from view, their intent clear. A turquoise slash of color across the lower half framed the title, and he had to smile.

He ran his fingers across the pages then held it up to show Davide over her shoulder. "Fitting, yes?"

Davide shook his head, joining Bailey's breathless laughter. "Perfect."

Cam gripped Bailey's curving hip firmly in one hand. "*Pleasure's Edge*. Don't you think that title is perfect, baby?"

She'd stopped laughing. "I . . . I guess."

"You guess? But you don't know because you haven't felt it. The dangerous edge that can make the pleasure that much sharper, that much more intense. But you will."

He rubbed the cool, slick cover along one lush, round cheek and she jerked. He feathered open the book and let the pages caress her skin and she shivered. He tapped her lightly, ever so lightly, with the flat of the book and she pressed back against him.

Whether she knew it or not, she wanted more. She was made for this.

"Davide? Would you like to taste her?"

Cam had a harder time saying that than he thought he would. Maybe because it was their first time. It had been difficult for him to watch Bunny kiss her, because *he* hadn't gotten to yet. Usually getting a woman to submit to his siren-like friend was a highlight of his night.

Not that the sight didn't have his cock aching. But he found he was more possessive of Bailey than was usual for him. He would just have to console himself that Davide might be the first to suck those breasts into his mouth, to taste her sweetness, but Cam would be the last.

The last. He wouldn't think about why those words gave him such satisfaction.

Davide's response brought him back into the moment. "I was wondering when you were going to ask."

He watched Davide kiss Bailey's forehead. The master of seduction at work. Since boarding school, no woman had been able to resist him.

When Davide's head bent to take one perfect, rosy nipple in his mouth, Bailey shuddered in pleasure, her knees buckling.

Cam held her firmly and spanked her right cheek with the back of the book.

She straightened with a shout of surprise and Cam smiled. That got her attention.

He watched her look over her shoulder and meet his gaze. "Did you actually spank me with a romance novel?"

He stared her down and lowered the book with a hearty smack on her left ass cheek. "What?"

She bit her lip, her eyes glistening, face warming right along with her edible ass. But her attention was on him, more than the man moaning against her breast.

"I said did you—*oh*!"

He spanked her again. Then he gently caressed her with the pages, stroking her lower back with his knuckles. "In case you were confused, the only words I want to hear you saying are please, more and yes."

Her stubborn chin came out. God, he wanted to bite it. He wanted to bend her over and fill her until neither of them could walk away.

Cam tapped the book with his hand and raised an eyebrow. "Do you like what he's doing to you, Bailey?"

Her green eyes flared. "Yes."

"Tell him you want more."

She bit her lip, but after a moment of silence she said, "More."

Davide immediately complied, taking her other nipple between his fingers and twisting until she moaned.

"Doesn't that feel good, baby? Do you want to be spanked again?" She glared at him, but she couldn't hide the excitement in her eyes. Excitement that only increased his own. "You know all you need to say."

"*Please.*"

* * *

She was drowning in sensations. The rasp of Davide's tongue and the pressure of his fingers. Cameron's gentle caresses followed by the stinging heat marking her ass, making every inch of her skin tingle. Even the air in the room felt like a lover's touch. Every cell in her body felt alive. Alert.

She loved it.

Cameron dropped the tome at her feet, and she stared down at the lovers on the cover. She would never look at a book the same way. How could something so innocuous become a tool for pleasure? And why had he dropped it?

His large hands were gliding over her back, her ass, between her cheeks. She pressed her hips back against him in a silent plea. She wanted more. She'd said please. Did he want her to beg again? It surprised her how much she was willing to.

What had they done to her?

"Cameron. Cam. Please."

She heard him groan. "Oh, I love hearing you say that. I really do. Sassy, defiant Bailey, begging me to spank her ass."

A sharp crack of sound and there it was. Fire. Blood-rushing, heart-pounding awareness. Need.

Bailey arched her back, pushing her breast deeper into Davide's mouth. God, Davide's beautiful mouth. But it was too sweet, too gentle. She needed more of that pain.

"More, Davide. Please, I can't—"

He smiled against her skin, then scraped his teeth roughly over the top of her tender nipple.

Just as Cameron slipped two fingers between her legs and inside her soaking sex.

"Oh God."

"So wet. Davide, feel how wet she is." Cameron's voice was rough. His heart beating hard against her back. His thick erection pressing against her hip through his thin linen pants. And those fingers were thrusting deep, curving against her g-spot. *Yes. Yes, there.*

Davide lowered his hand and she felt his fingers slip through the wetness on her thighs. He moaned, his mouth still full of her, sucking harder as he slid one finger in to join Cam's.

Both of them inside her, stretching her. It shattered her composure. It wrecked her resistance. It wasn't enough.

Her hips rocked between them, unconsciously pleading for more. She knew what came next. She wanted it desperately.

"Cam?" Davide lifted his mouth to look over her shoulder. There was a matching desperation in his voice. Cameron must have heard it and agreed, because both men removed their damp fingers and lifted her body into the air.

"Put your legs over the— Yes, that's right." Davide praised her, making sure she was balanced on the rung before he stepped back and unbuttoned his pants.

He pulled a condom from his pocket, then he let his pants fall, opening the foil package with his teeth and rolling it down his beautiful dark cock. It was just as perfect as the rest of him, but Bailey still gasped when she got a clear view.

He smirked. "You should see the other guy's."

Cam spanked her still-tingling cheeks to get her attention. "She will," he promised.

He was naked now, too. His cock heated her lower back, she could feel its size and she let out a shaky breath. Could she really take both of them? God, she wanted to.

Davide noticed her expression and his gentled. "Just breathe, Bailey. Just feel."

As if she could do anything else but feel. The cool metal beneath her thighs, the leather of the belt around her wrists, the heat of two male bodies surrounding her, focused on her.

"You know I never understood the purpose of these things—not enough rungs. Now I know. Wrap your legs around me, beauty." Davide kissed her chin, her forehead as she obeyed. Then he placed his lips on hers.

Another kiss. Uniquely his. His mouth worshipping hers, making her feel beautiful. Alive. Special.

When he pulled back he studied her features with a kind of wonder. "We were not expecting you at all, Bailey Wagner."

Before she could interpret his expression, or find the brainpower to speak, Cam was gripping her hips again.

"Now, Davide."

Bailey leaned her head back onto Cameron's shoulder, looking up at that dimple on his chin, the one that had so distracted her.

She wished he'd kiss her again.

Her eyes closed and she cried out softly as Davide pressed the head of his cock against her sex, filling her slowly. Teasingly.

"Please."

Cam kissed her temple. "Patience, baby. You'll have what you want soon enough."

By the time Davide's narrow hips were pressed against hers she was gasping. So full. It had been such a long time. And never like this. It had never been like this.

She tightened her thighs around him, trying to thrust her hips against him, but Cameron's grip was firm.

"Not yet, Bailey. We're not done yet."

She heard another packet tear, then felt thick drops of liquid dripping between the cheeks of her ass. Fireworks were flaring inside her body. Anticipation was killing her.

Bailey had experimented before. Her first boyfriend had been bisexual, after all. She'd liked it. She even used a plug every now and then, when the empty ache demanded to be filled.

When Cameron stroked the sensitive skin and asked her if she'd ever been touched there, ever been taken, she nodded.

It made him pause long enough that she knew he didn't like her answer. How did she know him so well already? He'd wanted to be her first. She took a deep breath and tried to control her quivering lips. "I've never had two men at once before. And no one has ever dared to spank me."

That was the truth.

Davide caught her eye, his lower lip bloody from where he'd bitten it to stop himself from moving as he wanted to.

He winked and Bailey knew it had been the right thing to say.

Cameron spread the cheeks of her ass wide, massaging her, relaxing her muscles. Her skin was still hot from the spanking, and his rough fingertips only increased the sensation.

Her breath came out in a whoosh with the initial pressure of his erection against the tight ring of muscles. She shook so hard she could hear the ladder rattle.

"Easy, baby." Cameron's guttural growl instantly soothed her. He was just as lost in it as she was. Lost in her.

Her moan was low and long when he began to enter her. With Davide's shaft already filling her, the stretching, impossibly intense feeling was already more than she could take.

Her back arched and her mouth opened on a soundless cry as they stole the breath from her lungs. Deep. Full. Consumed.

"Fuck, Bailey. God, you feel perfect." Cameron stilled when they were finally both inside her. Completely. "You've got us, baby. Both of us. Can you take more?"

Her eyes popped open. More? What did he mean? How could she possibly take more?

Davide nibbled on her jaw. "We have to move, Bailey."

What were the words she was allowed to use? "Oh, yes. *Please.* More."

They began to move, and Bailey felt her world shift. It was as though she had separated from her body, watching the two men thrusting in a counter rhythm, focused on bringing the woman between them to the ultimate brink.

Lucky woman.

The man behind her lifted one of his hands from her hips and slid his fingers into the short spikes of her blonde hair, and Bailey came back to herself with a groan.

"Feel everything, Bailey. Feel the two cocks inside you. My hand in your hair."

He tugged and she whimpered, her neck arching until she could look up into Cam's dark gray eyes. He studied her face for a moment, his own a study in desire, before swearing and covering her mouth with his.

He was everywhere. Surrounding her. His taste in her mouth. His scent. His body. Everything Bailey was melted into him. Each nerve ending flashing with life. Each racing heartbeat sending liquid heat through her veins, pounding into her sex.

Cameron lifted his mouth. "Come."

One soft word. One gently spoken command. And her body obeyed.

Bailey saw dark spots and stars as she screamed out with the power of her orgasm. She could hear male voices joining her as Davide and Cameron climaxed inside her, but she couldn't focus on anything but this feeling.

She was everything. Every moment. She was shattered into a thousand tiny pieces on the ground.

She was crying.

The two men untied the belt, rubbing her arms tenderly back to life. Cameron took her into his arms and sat in a buttery soft wingback chair, murmuring soft nonsense, rocking her.

Davide sat at their feet and kissed her hip, offering silent comfort. She couldn't stop crying. It didn't make any sense. She'd just had the best orgasm of her life, just been taken by two beautiful men who'd been as turned on by her as she was by them. Why was she crying?

She tried to laugh, to lift her hand to wipe her cheeks. She hated this vulnerable feeling. Hated that they might see her as weak. "Wow. You two sure do pack a punch."

Cameron took her hand in his and placed his lips on her damp cheeks, kissing away her tears. "It's normal, Bailey. Letting go of control takes more strength than most know."

"So you make girls cry often, do you?" Her tone was sharp, but she felt cornered.

Bailey hated *that* feeling, too.

Cameron opened his mouth to respond, but ended up shaking his head. He hugged her closer, rocking her until she gave in and put her head on his shoulder. It was too nice to resist. Just a moment, until she could think again. Until she got back to herself.

Thank heavens this was only for one night.

"Where is the delicious Baby Love? Gone already?"

Cam looked up from the granite island in the kitchen. He'd been staring at the coffeemaker, lost in thought, for longer than he cared to admit. He reached for the carafe and poured Bunny a cup. "Back home, I suppose."

Bunny leaned both elbows on the counter, accepting the cup with a smile and inhaling deeply. She'd changed from her wild party attire and she was back in the uniform she liked best. Baby blue flannel shorts and a tank top.

She sipped. "Maybe it's for the best. You know local women rarely hold your attention for long."

"Oh, she holds my attention just fine. She's stubborn as you, smart-assed as Davide, as skittish as—"

"As you?" Bunny smiled up at him. "Sounds like a recipe for disaster. But then, I'm funny that way."

Cam watched his friend enjoy her coffee. She had been a model years ago, until a wealthy playboy, a jackass Cameron was unfortunate enough to share a social circle with, decided he wanted her.

When he was done, he'd ruined her, as only a man with ridiculous wealth and connections could.

Cam had dated her for a while, but they both realized they made better friends than lovers. She didn't trust men, and he, well, he never stayed around long enough to give someone the chance to trust him.

"She disappeared." He blurted it out, grabbing another cup for himself and slamming it on the counter. "Davide and I were with her half the night, and then she disappeared."

It wasn't long after that first time that they'd taken her again. And, as Davide curled up on the couch to recover, Cam had carried Bailey over to the wall of glass, pressed her against it and made love to her by himself for the first time, the desert sky full of stars around them.

It had been slow. Tender. Loving. The experience had blown him away.

He'd woken Davide and sent him to get some towels and a shirt for her to wear, while he'd gone to rummage in the kitchen for some food.

"I came back to the library and she was gone."

Bunny sighed. "It might have been something I said."

Cam froze. "What? When?"

"I wandered into the library and found her alone and looking a little out of sorts. You and Davide can be a heavy combination for any woman. Especially one who isn't used to your type."

"My type?"

He glared and she nodded. "You like a challenge. You and Davide both. I love you, you know that, but despite her sass she doesn't know it's just a game to you." Bunny shrugged. "The trouble with women. Our hearts are too easily involved."

Shit. "Bunny, if you were anybody else I would send you packing."

Bunny nodded. "I can see that." She waited until he met her gaze. "Was I wrong? She's different, Cam. I know that. You know that. She's a keeper. And you don't usually do those."

He did know it, damn it. But it wasn't enough. One night with her wasn't nearly enough. She was so responsive, so adorably prickly and heartbreakingly vulnerable at the same time.

He'd dated women for months and not felt as connected as he did with Bailey in just a few days. He was addicted. That realization terrified him.

Bunny was right. He didn't do keepers. He didn't do forever. He came from a long line of lotharios and cheaters. His grandfather had an apartment installed in his mansion to house his mistresses. His father and mother? They were still married, but they lived on separate continents and sent each other emails about their latest conquests.

When women in his world said they loved you, it meant as long as you give me what I want or only for now. It never meant forever.

Maybe Davide had been right. He should have been more cautious.

"I'll talk to the pilot today. We might be leaving for Switzerland sooner than I'd planned."

Bunny's expression was compassionate but sad as she set down her coffee and turned to go. "Cam?"

"Yes, Bunny?"

"I'm sorry I stepped on your toes, but I'm going to offer you one last bit of advice. Don't buy her any 'thanks for the fuck' jewelry, okay? She seems like the type who will never get over the shame of it if you do."

She reached up to touch the ruby pendant at her neck instinctively, and he nodded.

He was such a jerk. And a fool.

Bailey would be better off without him.

Five

She was better off without him. Without both of them.

Bailey tossed around on her lumpy mattress, deciding that would be her new mantra.

When the tall, Amazonian beauty had opened the library door, Bailey had been embarrassed, reaching for her dress to cover her well-loved body.

But embarrassment had soon given way to harsh reality. This was his world. A world, if Bunny could be believed, full of other women Cameron Locke had used and left. One at every hotel. One in every port. It was a game, she'd told her. A game Davide and Cameron played. The bigger the challenge, the more points. She'd tried to be kind about it, but it still stung.

Well, she hadn't been that much of a challenge, had she? Bailey pounded her pillow with a violence it didn't deserve. A paper tiger, that was all she was. Give her the slightest bit of affection and attention, and she caved.

What did it matter anyway? It was just sex. Sex she'd decided to have of her own volition. No one forced her to be in that Richie Rich sandwich. That was all her. And she'd already decided it was only going to be for one night.

So why was she such a mess?

Because it had been amazing. Beyond any fantasy. Beyond anything she'd experienced or imagined. Her body still ached and tingled a day later.

A whole day without seeing Cameron. Without Davide on the roof. A man had come in bright and early to fix the ladder to the attic, but other than that, no word. Nothing.

Not even flowers. Or a phone call.

Last night was obviously just another game night for them. And whether or not she wanted to admit it, it had been life-altering for her. "Damn it."

The sound of pounding feet and rattling, followed by a low hum of singing made her frown. The plaster on the ceiling shook, sending a powdery shower down on her forehead.

Lovely. She threw off her covers and slipped into sweatpants, just in case, mumbling all the way. "If there is a ghost up there, you are rude and loud and you better run. I've seen *A Haunting* five times, and I will so kick your ass."

She grabbed a flashlight and opened her bedroom door, sighing when she saw the brand-new ladder down, the attic door open wide and puffs of smoke that smelled like sage wafting down into the hallway. "Of course."

Because her week hadn't been exciting enough.

Bailey walked up the steps carefully, appreciating the solid strength of the new ladder. At least Cameron Locke was good for something. She'd gotten a fixed roof, a few orgasms and a new ladder. He may eventually decide to fire her, but for now, she'd be thankful for small favors.

"Am I turning in the right direction, Will? Wouldn't want these poor little souls getting lost on their spirit path cause I turned right instead of left."

A nervous feminine laugh and then. "Do you think aliens walk a spirit path, Elder? Even if they're, say, cloned?"

Bailey lifted one eyebrow. Then the other. She raised a hand to rub her eyes before opening them once more. Nope. They were still there.

Old Mr. Olyphant, slowly lifting one foot, then the other, in a strange jerky sort of dance. Ms. Littleton, moved right along beside him, holding a braid of burning white sage in her hand.

And Kaya's grandfather, Will, whom she'd met only briefly but would recognize anywhere, stood in the middle, a large, pleased grin on his weathered face.

"You are doing well, both of you."

Bailey's breath came out in an exasperated huff. "The inn isn't covered for Native American exorcisms, guys."

Ms. Littleton jumped a foot in the air, nearly tipping over. "Ms. Wagner. I'm so sorry. I saw them coming up here and I was just . . . curious."

Bailey bit her tongue to hold back a smile when Mr. Olyphant muttered, "Tattletale."

"No harm done. But lets call it a night, okay? The little ghosties will no doubt still be there tomorrow."

"No. They are gone. The children had lost their way, but these two brave *Bahana* danced them back onto the path." Will looked at her with dark eyes that dared her to disagree.

She shrugged. "Awesome. Hear that, folks? Now when you go home you'll have a fun story to tell people about your trip. But for now, don't you think Mrs. Olyphant will be wondering where you are?"

The older man grimaced. "Not likely. She sleeps like a rock and snores like a steam engine. But you're right." He glanced over at Will and smiled. "I will have a story."

Will nodded at him approvingly, watching the two guests hurry past Bailey and back down to their rooms, Ms. Littleton dragging the smoky sage in her wake.

After a few moments, when he didn't move toward the ladder, Bailey coughed. "Um, I'm not sure what you're doing here, but I think we should go downstairs and call Kaya to pick you up."

Will sat down on the wood floor of the attic, surrounded by old trunks and squares of insulation.

Bailey tried again. "It isn't really safe up here. I mean, wouldn't you be more comfortable on your own bed? I have a room open if you need it."

He pulled his leather satchel open and took out what looked like a carving of some type.

She shook her head, her shoulders slumping as she came over and sat down beside him. This was the grandfather of one of her best friends. He might be insane, but she still had to be polite. "So, hang out in attics often?"

His lips twitched. "You have a hard time being quiet, don't you?"

She sat up straighter. "What?"

He pointed the wood in her direction. "Everything about you is loud. Your hair. Your clothes. Always moving around, doing something. And you talk a lot."

"Careful, handsome. I'm susceptible to flattery."

Will chuckled. "You *are* funny. But you just hide behind the *Hano* clown. I have a feeling you are really a hummingbird at heart."

Bailey grinned. "I wish I knew what you were talking about. Maybe Kaya can explain it to me when we go downstairs and call her."

"Don't you want to know why you're a hummingbird?"

"I'd rather know why you were up here with my guests in the middle of the night." She watched his small knife fly over the wood, forming an image that was as breathtaking as it was foreign. "Sure. Why am I a hummingbird?"

Will nodded. "My people believe the hummingbird is a messenger and a blessing, the one who intervenes with the gods and brings rain. There is a story about two lost children, left behind by their parents during a time of famine." His voice was low and entrancing. She could see the children, alone and afraid.

Hell, she'd been that child. How many times had her mother left her alone while she flitted off to experience some new spiritual awakening? Or worse, dragged her along from state to state, from bad situation to worse? Until the day Bailey was old enough to choose not to follow. To make her home here.

Will continued his story. "One day the boy made a toy in the shape of a hummingbird for his sister, to distract her from their plight. She threw it into the air and it suddenly came to life, flying away and returning each day with an ear of corn so they wouldn't starve. When it realized the adults still weren't coming back to the village, it flew to the earth's center to ask the fertility god to bring life back to the land. So the children's parents would return. And the people would know abundance once more."

"That's a beautiful story, Will."

"Thank you."

She shrugged. "I'm still lost."

Will's expression was pitying. "I know."

"I mean," she said with a little glare, reminding herself over and over about the need to respect her elders. "I still don't get why I'm a hummingbird."

"The hummingbird travels between two worlds, doing good for other people, but having no time for himself." He stopped carving and stared at her solemnly. "Even if other people want to love him, he is too clever. He flies too fast to be seen. Which is sad, as I imagine that is the one thing he truly wants."

He was good. Like Kaya, who could always see past her armor, always see inside her. Apparently it ran in the family. Two worlds? Did he mean the one she'd made for herself and the one she'd rejected? Or hers and Cameron's? Either way, those worlds seemed too far apart to bridge, even if she were to try.

Will stood with an ease that belied his age. "We shouldn't be up here. It's not really safe."

"*Now* you agree with me." Her voice was a little quavery, but she smiled. She could see why Dani liked him so much. He was entirely too charming. "By the way, did you really get rid of ghosts up here, or were you just messing with the tourists?"

Will moved toward the ladder, placing his carving tools back into his satchel and spoke over his shoulder. "Oh, the lost spirits were real. I came to see you the other day but met your guest Mr. Vic Olyphant instead. He asked for my help so I agreed." He stopped mid-rung and looked up at her with a grin. "They're gone for now, but just in case they lose their way again, I would get rid of that painted trunk in the far back. They seem to like it."

"What in the hell do you think you're doing now?"

Bailey sighed heavily before looking down from the roof. She damned herself for the leap of joy her heart gave when she saw Cameron standing on the ground beneath her. But she couldn't let him know that. "It's called working. I'd explain it to you but after what I've seen I have a feeling you wouldn't understand."

When she'd woken up this morning with the lingering memory of a dream where she heard Kaya saying, *"Make a wish, Butterfly Maiden,"* she'd needed a distraction. Anything. Inspecting the roofer's work seemed like a good idea at the time. Now not so much.

She started down, knowing he wouldn't leave until she was on solid ground. She wouldn't admit she was secretly thankful for that fact. "What are you doing here, anyway?" It was a little late for a morning-after call. She bit her lip, thankful she hadn't said that out loud. Maybe she was growing.

"I don't pay you to do this." He sounded grim. And pompous.

When Bailey's boots hit the ground she whirled around, placing her hands on her hips. "Pardon me, sir, but this is exactly what I get paid for. I am the innkeeper. I *keep* the inn."

Cameron Locke was not a happy man. "You texted the list to my business mail. Anything that needs to be taken care of I can handle. You may keep this inn, Bailey, but I own it."

"Until you lose interest in this game and move on to another." Maybe she hadn't grown as much as she thought. But she was too mad to think. The man's mere existence was pushing her buttons.

Apparently she was pushing his as well. "Why do you care so much about this dumpy bed-and-breakfast? You could work for a five-star resort with your abilities. No clogged sinks. No ancient roofs. Hell, we could tear this place down and—"

She stepped forward and pushed him. Hard. "Don't you dare. This place is my *home*. It's the only one I've ever had and I will be damned if you raze it to put up another trendy tourist shop or parking lot."

He gripped her wrists so she couldn't push him again, his gaze sharpening at her words. "The only one?"

She tried to yank away from him, but he was too strong. "Let me go, damn it."

A strange expression passed over his handsome face. "I can't."

He was kissing her. Dirty pool. She couldn't keep her walls up when he kissed her. It made her think of being pressed between him and Davide. Of being taken. Spanked.

Damn.

She felt herself being lifted, felt the world moving beneath her. She lifted her head. "What are you doing?"

He answered her question with another. "What is it with you and ladders? Every time I see you around one I have this uncontrollable urge to fuck you. Open that door."

The shed? "Oh, hell."

She opened the door and he brought her inside, reaching to shut it behind him. They were in the dark. The smell of cedar and earth and Cam filling the air around her.

He dropped to his knees with her still in his arms and her legs automatically wrapped around him. She couldn't see anything, but she felt him. The heat of his body burned through her clothes. His breath was warm against her cheek.

Long moments passed in silence. Neither one of them moving or speaking. But his heart was racing. She could feel it against her chest.

One more time. She just wanted to feel the way he made her feel one more time. Whether it was a game or a mistake, she didn't care. She needed this. Needed him.

She bent her head and kissed his neck, her tongue slipping out to taste the salt on his skin. He groaned and she smiled, one hand dropping down from his shoulders to his belt.

He didn't stop her as she slipped the leather out of its loop and reached for his zipper. Didn't stop her when she used her other hand to press on his shoulder until he was lying back on the hard floor of the shed, with her straddling his thighs.

Here in the dark *she* was in control. She could touch him, taste him, however she wanted. She slipped her hand inside his pants and wrapped her fingers around his erection and his hips lifted instinctively, his indrawn breath sharp with surprise and arousal.

"Bailey, I—"

"Shhh." She refused to let anything spoil this. If he could still talk, she wasn't doing a good enough job at distracting him.

She scooted down his legs and bent her head, closing her lips over the head of his cock and sucking gently. Teasingly.

"*Fuck.*" Cameron's curse was rough, his breathing jagged.

Yes. She wanted him like this. Wanted him to feel as insane as he'd made her feel. Not that she was feeling that sane. His taste was addictive.

Her mouth opened wider, taking more of him, her tongue gliding along his shaft. Delicious.

He slid his hand into her short hair, but he didn't push her down or pull her away. Good.

She couldn't stop tasting him. The drop of pearly liquid at the tip of his cock made her want more. Made her sex soak in reaction and her hips rock against his legs, aching for friction.

She sucked her cheeks in, trying to take as much of him as she could, one hand cupping the tight sac of his testicles.

Cameron shouted and his body tensed. "Baby, please. *Please.*"

She lifted her head, struggling to control her breathing. "Please what?"

He hesitated, and for a moment she wished she could see his face. His eyes. That irresistible dimple.

"Please fuck me."

She shivered before standing up and stripping off her jean shorts and underwear. She heard him fumbling in his pocket, heard the tearing foil of a condom wrapper. She bit her lip in excitement, lowering herself over him again.

He gripped her hips to guide her, and she braced herself on his chest, her body sinking onto his shaft with a slow, deep rock of her hips.

"Ah."

"Yes, baby. God, that's so good."

There were no more words between them. Both of them too focused on the physical sensations. Both focused on one goal. Pleasure.

Bailey circled her hips, rocking against him, reveling in the stretch of him inside her. Maybe it was the darkness, but everything felt more intense, more intimate.

Just the two of them connected in a passion she never wanted to end.

She never wanted it to end.

She was a fool. She might have actually fallen in love with her sexy, fickle boss.

He lifted his hips upward in a forceful thrust and she cried out, her back arching hard. She couldn't hold on, couldn't concentrate. Her body was shaking with arousal, with realization, so close to the edge already she could hardly breathe.

Cameron rolled her over, obviously just as aroused, just as impatient. He spread her thighs wide and pumped inside her, deep, hard strokes that had her shouting his name until her voice was hoarse.

"Bailey, I can't wait. Come, baby. Come for me." His gruff command was all she needed.

She reached up, digging her nails into his shoulders as her orgasm ripped through her, shattering everything in its path until there was nothing but this. Nothing but him.

She heard him call out her name and then he was with her, clinging to her with his face buried in her neck. As lost as she was.

Vulnerable again. She hated this feeling. Hated that she lost herself when he touched her. That she may have lost more than she could afford to lose by giving into him again.

Namely, her heart.

"Does this count as a bonus point?" she asked with a lightness she didn't feel. "If so, you just jumped way ahead of Davide."

His trembling body froze above her, and she instantly regretted her words. Damn, damn, double damn why hadn't she sewn her mouth shut? Transcendental sex apparently made her chatty. And not in a good way.

He lifted himself off her and got to his feet. She could hear his clothes rustling, knew he was getting ready to leave.

She grabbed her shorts and slipped them on just as he reached the shed door, opening it up to let in the light.

Bailey blinked rapidly, her vision adjusting just in time to see a flash of pain in his expression before it closed to her completely.

"I shouldn't have come here."

For a long time after he left she stood there in silence, a pain in her chest. Maybe he was right. He shouldn't have come to Sedona.

He shouldn't have shown her what she'd always been missing. He shouldn't have made her think she might not like it when he was gone.

But no harm done, right? She crossed her arms defensively. In fact, his coming may have been a good thing. She was beginning to see all manner of flaws in her old five-year plan. A handsome, wealthy man like—well, like Ewan McGregor for example—wasn't for her. A man like that would seem perfect. Perfect body, perfect chin . . . but he'd only seduce her with spankings and orgies, make her fall in love with him and walk away. She should just stock up on batteries and call it a day.

An image of Will popped into her mind and she remembered what he'd said. If she wanted to be loved, she had to stop flying long enough to give it a chance. Long enough to be seen.

Darn interfering old man. What if he was wrong? What if when she stopped flying she got knocked down?

What if she was too afraid to take that chance?

Six

Cam stood at the wall of windows in the library, his pilot's itinerary in his hand, studying the landscape.

What was it about this place?

He was one of the few people who could say he'd been to nearly every beautiful destination in the world. He'd been to all the small towns that built up around the tourist trade, selling merchandise from the ridiculous to the sublime. He'd climbed mountains, camped in breathtaking rainforests and surfed in waters so blue they looked like another sky.

Why was this high desert town, which on the outside was so similar to all the others, so different?

He knew the answer. It wasn't the brilliant red spires or the crisp clean air. There was only one thing. Only one reason.

She was here.

The manager of a ridiculous little broken-down inn who dressed like a colorblind Las Vegas showgirl. The woman who took everything on without backing down, who helped out friends and strangers alike, but wasn't afraid to say no. Loudly. That woman had crawled beneath his skin.

He turned and glanced at the desk where he'd set the file marked B. Wagner. He'd forgotten he'd asked for it. When Davide gave him his mail this morning, and he'd opened the large envelope with her whole life inside, Cameron had hesitated.

He was still hesitating. Because she wasn't just an employee. She wasn't just another woman that he and Davide had shared.

She'd said that place was the only home she'd ever known, and those words had reached inside him and gripped his heart.

His family had a dozen houses, more hotels and businesses—but had he ever thought of any one place as his home? Had he ever cared about anything the way she did for that hovel?

The answers to why would be in that file. But the simple truth was, he knew she wouldn't want him to read it. That she wouldn't like him snooping into her life uninvited.

"The gang is almost packed and ready to go."

He nodded at Davide's comment, but didn't look away from the file.

Davide came closer. "Planning on reading that before we leave?"

"No."

"I see."

Cam pierced him with his glare. "You see what?"

Davide didn't back down. "I knew she was different. She affected

194

me, too. I just didn't realize how different." He ran a hand through his hair. "Hell, Cam, I feel like handing you the car keys and saying something about finally growing up."

"Smart ass."

Davide smiled cheekily. "That's why you pay me the above-average-but-could-be-better-bucks, right?"

He walked over to the desk and picked up the file. "If you're not going to read it, maybe—"

Cam was at his side, pulling the file out of Davide's hands before he could finish his sentence.

Davide laughed. "*Maybe* we should tear it up."

The sound of tearing paper had never been harder for Cam to hear. But it felt right. Bailey Wagner was more than statistics in a file. More than a fling. She was special.

Faster than he'd imagined possible, he'd fallen for her.

He just wished he knew how to tell her that. How to make her believe.

Cam tossed the pieces in the trash. "Pack the Jeep, Davide. It's time."

When her cell phone rang and she saw the name Fran pop up on her caller ID, she had to smile. The bartender at the Laughing Coyote was always a fount of gossip. Small-town gossip was Bailey's Achilles' heel. Well, one of them. The perfect thing to distract her from the fact that she was going to Dani's house to dump her pride and her troubles on the table and ask for her friend's advice.

But within a few minutes of listening to the breathless woman's report she'd changed her mind. She hated gossip. Gossip could go rot like the devil it was.

"What do you mean, *leaving*?"

Fran chuckled. "I know. Everyone is talking about it. We were hoping those big spenders would throw some cash our way, you know? A whole house full of moneybags and none of them come down the hill to spread the wealth. Although," she lowered her voice, "I heard a few people talking about an orgy the other night. Why weren't we invited, I ask you? I haven't had a good fu—"

"Thanks, Fran. I'm going to check it out."

The bartender gasped. "Oh, I didn't even consider . . . I wonder what it means to the inn, his leaving so quickly. Think he's gonna put it back on the market?"

"We'll just see about that." Bailey said a terse good-bye and hung up the phone, turning her small, sputtering car around and heading up the hill toward Cameron Locke.

After another sleepless night, after what happened yesterday . . . he was leaving? It was a little fast, even for someone with his reputation.

She wouldn't think about all she wanted to say to him. How he'd hurt her with his silence. Wouldn't think about the fact that she'd had the best sex of her life, that her wish for a threesome and to feel like someone saw her, wanted her, had come true—even though it didn't give her the happy ending Dani and Liam had found.

No. She wouldn't think about anything but the inn. *Her* inn. She wanted to make him an offer. The same one she'd tried to give Pikeson but he'd turned down.

She'd be damned if she let someone else have her place. The Enchanted Inn was hers. The first place that she felt a foundation underneath her feet.

He might take her heart when he left, but he couldn't have that.

Her heart. She still couldn't wrap her head around it. It was crazy, but she knew it was true. Apparently she'd gotten more than her mother's eyes; she'd also inherited her bad taste in men. Men who had a tendency to leave. But then, her mom had a tendency to leave too. To run away.

"Let's hear it for genetics," she mumbled, stopping at the edge of the driveway and watching his entourage file out like elite ants with designer luggage.

She saw Davide and she turned off her car, leaving her door open as she ran to catch him. "Davide!"

He winced a little guiltily when he saw her. Just the reaction you hope for when the handsome Italian sex god who helped rock your world sees you in the light of day.

Bailey shook off the self-pity. "Where is he?"

Davide pulled her onto the grass, out of the way. "Bailey. I'm glad to see you. I wanted to tell you—I found out what Bunny said to you. She had no right. It wasn't true."

She put her hands on her hips. "Which part? The part where you two have shared women before me? The part where you like a challenge?"

He wrapped his warm fingers around her wrists, reminding her of how she'd let herself be bound by them. How she'd trusted them. His expression was intent. "The part where it is a game. It's not. You weren't. I . . . It meant more than that."

She tilted her chin, trying to hold on to her determination. "Where is he?"

Davide's expression closed and he backed away. "I hope you'll forgive me one day, Bailey. Cam is already gone. I'm taking the next flight out. You should go back to the inn."

Her head whipped back as though she'd been slapped. It felt like she had. Already gone. God, it hurt like a physical wound.

She glanced over at the handsome men and women piling into the two limousines in the driveway. Bunny met her gaze over the hood of the closest one.

Guilt? For what? For being found out by Davide? For not warning her that Cam's lovemaking would feel just like that? Like making *love*?

She was barely aware of what she was doing. It was as though someone else was guiding her movements.

Turn around. Get in the car. Drive home.

She was on autopilot. She just needed to get back home before she lost it. Before she showed them all that everything she was—sassy, loud, eccentric—was just a show. That in truth, she was a damn mess. Lonely. Leave-able.

Bailey parked the car and headed toward the front door of the inn. She stopped in front of the neatly packed, clear plastic luggage.

"Ms. Littleton, leaving already?"

The woman nodded, and Bailey noticed that for the first time she wasn't wearing dark colors, and she'd let her hair down. She looked more human. "You look like you had a good vacation. Did you get what you were after?"

Ms. Littleton smiled. "Not exactly. But I did realize that it isn't my destiny to communicate with aliens." She made a face. "They're far too unreliable. I'm sure it has something to do with dimensional physics or something, but there it is."

Bailey's lips twitched. "Probably physics."

"But coming here has shown me what my true calling is." The woman looked around before leaning closer to Bailey. "Ghosts. I think I draw them. And with what I learned from that sweet Native American man, now I know how to help them find their spirit path."

Just when she thought she would break and never laugh again, Sedona made her smile. She was still hurting, she still wanted to curl up in a ball and cry out her heartache. But there was always hope. For Ms. Littleton. For her.

Bailey took the older woman's arm. "You might be right, Ms. Littleton. In fact, now that you mention it, I've got a trunk in my car with your name on it."

She lifted the hood of her pink Bug and Ms. Littleton gasped. "The trunk from the attic?"

Bailey nodded. "I was planning on taking it to Jerome, but now I think it belongs with you."

Ms. Littleton was nearly dancing in place. "What's inside?"

She hadn't even thought to look. She flipped open the rusted lock and lifted the lid. "Son of a—"

The spider. That giant, colorful spider that started all of this was sitting on a pile of old photographs and yellowed envelopes. What was it doing in the trunk?

Ms. Littleton oohed and reached her hand inside. Bailey gasped. "Wait, the spider . . ."

It was gone. She glanced over at the older woman, but she was showing no sign that she'd seen anything other than the photo she was holding. It was definitely old. The faded image showed two small girls holding hands, the taller one clinging to a small doll made of corn husks.

They were wearing decidedly mischievous smiles. She could almost believe those little devils would love hanging out in her attic, making her crazy.

"There are letters in here. Journals. This is a treasure chest. Are you sure you want to get rid of it?"

Ms. Littleton sounded so hopeful. Bailey smiled. "You'll enjoy it more than I ever could. It's obviously been here much longer than I have, and I'd really like you to have it."

After seeing her unusual guest off with a warm embrace and sending Cyndy home, Bailey finally made it to her room. She stared at her cream-colored walls for a few minutes. This was ridiculous. She didn't want to have a pity party by herself. It could get ugly. Maybe she should call up Kaya, tell her she was coming over and they should invite Dani. It was good to be around friends. Especially when you felt like your heart was breaking.

She'd just reached for her phone when a knock sounded on the door. "Miss Bailey? Miss Bailey."

The old guest who wouldn't leave. "Is that you, Mr. Olyphant? Come in."

She turned to see the old man, his back pressed against the doorjamb, looking over his shoulder suspiciously.

"What's wrong now?"

"I think we may need to call Will back. I'm guessing we have another spectral visitor among us."

She buried her face in her hands. Maybe they were mad she'd gotten rid of the trunk. Oh Lord. Was she really starting to believe in ghosts, on top of everything else? "Is it in the attic again?"

"Nope. This time it's in the empty guestroom next to ours. And its been making a heck of a lot of racket—turning the television on and off, running the shower, slamming things—that I thought you ought to know before Mrs. Olyphant decides we have to go to another inn."

"We wouldn't want that. What you're describing doesn't sound like a ghost." It sounded like an intruder. "You stay here, Mr. Olyphant."

"You can call me Vic."

Bailey smiled absently. "Thank you, Vic. I'm going to go check this out."

She looked down at her sundress. White eyelet lace on top and pink zebra stripes on the bottom wasn't exactly ghost-hunting garb, but maybe the bright colors would intimidate them into crossing over. At least she was wearing sensible flats.

She grabbed the bat behind her dresser. The one she kept for this very occasion.

She walked down the hall toward the last room, feeling sorry for whoever was inside. She was not in the mood to be charitable.

Bailey whipped open the door, hoping to surprise the criminal and froze. Her mouth opened. Closed. Opened again.

"Right on time. I've just gotten to the good part. Although to be honest, this particular author has a *lot* of good parts. I had no idea romances were this . . . detailed."

She absently gave a thumbs-up and the shooing motion to Mr.

Olyphant, taking a step inside the room and closing the door behind her.

Cameron Locked was lying on the flower-printed coverlet of the queen-sized bed, his head propped up with pillows, reading *Pleasure's Edge*.

The book he'd spanked her with.

"Do you have a reservation?" *Shut up, Bailey. Don't chase him away until you find out what the hell he's doing here.*

Cameron smiled. "Afraid not. But I am a close, personal friend of the owner."

He set the book down and threw his legs over the bed. "Speaking of owners, as my last official job as owner of the Enchanted Inn, you're fired."

Her heart jumped to her throat. *"What?"*

He stood up warily, the smile on his lips not jibing with the vulnerability in his gaze. "Fired. You no longer work for me. I find there are some lines between business and pleasure that I have to draw."

She leaned back against the door. "I see."

His eyebrows shot up. "You see? Usually your tongue is a little sharper, Bailey. I was expecting more. Especially from someone I'm hoping will give *me* a job."

"If you keep speaking in riddles I may hit you with my little pink shoe. Or my big wooden bat."

Cameron smiled. "There's that spirit. The thing is, I went ahead and accepted the last offer pending prior to mine on the inn, since it hadn't officially been withdrawn. So a B. Wagner is now the owner of the Enchanted Inn."

"No."

"No?"

Bailey put her hands on her hips. "I'm not some cheap local you can throw a diamond tiara at to clear your conscience."

He strode closer to her, indignation bright in his eyes. "Number one, I didn't give you a damn tiara. I accepted your offer on the property. Two, if I *did* give a woman a tiara, I damn sure wouldn't make her pay for it and three, my conscience is clear. You left *me* that night, not the other way around." He hesitated. "Although I shouldn't have walked out like that yesterday."

Unfair. The more he argued his point the more his dimple stood out. She'd never gotten to lick it. "Oh."

"Oh?" He laughed, running a frustrated hand through his hair. "No 'why are you still here when most of your friends have gone off to live it up in Switzerland, Cam?' Just oh?"

She licked her lips and swallowed past the dryness in her throat. "You said you wanted a job?"

Cameron noticed her telling action and smiled, stepping closer until his arm was above her head against the door. "I do."

She was breathless. Her heart racing. He was so close, she couldn't resist lifting one hand to press it against his chest. "What are your qualifications?"

He kissed her, and Bailey felt her bones turn to jelly. God, he was good at this. Good at taking away her control.

It was his fault she was unbuttoning his shirt and running her fingers over his smooth chest. His fault that he took too long unbuckling his belt, making her slap his hands away so she could do it faster. She unzipped them and took his hardening erection into her hands, stroking him as he searched wildly for the opening of her dress.

He gave up, tugging down her top and slipping his hand under her skirt. He lifted his mouth from hers and bent his head to her nipple, sucking it hard against the roof of his mouth as he pulled down her underwear.

Bailey moaned. "That's a nice qualification. What else can you do?"

He smacked her bottom in warning, handing her the condom to slip on his cock. She fumbled, but finally slid it down and in an instant he was there. Gripping both cheeks in his hand and lifting her up against the door.

Cam pulled his lips away from her nipple with a groan of regret, looking up into her eyes as he lowered her onto his shaft. "I'm good with numbers."

They both inhaled sharply as he filled her. "Oh, baby you're wet. Mmmm. I know how to use most power tools."

He slung his hips high and hard inside her, and Bailey cried out, clinging to him as waves of sensation crashed over her.

"I give. The best. Deep. Tissue. Massage." He thrust inside her with every word, so deep she could hardly breathe.

Bailey was shouting, but she couldn't help it. "Oh *God*. That's a good one. I love that one."

Cameron's laugh was gravelly. "Thought you might."

For a while neither of them could speak. Bailey had been overwhelmed since she'd seen him in the room. She didn't know what to make of all he'd said. Right now she didn't care. She'd been so afraid that she would never get another chance to feel this way. Alive. Powerful. Weak. Whole.

His grip on her hips tightened and he powered into her as though he couldn't wait. As though he couldn't get enough. One hand lowered between their bodies to caress her sensitive clit, and the tender pressure sent her closer and closer to the edge.

He growled. "And this, Bailey Wagner, as much as you can take of this. I'll even share you with Davide once in a while. I'll give you whatever you need."

It was too much for her to take in. What he was saying, what he was doing. Too much.

She screamed his name when her orgasm swept her away, every part of her on fire for him. Belonging to him.

"I can fucking feel you coming around me. God, that's . . . Oh baby, I can't . . ."

His hips jerked against hers. Once. Twice. His big body shuddered against hers and he buried his face in her neck, muttering her name.

Baby Love

She pinched his shoulder then pressed her lips against it gently. "I forgive you, but only because of that last qualification."

Cameron lowered her back onto wobbly feet. "There's one more you might want to hear."

The tone of his voice had her meeting his gaze. She saw something in his eyes, in his beautiful GQ features, that gave her hope.

"What?"

"I love you."

"Why?"

He sighed heavily and leaned his forehead against hers. "You are the most difficult . . . I've never said those words to another woman in my life, and you want to know why."

"Please."

Cameron studied her expression, and he must have seen how important his answer was to her. "Because from the first second I saw you I wanted you, Superman underwear and all. Because you help people and smart-mouth them at the same time. Because pink drives me crazy . . ."

She rolled her eyes and he cupped her face in his hands, caressing her lower lip with his thumbs. "I couldn't leave. I thought about it, but it didn't even tempt me. I want my home, and all my challenges, to be with you."

She could see it in his eyes. Love. It happened so fast her head was still spinning, but she couldn't deny she felt it too. So much it scared her. But not enough to walk away from it. Not this time.

"Pink drives you crazy?"

Cameron looked down at her bunched up dress and grinned. "Baby, pink gets me *hot*."

"You're hired."

He picked her up and carried her over to the bed, tossing her onto the mattress with a growl. "I'm going to hear you say it back to me before I let you out of this room."

"Say what?" She batted her lashes with faux innocence, laughing when he threw his shirt over her head. She may be in love, but she wasn't stupid. She was ready for some more convincing.

"That's a beautiful kachina, Will. I'm sure Miss Bailey will love it. What is it?"

"Hummingbird."

Mr. Olyphant smiled. "If I let the missus see this she'll want one just like it. I better put it in Bailey's bedroom, just to be safe."

"I appreciate it. And I have something for you, too, Vic."

The old man's eyes bulged, and he looked around to make sure no one was in earshot. "Is it that thing we talked about?"

"The same."

He held out his hand and accepted the small, beaded pouch, a new sparkle lighting his eyes. "And you say a little pinch of this will . . ."

He waggled his bushy eyebrows and Will laughed. "Trust me. It's never failed."

Mr. Olyphant blushed. "Not that I need it necessarily, you understand. But all this love in the air"—he motioned down the hallway expressively—"gets a man remembering his youth."

The sound of a woman's laughter and a man's deep answering growl echoed toward the two old men.

"Indeed it does."

Sinful Pleasures

One

"So what you're saying is, if she loves me, she should understand why I need her to get those implants."

Kaya lost her serene smile and looked up from her reading table at the bane of her existence. "Are you my next appointment? If so, I think I've suddenly come down with a cold."

Jace smiled as he leaned into the open doorway. "No need to be that way, Kaya. Just having a little fun. Thought you might be sick of people wanting to hear that they're Cleopatra or Helen of Troy."

She was loath to admit he was right. Though, in their defense, some people came to the Crystal Vibrations Center, the New Age bookstore where she worked several days a week giving psychic readings, with an honest curiosity and an open mind, wanting to be a part of the magic of Sedona. But most just wanted an affirmation that they were right. Special. Cleopatra.

She wasn't about to let him know she agreed with him. "Why are you here?"

Jace walked farther into the room, making her uncomfortable. "I had an appointment, but I'm a little early. Any space in your schedule for me?"

She hesitated, and he sat down across from her, holding out his hands. "Come on, I'm curious. Aren't you?"

Another truth she'd never admit to him. It was hard enough they shared the same work schedule at the resort, her second job. Harder still that he was so close to Liam, the love of her dear friend Dani's life. This was usually the only place she could guarantee she wouldn't run into him. Why was he invading here?

Not even her dreams were sacred lately. He'd been in those as well. Especially since she'd seen those strange stars fall—since she, Bailey and Dani had made their wishes.

At least she hadn't seen the spider yet. Both her friends had seen a distinctly unique spider right before their worlds had been changed and their wishes came true.

Had it been the Spider Grandmother of the Hopi? Something deep within her said yes. Her friends had been given a gift. They'd been given love.

She studied Jace. Love was the last thing that came to her mind when she looked at his condescending smile. But she was curious about the half Navajo sous chef. Apprehensive, but curious.

She reached for his hands. She had always been able to sense things about people without touching them; emotions and thoughts like a warm breeze around her. Touching was a more powerful connection, the breeze occasionally becoming a whirlwind. She shouldn't touch Jace, but for some reason she didn't want to contemplate, she slid her palms against his.

Heat. Desire. Need.

Kaya's eyes closed and an image, similar to the ones that had been haunting her dreams, appeared in her mind.

Jace lowering her onto a bed, passionate intent clear in his beautiful eyes. She opened her arms willingly, pulling him closer for a hungry, primal kiss.

He lifted his smiling lips and bent down to press them against her neck. She turned her head, knowing her other lover wanted her and saw—

"Nick?"

She opened her eyes when Jace yanked his hands from her grip and stood so fast the chair behind him fell. "Nick, huh?" He forced a laugh, but Kaya could see his easy manner was gone. "If you tell me I'll find happiness with a giant, rock-loving redhead, I'll start doubting all those mystical abilities they say you have."

Kaya blushed. When it came to Jace, she doubted her abilities, too. She lifted her chin. "You wouldn't be the first pair of roommates we know to fall in love. Look at Dani and Liam."

His sexy lips twisted. "Funny." He tilted his head, his raven hair falling across his forehead. "So what, exactly, did you see about Nick, Kaya? More importantly, what did you see about me?"

"I'm ready, Jacie."

Kaya nearly jumped in her chair, startled. She saw a quick expression of regret from Jace before she turned to see one of the girls who worked in the shop downstairs. Tina? Was that her name?

"Excuse me?"

Tina smiled eagerly, her whole body practically vibrating like a perky, blonde Chihuahua. "Sorry about him. Jacie here got bored waiting for me to clock out for lunch and snuck upstairs. He's a little devil that one."

Kaya stood up, trying hard not to roll her eyes. "I won't argue with that."

"Kaya . . ."

The blonde came into the room, and grabbed Jace's wrist, tugging playfully. "I only have one hour. We're wasting time. You know how hungry I get."

Nausea welled up in Kaya's throat. She had to get them out of here. "Please don't let me keep you."

Jace was scowling when they left. Good. She hoped it took him exactly sixty minutes to get in the mood. Though she doubted he'd need that long.

This was a small town for having so many tourists. Kaya usually heard when Jace was seeing someone. Not that she cared. But there hadn't been any gossip in a while. She'd thought . . .

She started to pace the confining little room. The murals covering the wall portrayed starry skies and a lush desert landscape. But it was just an illusion, like so many things here. Including her visions about Jace and his best buddy Nick. A *Bahana* who liked to dig around in sacred sites and a Navajo who lived to torment her. Two men she had no business thinking about.

Jace, she hadn't been able to avoid—but Nick? Seeing him the way she did in her vision, through the eyes of a lover, didn't make any sense. She'd met him several times, of course, but she barely knew him.

She was fairly sure her grandfather would not approve. But then, there weren't many things in her life these last few years that he *would* approve of.

She placed her hand over her left shoulder, thinking of the tattoo she'd gotten a few years ago, the spiderweb that reminded her of her people's ways, as well as the connections every human being shared. One of her small rebellions.

Her gaze was drawn to the jar holding the crinkled green bills she received for giving readings. She'd sold her gift since she was eighteen in order to send money back to her aunt, who was raising Kaya's younger brother and sister. But it had gotten harder to stomach in the last few weeks, and she knew why.

Her grandfather.

He'd arrived about a month ago without warning, having walked for who knew how long from his home on Black Mesa. Then he just moved into her small cottage house in Oak Creek. No explanation.

When she'd called her aunt to tell her he wasn't missing, that he was with her, Aunt Pakwa hadn't sounded relieved. In fact, she'd been suspiciously closemouthed for a woman who usually couldn't wait to tell Kaya all the ways she was betraying their way of life. After that first call, however, Kaya couldn't even get her aunt to answer her phone. It worried her.

And her grandfather wasn't any better. He'd refused to talk to his daughter, saying he'd go back when it was time. In time for *Nimon*. For the festival.

That was only a few days away now. And Kaya still didn't understand why he'd come, why he hadn't said anything about her abandoning this lifestyle and returning home. He'd been acting very strangely. Even for him.

Her curiosity was killing her.

She didn't want to think about why she hadn't confronted him. He was her grandfather, a respected Elder of her people. And she loved him. Despite the years of tense separation, she always had.

A brisk knock on the open door had her spinning on her heel. She wasn't in the mood for a reading right now.

"I am having a really strong psychic vibe. Yes. Yes, it's coming through loud and clear. You will have lunch with two of your favorite people. The same favorite people whose phone calls you've been avoiding for the past few days."

Dani chortled, bumping the dramatically swooning Bailey with her hip. "Okay, Sassy, that's enough out of you."

Bailey lifted her eyebrows. "What? I'm just sayin'. *Food.*"

Kaya smiled. "Everyone's a comedian today. But food sounds good." Better than thinking about her grandfather. Or what she'd seen when she touched Jace. What she'd felt.

Her friends' happiness would be the perfect distraction for her restlessness.

Twenty minutes later, after they'd gotten a table in a serene little Japanese restaurant and ordered, Bailey finally stopped talking. And stared at her.

Dani was looking at her, too. Expectantly. Her expression was excited, as though she was holding back a secret.

A whisper of knowledge, a flush of emotion came to her on the wind, and Kaya gasped. "Dani, are you pregnant?"

The tiny, curvaceous woman paled and her deep blue eyes grew wide. "What? No! I mean, I don't think . . ."

She clapped her hand over her mouth, the white cast of her skin suddenly seeming to change to a greenish hue. Dani pushed back from the table abruptly, running for the bathroom, her brown curls bouncing wildly in her rush.

"Damn it."

Kaya jolted in her seat. "Damn it? I'm sorry. I should have waited for her to tell me."

Bailey shook her head, grabbing the sake their quiet server had already placed on the table, along with the tempura squid slices and dipping sauce they'd ordered for their appetizer.

"That's not it, K. Here we were, our conversation all prepared, and you go and throw a fetal monkey wrench into our perfect plans. Not cool, Kaya. Not cool."

Kaya bit her lip. "That wasn't what you wanted to talk about. She didn't know, did she?"

Bailey glared at her until she'd finished chewing. "Obviously not. You and your Jedi mind tricks. Now she won't be able to focus."

"Yes, I will." Dani scooted back into her chair with an embarrassed shrug. "False alarm. Just needed to splash a little water on my face."

Bailey's expression softened. "Is it possible Kaya's right?"

"It's definitely possible. I just didn't think it would happen so quickly."

Kaya tilted her head. "You were trying?"

The blush that put the color back in Dani's cheeks was telling. "Liam says we waited so long to get together, that we have a lot of catching up to do. Besides, Liam's always known how much I love children."

Kaya heard the yearning and wonder in Dani's voice, and she understood the cause. After her ex, Sal, had shown up, she'd told Kaya and Bailey the rest of her secrets, wanting there to be no more barriers between them.

Dani had grown up in the foster system. It always threw Kaya, how apathetically the "civilized" world treated their children and their elders. The two most precious commodities a community had. Hope for the future and the wisdom to make it bright. Even though her own parents hadn't been a large part of her life, her extended family had always been there to see to her needs.

Bailey laughed. "You and the sexy chef never do things in the normal way do you? I love that about you."

Their server slid in and out like a shadow, depositing a large sample platter of tuna, unagi, tomago and snow crab.

Kaya's stomach growled, but she hesitated. "Should we go somewhere else?" Dani's constitution might not be able to take sushi today.

"Don't hold back on my account. I'll just eat the tempura." Dani bit into it and moaned. "I have to say it, I never thought a sushi restaurant in the middle of the desert was a good idea. I'm from Dallas, and they have some of the best sushi this side of Japan. But this place is fantastic."

Kaya slipped a tuna roll into her mouth, agreeing with Dani as the buttery fish literally melted on her tongue. She'd never had sushi until she'd come to live in Sedona. In fact, the mere idea of eating raw fish had sounded disgusting.

She closed her eyes on a sigh. She was big enough to admit when she was wrong.

Without lifting her lids to study her friends, Kaya spoke. "Out with it. If your plan wasn't about Dani's news, and we aren't going to talk about how she's now dying to tell Liam . . ."

She let the question hang in the air, knowing she wouldn't have to wait long. Not with Bailey around.

Surprisingly it was Dani who spoke first. "Wishes," she blurted out. "We wanted to talk to you about the wishes we made that night."

Bailey took a drink of water to wash down the wasabi she'd just slathered all over her crab, making noises of pain or agreement, Kaya wasn't sure which.

The wishes. She'd be lying if she said she hadn't been amazed by all that had happened with their lives since that night. All those connections. The Istaqa. The spider that only Dani and Bailey had seen. Kaya's dreams.

Since then, Dani and Liam had discovered they were far more than best friends, and they'd been protected from harm by a powerful Istaqa, a coyote spirit that they'd apparently shared more with than Kaya had first realized.

Bailey had fallen in love at first sight with the jet-setting Cameron Locke and gotten ownership of the inn. Though Kaya knew without a doubt which one mattered most to her now.

And Kaya had gotten . . . her grandfather. A grandfather who might be able to help her decipher all these symbols if he would only talk to her.

"What about the wishes?"

Bailey fanned her cheeks and smiled. "You tell us, Butterfly Maiden."

Kaya shifted uncomfortably in her chair. "What do you mean?"

"Everything's come true so far. Your dream, our wishes. Everything." Dani leaned forward, her eyes bright. "You're the last one."

"What she's trying to say is, you wished for a threesome, too, just for a second. Don't bother to deny it." She glanced at her nails and murmured to Dani. "My money says Jace is bachelor number one."

A small, high-pitched squeak made Kaya jump, then wish she could sink into the pretty blue carpet when she saw the server standing beside their table once more, a pitcher of ice water in her hands.

Bailey held up her glass. "Thank you, I'd love a refill."

When the rattled young woman left, Kaya took a deep, steadying breath. "Maybe we shouldn't get together to eat out anymore. You always end up traumatizing the poor waitstaff."

Bailey shook her head. "You're a waitress at the resort. Admit it, the more eccentric the customer, the more interesting your night."

"Interesting doesn't always equal good."

"Don't try to change the subject, since I'm pretty sure it's the reason you haven't answered our calls in two days." Bailey lowered her voice, and Kaya knew it was the only concession she'd make. "I wished to be seen, really seen for who I was, and Cam showed up."

Kaya couldn't help but smile at the way Bailey's voice changed on her new beau's name. But Bailey wasn't done.

"Dani wished to trust again. And she had to face her past, and find out the truth about Liam to discover that what she'd wanted was right in front of her. Just like Dorothy in the friggin *Wizard of Oz*."

Kaya knew where this was going. "And I wished for freedom to make my own mistakes, to find happiness. To not have to be what everyone expects me to be."

But her wish was more complicated than theirs. And impossible to have. Her whole life was about paying for someone else's mistakes. Her mother's. Yoki and Len deserved some security, regardless of who their fathers were, and who their mother *wasn't*. As their eldest sister, Kaya had formed an uneasy alliance with her aunt to make sure they had it.

She studied her friends' earnest expressions. On the surface you couldn't see it, why they were friends. They were all so different. Bailey loud and bright and fearless, Dani soft and warm and compassionate, Kaya seemingly aloof and serene. But inside they were so much alike. In one way or another they'd all learned early that they'd have to take care of themselves, and they all found it hard to trust that love would stay. Kaya had sensed it from the first. That they were meant to be friends. Knowing them had made her life here fulfilling. Their friendship and loyalty meant the world to her.

"Has Will made your kachina yet?"

Bailey rolled her eyes at Dani. "We're going off topic again, aren't we? I thought we were going to talk about our threeso—"

"Wait, kachinas? Dani, what kachinas?" Kaya held her breath, waiting for the answer.

"Will made a kachina for me. The bear kachina. He said it was a healer, just like me. He really helped me realize how I felt about Liam. And inspired me to get back into nursing."

Bailey chewed her lower lip thoughtfully. "Really? I got the hummingbird kachina. I thought it was just because he'd told me that story about how the hummingbird flies so fast no one can see it . . ." She snorted. "Getting into other people's heads must run in the family, huh, Kaya? Kaya, what's wrong?"

Her grandfather had given them katsinam? Kachinas he'd made *himself*? No. The man who had raised her aunt and mother would never do that. He followed the Hopi Way. He made kachinas for the young girls of the village, to help teach them about the sacred rituals of their religion. He'd made one for her when she was a child. Before she'd disappointed him by leaving their home.

What was he doing here? And why, the insecure child inside her cried, was he guiding her friends onto their paths when he'd hardly spoken to her since he'd arrived?

"I didn't know. He didn't tell me."

"Not to distract you from your family troubles . . . but what about Jace?"

Bailey's question was enough to pull Kaya out of her reflection. She raised her eyebrows and shook her head. "You keep trying, but that path leads to nowhere. Jace and I do not mix. Besides, didn't you pass him on your way up to get me today?" And the girl he was with? She curled her fingernails into her palm to stop herself from saying it.

Dani and Bailey shared a guilty look, then Dani shook her head. "Liam is positive Jace hasn't been seeing anyone. He and Nick have been teasing him about it."

That's what Kaya had thought, but she knew what she'd seen. "It doesn't matter. I have too much to do to worry about—"

"Having a life?" Bailey interrupted her. "Enjoying yourself instead of paying for other people's mistakes? Taking a walk on the wild side?"

Dani blushed. "Trust me, you'd like it."

Kaya pushed her plate away. "I love you both, but to be honest, I'm not sure I have a wild side." She thought about her visions of Nick and Jace surrounding her and sighed regretfully.

"Bullshit."

Kaya smiled apologetically at the couple a few tables away from them before glaring at Bailey. "Do I have to ground you before you'll behave?"

Bailey grinned, reaching into her purse to throw some money on the table. "No. You just have to come with us and do what I tell you to. And be prepared . . . old Gramps may not approve."

Kaya didn't want to think about why that fact made the idea more appealing. Or why she got up to follow her friends without arguing.

Dani slid her arm through Kaya's and grinned. "Bet you didn't see this one coming."

She hadn't. She should probably be worried.

"Motherfuckingsonofabitch!" Jace dropped the knife and instinctively stuck his bloody finger in his mouth, heading toward the sink.

He turned on the cold water and slipped his finger beneath the forceful stream, watching his blood spin down the drain.

Every day. Every fucking day it was something. He'd come to this resort with eight years experience in kitchens under his belt. His knife skills were flawless, his mastery over every piece of equipment, every skill on the line, perfection.

He'd moved to Sedona almost two years ago, and since he'd gotten this job, it had been one thing after another. A burner he'd turned off himself turned on again when he was in the middle of cleanup, burning his wrist and leaving a scar. Pots fell off their hooks. Once he'd even gotten locked in the walk-in refrigerator. And every day with the knives . . .

Anasazi.

The Navajo word for ancient enemy. His Anglo father would chuckle, but Jace was convinced it was because he was part Navajo. This resort was on Anasazi sacred land.

It sounded insane, thinking that the spirits of a long dead enemy were making mischief in the kitchen, but Jace knew better than anyone that sometimes the things you thought were bedtime stories or superstitions to scare children could turn out to be very real.

"Kitchen attacking you again?"

Jace didn't look up from the sink. "Think of the devil and he appears. You aren't supposed to be back here, Nick. What's up?"

"Stax is gone."

Jace smiled, slipping his good hand into the pocket of his chef's coat and pulling out a small tube of superglue. "Good riddance. I thought that guy would eat us out of house and home. Or slit our throats in our sleep."

He glanced up to catch Nick staring at his finger in fascination.

"What are you doing?"

"Better than a Band-Aid." Jace smiled as he coated his finger with the sticky substance. "An old chef's secret. Works better than duct tape. And don't change the subject. Why do we care that Stax is gone?"

"He left before he could help me . . . find what I was looking for."

Nick didn't have to tell him. He'd known his friend long enough. The cure. Nick was looking for a cure for what he was. Stupid bastard. If Jace had that "disease" he, for one, would revel in it. The trouble he could get into . . .

Jace shrugged. "Like Kaya said, he's Istaqa. A coyote spirit tied to this land. He belongs here. I don't think he's gone far."

Nick rubbed the back of his neck in agitation. "Maybe. But the man sure knows how to cover up his tracks. Can't seem to sniff him out. And I was counting on him to finish the translation."

The reason Nick had moved here in the first place. When Jace had decided it was time to meet his mother's people, to learn about the culture and life of the woman who had died giving birth to him, Nick had taken that as a sign. He'd accepted a job doing research in conjunction with the Coconino National Forest, thinking it would give him answers. And the opportunity to study the site that matched his unusual artifact, the engraved prayer stick with strange symbols he'd brought back with him from his trip to South America.

Jace had been glad of the company. Someone familiar in this foreign landscape, so different from the bright lights and excitement of Las Vegas, was welcome. Especially since his family "reunion" had not gone well.

Yet, they'd both stayed on.

He understood Nick's reasoning. When only one person knew and accepted what you really were, you had a tendency to stick close. But Jace had stayed for another reason altogether. And her name was Kaya.

Jace shrugged. "Maybe it's not time to finish it."

His friend harrumphed. "Spoken like a native of Sedona. I think this place is rubbing off on you. I remember a wild man who didn't think about anything but the next party, the next paycheck and the next piece of ass."

"Maybe I've grown up."

Or maybe the only ass he could think of lately belonged to a woman who would just as soon kick him as look at him. He was, she had told him with her actions and sharp-tongued words, everything she abhorred in a man. Flippant, uncaring and egotistical. His Navajo blood was just the icing on the cake.

She did have a sweet ass, though. And the rest of her was just as tasty. She was tall for a Hopi, slender and golden, with eyes that saw right through him. Through everyone.

Kaya. He'd been watching her, maybe more than he should. She'd lived here for years but he could count her friends on one hand. She worked two jobs, and he knew she made a good living from both, but you wouldn't know it from the simple way she lived.

He wanted to be there when she finally let go. He'd fantasized about it. But so far the only thing he incited in her was anger and irritation. At least when he got her riled, he saw fire in her eyes. That gave him hope. Although the Tina incident probably hadn't helped his standing.

"Stop."

Nick's low growl made Jace freeze. "What?"

"You're thinking about her again. I can smell it on you."

Jace sighed, slipping a single finger glove over his wound. "My bleeding break is over, and the lunch rush is almost here. And stop with the smelling. It's creepy, man, seriously. My thoughts are my own and if they have a particular odor, I don't want to hear about it."

It didn't help his mood that Nick wanted Kaya, too. Had from the moment he'd seen her. Just like Jace.

They'd been best friends since senior year in high school, and in all that time this had never happened. That he knew of, anyway.

If he was honest he knew Kaya was more Nick's type than his. Jace preferred perky blondes who wanted a good time. The perkier and blonder the better. It was Nick who loved the quiet, introspective ones, the dark-haired moody girls who wouldn't know fun if it jumped up and bit them on their granny-pantied rear ends.

Or at least he *had* loved them. Jace couldn't think of a single woman Nick had dated in the last five years who'd lasted more than a night—when he dated at all.

He was a different person now. Still Jace's friend, but different.

"Go brood somewhere else. Liam, the traitor, is home relaxing since he abandoned ship. He'll keep you company."

Nick smirked. "He can't help that he's rich, Jace. You shouldn't hold someone's genetics against them."

"Hah. All the times we played poker with a ten dollar max. I could have looted his ass, then I'd be the one living the high life with sweet little Dani, and he'd be getting attacked by his own knives."

Nick turned to leave, chuckling. "No, he wouldn't. The resort only hates you, Jace. Remember?"

He remembered. The resort. Kaya. It was a damned epidemic. And he was sick of it.

Two

Her grandfather was trying to drive her crazy. That was the only explanation.

Maybe it was a good thing he wasn't around. Her hand came up to touch her hair. She couldn't believe she'd actually done it. With the same adrenaline rush she'd felt when she decided to get her tattoo, she'd watched as the hairstylist cut her long black hair in a simple shoulder-length bob, coloring it with rich, henna-red highlights.

Her grandfather definitely wouldn't approve. If she could ever find him. She'd returned home, ready to confront him, to find out what he was up to and how her friends were involved. At the very least listen to a lecture about how far she'd wandered from the Hopi way. But, although she could smell the ceremonial smoke, he was nowhere to be found. On her patio there was a circle of cornmeal and a *paho*, a small prayer stick decorated with one perfect feather, but no grandfather. It was as though he'd just left what he was doing moments before.

But these types of ceremonies usually took place in *kivas*, the underground rooms where men gathered and shared the secrets of the ancestors and the knowledge of the kachina.

Not in her tiny little house.

She'd waited up for him, but he hadn't come back. Was he up to more mischief? Maybe matchmaking for Fran at the Laughing Coyote? At this point she had no idea.

Now it was morning and she'd barely slept, and still hadn't connected with her grandfather. She knew he'd been here. His blankets were mussed and the smell of sage still hovered in the air. That made her feel a little better. At least he hadn't gone missing again. He was just steering clear of her.

Was it because he knew when she had finally fallen asleep her dreams were less than peaceful? That they had nothing to do with her worry for him, and everything to do with Nick and Jace?

She stepped outside and walked onto the path behind her cottage. She'd found it the first day she'd moved here. It was one of the reasons she loved this place. The trees and brush that shielded her house led to jagged red rock. She came here to find answers. To think.

It had only been a moment. Just an instant that she'd thought about being with the two men before those stars had fallen. Despite what Dani and Bailey had said at lunch yesterday about it being her turn for a threesome, she didn't think her path included either Jace or Nick, let alone both.

There was a reason some things remained fantasies. But the line between what she felt in her visions and dreams and what she was feeling now had been blurring so much lately, she wasn't sure of anything.

She'd also noticed how much more she felt around Dani and Bailey now. Their satisfaction. Their joy. Their secrets. Did that have to do with that first dream?

I dreamt about you, about all of us. I saw stars fall and I heard a voice say, "Wish, Butterfly Maiden." Then I saw three paths merge into one . . .

Were they more connected than she realized? Beyond mere friendship? Beyond their wishes? Or was it just envy because she'd been alone too long?

If only her grandfather would talk to her. Maybe he would know what it meant.

As soon as she thought of him she heard his voice. Clear as a bell. Singing a chant she remembered from her childhood. He must be here.

She moved farther down the path . . . there . . . no *there*, beyond that rise. She walked faster, determined not to let him get away this time.

He *would* talk to her. Or she would take a page from Bailey's rulebook and bop him on the head with it.

He'd picked up her scent the moment she arrived. No one else in the world smelled like that. Within moments it grew stronger, and with each breath his muscles tightened.

How could he concentrate on the task at hand, looking for Stax, when she was so close? Taunting him. Making him long to bury himself inside her. To see if she tasted as right as she smelled.

Don't act like an animal, Nick. Remember what Stax taught you.

He willed his heart rate to slow. The Istaqa had, in between being a giant pain in his ass, given him a few lessons in control.

"I was born what I am. I don't see myself as split in two. But you, if you are to survive, one side must be dominant. Your mind is too fragile to war with itself. Concentrate. You can control it. If you don't, you will go mad before you find your answers."

He could hear Stax as if he were right behind him, reminding him of his weakness. Control. He remembered when he thought he had it. But that illusion had been ripped away from him five years ago.

Kaya's scent deepened, grew richer, as though she was . . . aroused. Moments later it changed again, turning to worry. He suppressed the growl that threatened to erupt from his throat. Who was it? Was someone touching her? Had they hurt her?

He let his mind expand, sensed everything around him with his enhanced abilities.

Nick's body hardened, all the blood rushing to his cock when he thought about her. He knew Kaya had abilities as well. Not the same as his, but he wondered if she could feel him. How desperately he wanted her. How difficult it was to hold himself back, though he had a thousand good reasons to do so.

The most important reason of all, even more than this curse he'd been given, was Jace. His best friend. Jace wanted her for himself. Had since he'd met her at the resort restaurant.

He knew Jace better than anyone, and not so long ago, he hadn't believed the man had a monogamous bone in his body. Hadn't thought he would last a week without a woman in his bed. But in the last couple of years, Jace's partners had become more sporadic, until, without any fanfare or explanation, he'd stopped bringing women home altogether.

Jace didn't have to tell him why. Nick could sense it. And he recognized the same truth in himself.

It was her. The woman who didn't seem to know either one of them existed.

From the corner of his eye he saw a blur rush past him. Kaya?

Nick could not resist his instincts. He followed her.

She was moving fast, deep into the desert hillside, but he was faster. He found himself pulling back, keeping just out of sight. He made no sound she could hear. Stealth was a gift of his curse.

He watched her long, loose skirt flying out behind her, clinging to her lean, golden legs, her simple peasant blouse flashing nearly sheer in the sunlight. Had she dyed her hair?

Nick tried to tamp down his desire. This wasn't foreplay. He was no better than a mindless beast. She was looking for something, someone, and all *he* could think about was sex.

He stopped when she hesitated at the winding, clear water of the creek, watching her from behind a wide-trunked cottonwood. She whirled around, her brow furrowed in confusion.

"Is someone there?"

He held his breath.

Kaya knelt beside the water and rubbed her temples. "I'm not sure what's wrong with me."

Nothing. Nothing was wrong with her. Except she had on too many clothes.

She froze and looked up. "There you are again." His sensitive hearing picked up her mumbled, "And you are definitely *not* my grandfather."

Nick almost chuckled. He was suddenly reminded of a childhood story, *Little Red Riding Hood*. He supposed he was the big, bad wolf in this scenario. And with those new, ruby streaks in her normally blue-black hair, she looked even more edible. He *did* want to eat her. Wanted Kaya for breakfast, lunch and dinner.

His imagination vividly drew out the scenario. He closed his eyes and saw her spread out on his table, his head between her thighs while he feasted. She cried out as he drank her down, swallowing every last drop of her arousal until she was begging. But he knew he wouldn't be able to stop. It would never be enough.

And when he was finally able to pry himself away from the sweet, uniquely Kaya-flavored arousal, it would be to fuck her. To take her there on the table, on the floor. To turn her over and have her in the way he'd dreamt of so many times.

His eyes opened with a snap at her moan. He took a deep breath and shuddered. She'd felt him. His thoughts. His arousal.

Did she realize? With her eyes closed, her hips rocking slowly, tormenting him, did she know where it was coming from?

Her long, slender fingers slid up her blouse, gliding over the curve of her breasts, the nipples so dark he see them through the fabric. She shivered delicately, her cheeks and throat tinged with color. With need.

The beast in him smiled, wanting to test it. Wanting to see how much of him she could feel. Before Nick knew what he was doing he'd unbuttoned his jeans and slipped his hand inside to grip his cock. Hard, hot and ready. The way it always was around her.

Can you feel this, Kaya? Can you sense how much I want it to be inside you? How much I want to watch you pleasure yourself?

A silent howl of victory echoed in his ears as he watched one of Kaya's hands drop to her lap, her knees opening, fingers pressing between her thighs, soaking the thin material of her skirt.

He was doing this. He was making her feel his arousal. Making her hips thrust against her fingers, the fabric rubbing against her clit, the lips of her sex.

He stroked himself to her rhythm, fist tightening as he imagined she would when he was inside her. She'd take everything he had to give and more. She'd be just as greedy as he was. She'd want to claim him, own him, taste him.

A vision of her lips wrapping around his cock had him straining. *Faster, Kaya. Faster.*

Through the red haze of lust he watched her comply. She was a goddess. Spreading her knees and reveling in her power. Her sexuality.

Even fully clothed she had the ability to wreck him. It was the most erotic thing he'd ever seen, and he knew this image would be branded in his mind forever.

Kaya coming undone.

She cried out, her movements swift now, one hand pressed against her breast, one massaging her sex as she rocked against her invisible lover.

Him.

He was so close. To losing any shred of control he had. To

coming. To leaving his hiding place and pumping himself to blissful release inside her.

"*Yes.* I've never felt . . . don't stop."

They were whispers barely spoken through her panting breaths, but Nick heard.

I won't, Kaya. I won't stop until you come. And you're going to, aren't you? You're going to come so hard for me you'll cry out with it. So hard you shatter. And while you do, you'll be feeling me inside you, filling you, making you take everything I am. Show me now, Kaya. Show me how beautiful you are when you come.

Her voice broke through the tense silence like a summer rain. She cried out her pleasure, and he couldn't help but join her. Lightning jolts of release flowed through his body, rocking him to his core.

All the while he watched as her stunning features were transformed in climax. He'd been right. She was a goddess.

His tongue flicked out across his lips and he tasted her climax in the air. And he would kneel at her altar to have more.

Kaya shook her head and he went alert. She was looking around, lost and confused. Ashamed. How could she be ashamed of that? It was natural instinct. She was born for it.

She stood and straightened her clothes with shaky hands. She backed up, heading back down the path, toward the safety of her rented cottage.

No. She couldn't leave him. She belonged to him. He wanted more. More.

She turned to run as if the hounds of hell were on her heels and he scented the one thing that could stop him. Fear. The need he'd sent her had been too strong.

Nick stripped off his clothes grimly. He wouldn't follow her. Not after that. She'd seemed so vulnerable, all he wanted to do was take her in his arms and promise her that nothing would hurt her again.

But how could he keep that promise when he knew what he was?

Cursed. Untamed. And a bastard to boot. How else could he explain the way he'd pushed his feelings on her so passionately? He'd wanted her to feel him. To feel how much he wanted her. All the things he'd imagined doing to her night after night, for so long.

He was a selfish bastard.

But, a voice inside him whispered, *she responded. She wants you, too.*

God help her. Because he wasn't sure he could let her go for long. Not after this. Not when every cell in his body was crying out one word in a single, powerful voice.

Mine.

He folded his clothes and placed them at the base of the tree. Then he let it take him over. His curse. His own personal demon.

The wolf.

Running deeper into the wilds, he started to howl. He'd found her. He'd tasted her. She was his mate.

But Nick knew the wolf's elation wouldn't last. Not when the man inside was still convinced he couldn't have her.

We'll see about that.

Three

"Kaya, sweetie, can we switch tables? I don't think I can handle all the testosterone at mine without dumping braised buffalo in their laps."

Kaya smiled gratefully at the flamboyant waiter who shared her shift, his machinations distracting her from her chaotic thoughts. "I'm getting a shifty vibration. What are you up to this time? You usually love a challenge."

He sighed. "That's what I get for being scheduled with my own personal psychic friends network. You want the truth? There's a person sitting in your station that I recognize—a person I want to sing to me as we sit atop a glittering elephant and drink absinthe."

She sent him a blank look and he rolled his eyes. "I forget you don't go out enough to get that movie reference." He slid an arm around her shoulders. "Hang on to your bra straps. It's Ewan McGregor."

"What?" *That* name she recognized. But only because Bailey had said it nearly every day since she'd known her. Until she'd met Cameron Locke, that is.

"Where?" She went to the swinging doors that led from the kitchen into the dining room and craned her neck. "Which table?"

She had to call Bailey. Never mind that she'd decided to avoid her friends for the moment, at least until she was sure they wouldn't convince her to pierce her eyebrow to match her new wild hairstyle, or they'd worked off some of their excess . . . emotions. The last thing she needed was to accept a dinner invitation with the two new couples, sensing what Dani and Bailey felt for Liam and Cam up close and personal. She felt like a hormone factory as it was.

And whatever she'd experienced in the woods had only agitated her more. Made her aware of needs she'd barely admitted to herself. She'd never felt so connected. And she had no idea who it was—*what* it was—that had done it.

But this went beyond discomfort. Sitting at her table was what Bailey had called her Holy Grail. Her Moby Dick. Her Ewan. And he was at the resort.

She had to tell Bailey.

She turned and bumped into a wall. A wall that smelled fantastic, and looked a lot like Jace's chest. Not that she'd noticed his chest. Or dreamt about it.

He looked down at her curiously, his gaze narrowing suspiciously on her hair, but spoke to the man beside her. Jerk. "What's up, Wally?"

The waiter crossed his arms over his chest. "Gloom and despair for me, but Kaya is feeling no pain." He winked at Jace. "She's having the Alyssa Milano moment."

Kaya glanced back and forth between the two men, confused. "What does that mean?"

Jace shrugged. "This resort caters to the stealthy wealthy, you know that. Politicians, CEOs, movie stars; if they come to Sedona, they come here. And if one of the kitchen or waitstaff have a particular admiration for one of these guests, that's what we call it."

Kaya frowned. "I've worked here longer than you, so how do you know that and I don't?"

Wallis opened his mouth but Jace held up one hand. "We'll compromise. You go see what he wants as an appetizer, and I'll explain this to Kaya. Let's get out of the flow of traffic, shall we?" He touched his hand to the small of her back and guided her farther into the kitchen, near the large, heavy door that led to the back of the building.

Why wasn't she pulling away? She disliked Jace, dreams and visions notwithstanding. Didn't she? Besides, he was dating that Tina woman, no matter what Dani had said to the contrary. But his hand was burning through her uniform. Making her tingle.

"You don't know because everyone else knows you don't care. Kaya works. She doesn't have a television, doesn't go to the movies. She doesn't participate in politics and she's not interested in the latest NBA star." His attention kept returning to her newly cut hair. "Until today I'd be willing to bet she never let a stylist touch her hair. She would never have the Alyssa Milano moment."

She wanted to be mad at him, but instead she felt a little sad. The person he'd just described was not who she wanted to be. That woman sounded lifeless, bloodless. Cold. Even the Hopi who lived on the reservation had more fun than that. Lived more. Was that how people saw her?

Jace flinched. "Hell. Don't look at me like that, Kaya. Tell me I'm an asshole. Stick your nose in the air and look down on me. Anything."

He pulled her out the door so fast she hardly had a chance to blink. The cool air shocked her and she closed her eyes, letting it soothe her heated cheeks.

"I'm sorry, okay?"

She couldn't keep her lids down. "Did you just apologize?"

Jace offered her a sideways smile. "Don't let it get around."

Kaya leaned back against the wall of the building, studying him. He *was* handsome. Almost beautiful, though his features were too sharp for that. Dark and tall and strong . . . and arrogant. Cocky.

She wanted him.

A door had opened inside her over the past few days that she wasn't sure she could close. Wasn't sure she wanted to close. Behind it were all the selfish needs and desires she'd repressed, hidden away. They did nothing to help her fulfill her obligations. Nothing to honor her family. But they were hers, they were strong, and they wanted out. Wanted what she'd felt in the woods again.

Wanted to know how it would feel if Jace kissed her.

She smiled. "Why Alyssa Milano?"

Jace tilted his head, taking one step closer. Two. "The story goes that many years ago, she came to the resort. One of the line cooks had been in love with her since he was ten years old. He had posters on his wall, he belonged to her fan club, the perfect fanatic."

He placed one hand on the wall above her head, leaning closer. "He begged the chef to let him make her something he'd been working on. Something special that wasn't on the menu. It was approved and he was in heaven, creating the perfect dish for the woman of his dreams."

"What happened?"

Jace laughed softly, his gaze tracing a path across her cheeks, her lips. "The same thing that always happens when a man is confronted with a beautiful woman. He made an ass out of himself. She asked to come back to the kitchen to thank the line cook personally for his masterpiece, and he couldn't believe his luck. He saw her, but they were separated. By the grill station, the sauté station, the serving line. But he had to get to her. He raced past the cook in sauté, who was, at that very moment, flambéing tequila shrimp. When he bumped into him the chef wheeled around, the pan filled with flaming shrimp still in his hand."

Kaya covered her mouth, seeing events unfold in her mind as he told the story. Trying hard to slow her racing heartbeat as it reacted to his nearness. "Oh, no!"

Jace nodded, pressing his forehead against hers. "Oh, yes. He lit up like a bonfire. They put him out pretty quick, but by the time the smoke cleared, Alyssa had been whisked away, never to be seen in the kitchen again. *Voila*, the Alyssa Milano moment."

He tugged her fingers down, his beautiful brown eyes narrowing on her mouth as she said, "I wasn't having that moment."

"No? Not a member of Mr. McGregor's fan club?"

"No."

Poor Bailey. She wasn't going to get a phone call right now. Because there was no way Kaya was moving from this spot. Not yet, anyway.

"I took Tina to lunch. That's all."

She wasn't happy he reminded her. Jace sighed and pulled back enough to look directly into her eyes. "She's the cousin of a friend. She just moved here a few months ago, doesn't know many people and for some reason, she's latched on to me."

She lifted an eyebrow. "It's none of my business."

Jace licked his lower lip sensually, his long lashes shielding his eyes. "It could be."

He was going to kiss her. The thorn in her side. And she was going to let him. She would probably even kiss him back. She wasn't going to be that predictable, passionless woman he'd described.

He smiled, dipping his head. "Then you won't mind if I—"

The low, threatening growl behind Jace cut his sentence short. He glanced over his shoulder and swore. "Kaya, I want you to get inside. Slowly now, don't make any sudden moves."

She took one small step up toward the door, seeing a large gray timber wolf behind Jace. He was huge. His sharp teeth were bared threateningly in Jace's direction.

And he looked familiar. "Stax, Jace. He was the wolf with—"

"Go."

"But if he's like—"

"Kaya. Go. *Now*."

*   *   *

"Are you happy now, Nick? Good job. You cock-blocked me. Anything else? Wanna steal my lunch money? Slash my tires?"

Jace was pissed. For the first time since they'd met, Kaya was looking at him the way he'd wanted her to. The way he'd imagined when she'd become the star of every sexual fantasy he had. Kaya as the prim schoolteacher. Kaya as the strict dominatrix. Kaya on her knees, in his lap, anyway he could get her.

Nick just stared at him accusingly from behind the eyes of his wolf. Jace had learned the Navajo people believed shape-shifters were witches, evil, but he knew better. Nick wasn't evil.

Though he *was* a prick.

"No talking then? Well, how about listening. You want her? Fine. So do I. And I think she wants me." The wolf snarled. "Well, what do you think we should do about it?"

Jace knew what he wanted to do. Vulgar or not, he was so on edge, wound so tight, he could probably punch a hole in the wall with his cock. He wanted Kaya. Hell, he *needed* her. It didn't make any sense, and God knew she never gave him any encouragement, but there it was.

And there Nick was. Making him feel guilty.

He glared down at his friend. "I didn't ask for this, you know. I wasn't raised Navajo. I was raised on roulette and the fine art of cocktail waitress tipping. Why did *I* get stuck with the fuckin' skinwalker?"

The wolf stalked closer, real rage in his eyes now. And hurt. Jace hit the wall and Nick turned away, his powerful body disappearing with a speed and grace that only ticked Jace off more.

He had that gift, that ability, *and* he wanted Kaya? Fuck that.

May the best man win. And he did mean *man*.

He walked back into the kitchen and started up on the line. Not making eye contact with anyone, not even when the restaurant attacked again, dumping the olive oil beside him on the floor. Breaking the handle of his favorite skillet.

He was hyperaware each time Kaya came back from the dining room. Knew she was trying to catch his eye. That she was curious about what had happened to the wolf.

But if he talked to her right now he'd lose it. Worse than the line cook in his story. And he didn't want to fuck this up. She was too important.

Why? Because she resisted him when so few women did? At first maybe that was true, but it was more than that now. So much more.

Was it because Nick wanted her? Rivalry? He'd like to say yes, but the truth was that poor bastard deserved someone as amazing as Kaya. Someone who understood him in a way no one else, not even Jace, ever could. Kaya could have been that person for him.

But Nick preferred to maintain his distance, to want her tragically from afar, while Jace tried to harass her into giving him some attention.

Jace wasn't sure why, but she was paying attention now. And it was too late to hold back, even though he had a feeling his desires might be more than she was ready to handle. And it was too late to be a gentleman and step aside.

He offered up a silent apology to the Anasazi.

And Nick.

* * *

Kaya was exhausted. It was one o'clock in the morning, and the strangest day she'd ever had was over. All she wanted was a nice long soak in the tub. She didn't want to go looking for her grandfather, didn't want to figure out why Jace had decided to avoid her, or why that wolf had suddenly appeared, the one she was sure she recognized. Or why it felt . . . so familiar.

She'd found out from the manager that Bailey's idol had reservations to be at the resort for four days, so she consoled herself she hadn't completely ruined her friendship with Bailey by not calling. A phone call she should have made instead of attempting to be seductive.

Too bad it hadn't worked. She'd almost walked on the wild side. Maybe it just wasn't in the stars for her the way it was for Dani and Bailey.

And she still hadn't seen that darn spider.

There was another possibility. Maybe she hadn't really meant her wish. Without her responsibility to her brother and sister, whom she adored, what would she be? Without having to work two jobs, what would she do? What did she want? She didn't know the answer to any of those questions. And the truth of that bothered her.

When she was younger her grandfather had told her she was meant for great things. Was this why he avoided her? Because he saw now that she hadn't lived up to that potential?

Kaya clocked out then leaned against the serving line with a sigh as she ran a hand through her hair. She really needed to stop feeling sorry for herself.

"Everybody's gone."

She jumped, her hand tangling momentarily in the thick strands. "*Ouch*. Don't *do* that."

Jace. His chef jacket was unbuttoned, his hair was mussed, and Kaya's heart, despite herself, started to race. He spoke again. "Everybody but us."

His expression was unreadable as stone. Was he waiting for her to leave so he could lock up?

"Just let me get my bag."

Jace shook his head. He strode toward her, slipping his arm through hers and walking her backward into the kitchen manager's office.

He didn't say a word as he lifted her onto the desk. He took off his coat and pulled the white T-shirt he wore beneath it over his head, revealing his smooth, muscled chest. Then he just stood there.

Nothing witty or sarcastic to say. No joke to ease the tension. No seduction. He was just . . . waiting.

For her move.

Kaya wasn't sure what to do next. She was raised in a different world with different rules. Rules she'd regretted breaking in the past.

She wouldn't regret this. Her dreams. How she'd felt when she touched him, or this afternoon, the anticipation she felt now. The heat. She didn't want this to stop. She wanted more.

She studied his chest, watched it rise and fall with his breathing, watched his muscles flex as he held back. She licked her lips and he groaned.

Her fingers lifted to the top button of her white dress shirt and released it from its catch. A muscle beside his eye twitched.

Kaya smiled. It felt good. Better than good. She allowed her mind to open. Allowed herself to feel his desire and gasped at the intensity of it.

She unbuttoned the second button. The third. It was killing him, this waiting. She felt the need bubble over inside him, felt him give over to it just seconds before he moved.

Then he was there, kissing her, ripping open the buttons of her shirt to reach her bare skin. She couldn't get close to him. Her slim black skirt had no give.

Kaya reached down to the side seam and, without taking her mouth from his, tore it up to her hip.

Jace lifted his head at the sound, looking down at her handiwork before meeting her gaze. His smile of delight was answered by one of her own. Then she gripped his hair in her hands and tugged until he kissed her again.

She saw the images in his mind. He wanted her to wrap her legs around his waist. She did, and moaned. His erection, hard and hot, fit against her perfectly. Or would, if they weren't wearing so many clothes.

He seemed to come to the same conclusion, slipping his fingers inside the waistband of her cotton panties and ripping. She thought she could easily become addicted to that sound.

She sensed his excitement as if it were her own when he ran his knuckles over the fine triangle of hair covering her sex. It was sensation on top of sensation, her feelings and his.

Had she ever truly been connected until today?

Kaya heard another tearing sound and opened her eyes when he broke their kiss again. He took her hands in his and guided them to his shaft, showing her how he wanted her to slide the condom on.

Her fingers caressed the bare, velvet-ridged skin at the base and he trembled. He liked that.

She did it again.

"Kaya." That was all, just her name, but it came with so much emotion she reeled from it.

He bent his head, leaving one scraping bite along her nipple through the fabric of her bra. "Kaya."

"Jace, please." *Don't make me wait. Don't make me feel things you don't mean. Show me what I've been missing.*

He reacted as though she'd spoken aloud. His hands dropped, arms slipping under her knees and lifting them up until she had to lean back on her hands, the smooth-grained wood beneath her palms.

He looked down at her and swallowed. "I knew you'd look like this. Be like this."

He'd fantasized about her; Kaya saw it in her mind. But she was just as open to him now. She was already so wet she knew he could see it. He knew how excited she was. How ready.

Jace didn't need any more coaxing. She felt the head of his erection slip through her arousal, then fill her slowly. One inch at a time. Pleasure followed, filling her along with the weight of his swollen flesh.

Why was he torturing himself? And her? She knew what he wanted. The hard, frenzied ride he'd imagined. She wanted it, too. She needed it.

A whisper of words came to her from his mind. Words that would take away all his hard-fought control. "Fuck me, Jace. I want you to."

She only had a heartbeat to feel embarrassed before, with a roar, he let go of his control. Thrusting deep and hard inside her. As wild and passionate as she'd dreamed.

"*Yes.* Oh!"

That was it. That feeling *he* already knew would come but she'd never known during the short-lived, unsatisfying relationships in her past.

He loved the feel of her around him. She was tight around him. Deliciously tight. Don't think about how tight. Fuck, he wouldn't last long.

His thoughts were heightening her desire, wrapping around her until they were another caress. More fingers gripping her flesh, more lips gliding across anything they could touch.

Energy filled her body with every deep, slinging thrust of his hips. Brilliant, infinite. Enough to power a universe. "Jace."

"Say it again."

"Jace."

He pushed her legs up until she slid onto her back, until her knees were against her shoulders and she was spread wide, for him.

He was deeper now. So much deeper. And he was grinding against her clit with every stroke, driving her wild. Driving them both wild.

"Again." He groaned.

"Jace, oh, Jace that feels *so good.*"

"*Yes.* Kaya, I need you to—"

Come. Please, baby, come for me. I want to feel you squeeze my cock when you climax. I want to hear my name as you fly. I need to hear it. I'm so close—

"Jace!" The energy burst up her spine and out through her head, her fingertips. Energy and a pure, dazzling pleasure, unlike anything she'd ever felt before.

She reached for him, gripping his arms, his shoulders, anything to keep her connected to him as she flew.

He shouted her name over and over. When he found his release she felt it. It tore through her with the force of an explosion, sending her soaring again. Higher than before. With Jace.

Jace.

Four

Meet me at our sacred spot tomorrow. You remember where. We will talk.

Kaya stuffed the note back in her jeans pocket, adjusting her small backpack filled with water, some granola bars and a first aid kit. She wasn't sure what she would find here. She'd driven north toward Flagstaff, then parked her beat-up red truck and headed into the forest.

When she'd arrived home last night, thoroughly debauched and a little shaken, this note had been waiting for her instead of her grandfather.

The old man had gone wandering again.

As if she didn't have enough to worry about after having a transcendent experience with Jace. An experience that, if she was truthful with herself, she always knew he would give her. Wasn't that why she'd kept him at bay for so long?

It was insanely satisfying. But this wasn't exactly how she'd pictured spending her morning after. Surrounded by green, lush foliage and mountain peaks, hip-deep in childhood memories.

She'd been her sister Yoki's age, just a little older than ten, when her grandfather first brought her here. Her mother had left again, and Kaya had already been learning how to take care of herself, trying to make sure her aunt had no reason to punish her.

Her grandfather had woken her up very early, and they'd driven down the road, singing songs to the rising sun and laughing.

The walk had been long, but he tried to explain along the way how important this place was for the people. For her. He held her hand and told her about the plight of the Hopi. How they tried to worship and build their prayer shrines in holy places. Placing their *pahos* and *piki*, the ceremonial food, in the hopes of their prayers being heard.

He told her how the Navajo sought to stop them at every turn because of their jealousy and greed. How the government blocked them from their holy sites, stopped them from gathering ceremonial supplies, and had even, just a year or two before she was born, defeated the Hopi, the Zuni, and even those stubborn Navajo when they tried to stop a ski resort from being built on what they called the San Francisco Peaks.

"The dwelling place of the katsinam, Elder Sister. Where our protectors, those who bring us rain, and the greatest of our ancestors reside after this life. We stand in its shadow. It guides us to our sacred site."

She remembered feeling overwhelmed. Was everyone against them? Even the children she met when they journeyed into town?

"Not everyone. But a Hopi must live apart. It is not an easy life. Some, like your mother, cannot follow our path. But Ma'saw has told us we mustn't stray from the old ways. We must not forget."

They'd made a small shrine near a cave where her grandfather told her some of their people had found shelter before they came to their true home.

It had been a special day for Kaya. Her grandfather had looked down on her with all the hope and love she'd always wanted to see in her mother's eyes. The same love that she'd watched dim in him when Kaya had decided to leave their land.

She saw the cave and searched the forest floor around it. There it was. The small pile of stones that held her prayers and hopes for love and the well-being of all Hopi. So many years and it was still there.

"I want you to have those pictures develo— Kaya? What are you doing here?"

She whirled around, shock filling her as she watched several men exiting the cave, none of whom were her grandfather. "Nick?"

He didn't look too happy to see her. But then, it was hard to tell with him. He never looked happy. At least he'd shaved off the beard he was growing the last time she saw him. He had a good face. She'd always thought so. And an impressive body. Broad-shouldered, thickly muscled. But he seemed unhappy.

Why did that bother her? It always had. She'd see him at a party or speaking to a tribal member at a festival and wish he would smile. Wished she could make him smile. She barely knew him, but for a while she'd felt that they were so similar. Both separate and alone, despite their friendships.

Her dreams had shown another side to him. A more passionate

side. A side she shouldn't be thinking about, considering what she'd done with Jace last night.

She shook off her strange thoughts when she saw a member of the Zuni tribe she'd known since childhood. She raised her eyebrows. "Aalek?"

His smile was genuine and wide. "Kaya. You look well."

She couldn't help but grin. "And you. Have you seen my grandfather?"

His brow furrowed in thought and he shook his head. "No, and we've been here all morning. Was he headed this way?"

If her instinct was right, then no. He'd done it again. Why was he avoiding her? Had she offended him so much that he had to send her on wild goose chases just to escape her?

"Kaya, are you okay?"

She nodded at Nick, not trusting herself to speak.

He turned toward Aalek abruptly. "Go ahead and take these back to the office. I want to get a few more soil samples and rubbings of the glyphs, then I'll join you."

Aalek nodded and waved to her before disappearing into the trees.

"He works for you?"

Nick nodded. "With me. He makes sure the sites are treated with the proper reverence, and he's able to guide me around sacred places"—he pointed to her small pebbled shrine.—"like this one."

"Oh. Why are you here? I mean, at this particular site?"

She'd known he worked for the government, ensuring that ancient and sacred places like this one were evaluated and protected.

She also knew it was people just like him who'd given away most of her heritage by complying with that government.

Why was Jace friends with this man? She stopped herself. A few days ago she'd wondered how anyone could be friends with Jace and felt sorry for Nick, and now look at her. Who was she to judge anyone? That was her aunt talking. Not her.

He made a noise and she realized he'd been trying to get her attention. "If I'm already boring you it doesn't bode well for the rest of my explanation."

She laughed. "I'm sorry. I am interested. Please."

His lips quirked and his hazel eyes sparkled. She thought he was handsome, in spite of herself. She always had. So different from Jace. He was a silent figure that drew her attention, where Jace was loud and almost belligerent in his charm.

Nick had hair like the red-haired kachina of the Hopi, but cut very short, almost militantly short. And a strong, square jaw, with a curving scar on his chin. Was that why he sometimes wore a beard?

He ducked his knees until he was level with her gaze. "Am I right in assuming you know the history of this cave?"

Her grandfather had told her stories of the people who used to live there. People that he claimed were special. She nodded. "Enough."

"Well, I'm studying the petroglyphs that were found only recently, in a much deeper tunnel of the cave." He shrugged. "That, along with the soil around the area, to determine the exact date people may have lived in that section and made those drawings."

She didn't know about any drawings. Her grandfather had never told her. Maybe this trip wouldn't be for nothing after all. "May I see?"

His expression showed surprise. His emotions were, oddly, guarded. From her? Or from everyone?

"Of course. If you'd like."

She walked into the cave and took a deep breath. Damp earth and moss. She sent a silent prayer of reverence and thanks to those ancestors who'd walked this path before her and followed Nick closely.

There was light coming from a narrow tunnel. "Down there?"

How could someone as big as he was even fit?

He glanced over his shoulder, catching her wide-eyed gaze. "It's a bit of a squeeze, but worth it, trust me."

She felt a wave of assurance coming from him and she stumbled in surprise. How did he do that? Just drop the wall of his emotions and blanket her with one of his choice? "Nick? Where are you from?"

"I lived in Nevada for a while. It's where I met Jace. Before that, believe it or not, I lived in Oregon. One of the most beautiful places you could imagine." He made a face. "When it isn't raining, that is."

His guard was up again. And so was her curiosity. "Why did you decide to do this? Geoarchaeology, I mean."

"I kept switching my major between the archaeology and geology." He gestured for her to bend down as the roof of the tunnel dipped for several feet. "My professor told me it wasn't common, but I could do both, and I'm glad I listened. I think you have to understand the whole picture before you can truly know what happened in the past. Not just what the Earth was doing, but what the people were doing and how it affected the world around them."

"That sounds more like philosophy than science."

There was a smile in his voice. "More like a passion."

He stopped and Kaya bumped into his back, her body pressing against his for an instant. Everywhere she'd touched him her skin was tingling. He was so warm. And he smelled like the forest. Only deeper than that. Untamed.

She shook her head. *You aren't making any sense, Kaya.* She'd just had fantastic sex and it had addled her brain. She was *not* aroused by Jace's attractive but grim roommate.

"Here it is."

He knelt down and she followed, though she tried not to touch him in this narrow space.

"Unbelievable."

The drawings were pristine. As though frozen in time. No weathering, no fading. "They could have just done this."

He traced the edge of it with his wide, callused fingers. "I know. It was deep enough in here that the cave effectively sealed it from the ravages of time. It's also, according to Aalek, a bit unusual. Do you agree?"

Alertness. Awareness. Was she feeling that? Or was he? She tried to focus on the petroglyphs.

They were definitely familiar. "This is information. The one that looks like a square maze? That's Tapu'at. Mother and child, or the symbol for Mother Earth."

She pointed to the next. "These are a record of their migrations. How long they wandered before they found this place."

She dug her knees into the dirt, thankful she wore jeans as she leaned in for a closer look. Was it a person or an animal? She tried to remember all she'd learned from her grandfather. Though if she was honest, she'd learned more from the books she'd purchased about her people since she'd left home. "If this was Hopi, the clan symbol should be there. But it's not one I recognize."

Caution.

"I've seen it before." Nick spoke absently, but she knew he was waiting for a reaction. "From what I understand it's a representation of, for lack of a better word, a skinwalker."

Skinwalker. She instinctively shied away from the word. Shifters, not like Istaqa, coyote protector, but more akin to witches and long-banned ceremonies, where people would change into crows, coyote, wolves.

Wolves. Like the wolf who'd been with Stax? The one outside of the resort last night?

"There's more farther in. More specifics. But I have a feeling you don't want to know any more. No doubt you'll want to get back to Jace."

She nodded, unable to tear her gaze from the image. "Yes. I mean no, you're right I've had enough."

Ask it. Ask.

"Were you at the restaurant last night?"

"Yes."

Kaya was afraid to move. "Outside?"

"Yes."

"Why did you say that, about Jace and me?"

She looked up at his tormented face. "Because I saw him nearly kiss you last night. And today, I can smell him on you."

It couldn't be, and yet, so much about him made sense now. Including his relationship with the Istaqa, Stax. "You're the wolf."

"I'm the wolf." He narrowed his eyes. "Why aren't you running?"

Kaya had just been wondering that herself. "I'm not sure. I'm surprised. I had no idea. But I don't think Stax, for all his mischief, would befriend a soul-stealing witch." She inhaled sharply and thought of Dani. "Do you know what he did with Sal? Is Dani in any more danger?"

"You're sitting in a dark cave with a man who can change into a wolf, and your first thought is for your friend." He shook his head. "She's in no danger. I'm not sure what happened to that asshole after I dragged him to the base of the mountain, but I'm sure he won't be back. Stax has a particular fondness for her."

She sensed him sending her admiration. It was getting easier to distinguish his pushing, the feelings he was sending on purpose, from his normal reactions. "How do you do that? Are you telepathic as well?"

He was still looking at her as though she were a strange creature under a microscope. "No, but I can project. I think it's part of the heightened senses thing. And instinct."

"You think? You haven't always been like this?"

She didn't need to use her abilities. The bitterness came through clearly. "No. Five years ago, I was cursed. Since then I've been searching for a way to reverse it."

Was he dreaming? Was he really kneeling in a cave with Kaya, her exotic, flawless features locked in a captivated expression as he talked about being a wolf?

She hadn't run. She could have. He wouldn't have stopped her.

God, he loved that she hadn't.

From the moment she'd arrived at the cave's entrance, he'd known. He'd gone running all night, driven wild by the thought of Jace kissing her, and the next day she arrived like a gift from heaven. But she'd already been claimed by his best friend.

Was it strange that his feelings for her hadn't changed? It was impossible to want her more, and yet, with her reaction to his secret, he did.

She was spectacular.

And she wanted to know how he had been cursed.

"I was foolish and eager, like most in my profession. I wanted to understand the tribe I was living with for a few months in South America while I studied one of their ancestral temples, wanted to live as they did. More than that, as they used to live."

He grimaced. "I didn't know that I'd aligned myself with a man who was no ordinary guide, but one that was a leader of a certain cult within the tribe. A feared cult. And no one told me.

"The guide invited me to a late-night ceremony. There was drinking, chanting and revelry. They made me drink out of a special cup. A mixture that would connect me with my animal spirit, to see if it chose me."

He looked down at her and quickly unbuttoned the top few buttons of his shirt, dragging the cloth out of the way to show her the start of the scar. "I thought they were talking in metaphors. Apparently I was wrong. I was so surprised to see a timber wolf in that region. But it made sense in my drug-induced state. I saw plenty when I went camping when I was young. I admired the wolf. And it chose me.

"When I woke up, no one would speak to me, and I was escorted out of the village and given my things. One of the chief's wives slipped a prayer stick into my bag, I think she was trying to help. To warn me."

He sighed. "It didn't take long before I discovered I'd been given more than a hangover from that ceremony. That I'd been cursed."

Soon enough he'd discovered what he was. What he could do. And the only person who'd been there for him, who'd always been there for him, had been Jace.

He started to close his shirt but Kaya stopped him. She came closer and unbuttoned it completely, spreading it across his wide chest to study the long parallel scars running down one side of his body.

She touched them, her fingertips just skimming across the raised flesh, and Nick nearly howled in agony at the pleasure of her touch. She was so close. But she wasn't his. She'd chosen Jace.

"I've heard skinwalkers have to wear the pelt of their animal to change. I've never heard of anyone but a god, or a messenger of a god, having the ability to do it without using witchcraft."

She was talking to him? She actually wanted him to *concentrate* while she was touching him?

"There are some stories, scattered, about a people who were punished. They searched for a cure. Maybe they found it. Maybe these petroglyphs could help."

Couldn't she see how her nearness was affecting him? Couldn't she hear it in the rough growl of his voice?

Nick inhaled sharply when her hands wandered to the base of the scars along his sensitive side. Wasn't this what he'd wanted the other day when he'd watched her? When he sent her his fantasy? Wanted her to touch him as gently and lovingly as she'd been touching herself? Wanted her skin against his? Her acceptance?

Her hand paused and she bit her lip. "You're projecting again. It feels like . . . on the path by the creek . . . that was you, wasn't it? You sent those feelings, those images to me."

Would she run now? "I didn't mean to. I just . . ."

"You just . . . ?"

"I wanted you, Kaya. So badly I couldn't see straight. Then, when I realized you were reacting, I took advantage." He held his breath, her sweet scent, so uniquely Kaya, still in his lungs.

She looked up into his eyes then, her own dilated and hazy with something he was afraid to name. "I've never felt that connected. Not like I was feeling someone else or sensing someone else's emotions, but more than that. You showed me myself through your eyes and I was beautiful. Sensual. Exciting. Not cold or lifeless. And it felt true."

"You *are* all those things, Kaya. I've been trying to stay away from you. Trying to find the answers to why I am what I am. But all I can see is you. All I dream about is you. And since you came for me the other day, it's gotten worse."

Why had he said that? Jace. Think of Jace. Jace wanted her. He'd had her. She was his.

Nick shook his head. "We have to go."

But Kaya wasn't done tormenting him. "We should," she agreed softly. "I just need to—" She bent her head and pressed her lips against his scar, above his heart. "You're so warm," she murmured, her tongue flicking out to taste the long-mended flesh.

Nick bared his teeth. "Do you think I can't smell you, Kaya? That I can't scent your body heating? The liquid honey already soaking through your jeans?"

He gripped her shoulders with shaking hands, pulling her mouth away from his skin. "Even before I had this animal inside me I would have chased you. Don't be fooled into thinking I was ever harmless." He made a sound of frustration. "You had Jace inside you. Loving you, fucking you the way he's always wanted to. The way *I've* always wanted to. He's my friend; you can't have us both."

She looked shocked at his words. Nick knew she wasn't faking her reaction, that she'd been surprised by the strength of their attraction and how it affected her. His wolf cried out in joy that she wanted him. His mind was spinning, struggling with what he should do, and what he wanted to do.

"Why?"

"Why what?"

She caressed his stomach with her fingers. "Why can't I have both of you? Where is that written?"

He closed his eyes. "Kaya? I'm hanging on by a thread here, honey."

"I know it sounds crazy. I was just with Jace and I've never felt like that. He was so tender." Nick jerked beneath her touch instinctively, not wanting to hear it.

Her fingers curled into his flesh. "But you. In the woods—this close—you make me feel something I've always been too afraid to name. Something I didn't understand until today."

She leaned closer until her lips were pressed against his neck. "In my life I've never had time to think about what I want, but you . . . with you I can't avoid my feelings, my desires. Besides, I think I wished for this."

How did she do it? Say exactly what he wanted to hear. No push this time, no misunderstandings. Kaya wanted him.

And Jace.

Son of a bitch.

He lowered her onto her back, careful to keep his weight from crushing her. "Don't think I'll turn you down, Kaya. Getting inside you is all I can think about." He swore long and fluently when she wrapped her legs around his hips. "Not like that. Not without Jace knowing."

The flicker of disappointment in her beautiful doe eyes had him snarling. "But maybe I can take something for myself. A little taste?"

The small space was full of heavy breaths and rustling as Nick unzipped her jeans and pulled them down to her knees. He gripped her hips and flipped them both with an agility he found himself reveling in. He could give her this. Give himself this.

He was on his back, the ground cool beneath him. And she was kneeling over him, her body lithe, beautiful. Her hands reached out to grip the walls as he pulled her up his body until the sweet, full lips of her sex were over his mouth.

"Nick?" The tremor in her question thrilled his wolf. She felt it. His power over her. Knew what he was about to do.

"No one smells this sweet, Kaya. Only you. God, I'm fucking drowning in your scent and I haven't tasted you yet, haven't even kissed you." He met her aroused gaze and smiled. "Let me kiss you now."

Kaya hesitated only briefly before nodding.

With the first taste of her he could hear the wolf inside him rumbling with pleasure, with the need for more.

She was so wet, her taste soaking on his tongue, the air around them saturated with her desire. Kaya. He stiffened his tongue and filled her tight little entrance, wanting to feel it stretch around his cock, but loving her flavor too much to lift his mouth.

He could hear her moaning. She liked that. She loved it. Could she take more? Could she take more of him? Two men at once?

The idea, strangely, only made him harder. Imagining Kaya being filled front and back. Hearing her cries ringing in his ears, knowing he had helped to drive her over the edge.

His nose was pressed against her clit, his tongue curling deep inside her, drinking her greedily. He took one hand off her hips and slipped it between them, lifting his mouth long enough to press two thick fingers inside her, spreading them with each thrust, stretching her.

"Yes. Oh, yes."

He smiled as she started to rock mindlessly against him. "You like that, Kaya? Can you take more? If you want both of us, Jace and I, you'll need to."

She tensed, nodding with a needy groan. "Anything."

Spectacular. He'd always known she was. He removed his fingers, now covered with her sweet, rich honey, and traced a line back and up to her ass.

This. He wanted in. He wanted to claim her in the most primal way he knew. Every way there was.

He lapped at her damp thighs and nibbled with his teeth while his fingers massaged her anus, readying the ring of snug muscle that would hold him so tight he might bruise her.

"You'll take me here, Kaya, won't you? You said anything. Breathe out, honey, that's right. Relax. You'll take all of it, all of me back here. And then you'll let Jace take you"—his tongue slid around her sex—"here. Imagine it, Kaya. Imagine me here."

He sensed the pop of release as his fingers pressed inside. She was tighter than he'd imagined. So tight around his fingers he almost lost his control in that moment.

She shouted his name. In surprise. Desire. Confusion.

Nick chuckled against her clit. "Oh, yeah, honey. You're going to love it. Love how we make you feel."

Kaya cried out again and he knew she was close. He growled out a command. "I need you to come in my mouth, Kaya. I need to swallow you right down my throat with my fingers in your ass. *Give me.*"

She rocked against him and he could taste the richer flavor, still Kaya, but more, as she climaxed with a cry. He wanted to bend her over and get inside her. Instead he licked and sucked and swallowed, thrusting his fingers between her cheeks until she was whimpering weakly, her body shivering with sensation overload.

He would take her home. "We'll take care of you, Kaya. We'll make it good."

We. The more he said it, the better it felt. His best friend. His woman. He wondered that he wasn't more possessive.

If it were any other man, Nick might rip his heart out. But Jace was different. He trusted him completely.

As he dressed the limp Kaya and took her out of the cave and back to civilization, he hoped Jace felt the same way.

For everyone's sake.

Five

Jace's mind was officially blown. He parked in his driveway, not seeing anything as he strode, lost in thought, toward the door.

He'd just had the weirdest conversation with Liam and Cameron Locke, Bailey's new millionaire squeeze.

Jace liked Cam. And his associate Davide, despite the fact that the women in town all sighed loudly whenever he passed by. Jace had joked that he finally had some competition.

But he didn't care about that anymore. His experience with Kaya had cracked the wall he'd kept up around his heart. The one that had protected him when his father had married and starting having children that looked nothing like Jace. The one that had soothed him when the very family he'd initially come back to Arizona to see, to learn from, still hadn't accepted him as more than a distant acquaintance in two years.

He felt vulnerable. And guilty as hell.

Nick loved her. He'd be a shitty-ass friend if he hadn't sensed it. There were a million reasons why what he and Kaya did last night wasn't wrong. And only one reason it was. His friendship.

What Jace felt for Kaya was more like love than any emotion he'd experienced. It was hopeful, it was crazy, it made him hard and confused, and kept a goofy grin on his face when he went to see the guys.

"I know that look." Liam had smiled slyly. "See it every morning in the mirror. And you called *me* whipped."

Jace snorted. "Shut up, jackass."

Cam was smirking. "Oh yeah, he's got it bad. Bailey was right." He glanced at Davide. "Don't tell her I said that or I'll never live it down."

Jace had been confused. "Bailey? What was she right about?"

Cam shook his head. "She made me swear not to tell anyone about the wishes . . . I mean . . . shit."

Liam clapped Cam on the shoulder consolingly. "Men aren't made to keep secrets, Cam. Dani made me swear not to tell, too."

Jace had run his hands through his hair and tugged. "Are you trying to make me beat you? What the hell are you talking about? And what does it have to do with my sleeping with Ka— *Fuck*."

He hadn't meant to say it. Maybe Liam was right. Men weren't meant to keep secrets. "Just tell me what Bailey was right about."

"She said it was Kaya's turn to get her wishes. And she laid money down that you were one of the two in her threesome." Cam's smile grew when Jace went pale. "Need to sit down?"

"Yes. Yes, I do."

Davide had reached for a canvas chair and slipped it behind him before Jace fell.

He couldn't quite believe it. "*Kaya* wished for a threesome? Our Kaya?" *My* Kaya?

Liam sat down on the ground by the pool and reached into the cooler, tossing them all a cold beer. "It's after noon. And I think you need this." He'd flicked off the bottle cap and took a healthy swig. Then he caught Jace's eye. "They all did. All three of them. Dani, Bailey and Kaya. Remember that poker night?"

Jace nodded, still having a hard time processing that his sweet, cool, workaholic Hopi wanted a threesome. Then again, she hadn't been cool the night before. She'd burned him alive. It was the sexiest encounter he'd ever had.

Cam drew him back into the conversation, clicking his beer bottle in salute. "They all got their wishes, too, didn't they? Or, from Jace's floored expression, most of them did."

"Wait a minute, seriously?" Jace leaned forward, looking at Liam. "Cam I can believe—no offense, but he seems the type and I always had Bailey pegged as adventurous—but Dani? You shared her? With who?"

Liam took another deep drink before answering. "Stax."

"Holy shit, man."

"I know."

Cam's eyebrow went up. "Now I'm confused. Who is Stax?"

Jace and Liam answered together. "Nobody."

Liam shrugged. "Just one time. It's what brought us together."

Jace glanced at Cam, who pointed with his bottle toward Davide. Jace swore. "I thought you were friends."

Davide smiled. "We are. Good enough friends that he trusts me. Knows I would never hurt him. Or Bailey."

Jace couldn't believe he was having this conversation. He'd come from the sin capital of the world to a small tourist town. People communed with spirits in Sedona, they didn't participate in orgies.

Kaya had wished for a threesome. Instantly Nick came to mind. His best friend. They both felt the same way for Kaya. But she hardly knew Nick. Was there any attraction? "Fuck. What else did she wish for? I should be prepared."

Liam shook his head. "The rest was private. Honestly, from what Dani told me, they'd been joking about the threesomes. But she swore everything they'd wished for had come true." He smiled, more contented than Jace had ever seen him. "The mother of my unborn child never lies."

Now Jace stood in his kitchen, his mind in turmoil. He wasn't used to sharing. One time, like Liam had done, or once in a while, which seemed to be Cam and Davide's situation with Bailey. But could he share Kaya when he'd finally gotten her in his arms?

Did he want to make sure her wishes came true?

He sighed and headed to his bedroom. He needed to shower. Needed to think. And then he needed to find Kaya and ask her what she was thinking when she'd made that blasted wish.

And *who*, exactly, she'd been thinking of.

"Took you long enough."

"Kaya?" Jace blinked. She was sitting on his bed, her back against a pile of pillows, a small towel draped over her . . . and nothing else. She was using another to pat her hair dry. She must have just showered. In his bathroom.

She made an apologetic face. "Sorry. I was covered in cave gunk, which isn't as exciting as it sounds. We thought a shower might be a good idea before you got home."

"That's ok— We? Whose 'we,' Kaya?"

"I am."

Jace felt his blood pressure rise. Nick had one of *his* towels wrapped around his waist, another around his neck. "Plumbing broken in your room, buddy?"

Nick smiled, his teeth gritted. "Nope."

Jace stepped farther into the room. "Then I suggest you go back there and leave us alone."

His friend's gaze narrowed. "Nope."

Jace looked back and forth between them, both nude, both freshly showered, and he laughed roughly. "I get it. Has this all been a setup, Kaya? After all these years you drop your ice princess routine, change your hair, sleep with me, and then come to my house and fuck Nick, too? I didn't know you had it in you."

Kaya paled visibly, her head jerking back as though she'd been slapped. She scrambled out of the bed, holding the towel protectively against her. "No, Jace, I'd never . . . I'm sorry. This was a bad idea."

She tried to run out of the room but Nick was fast. He grabbed her shoulders and pulled her back against his front, pressing his mouth to her temple before glaring at Jace. "You're a bastard. You know her better than that."

"Do I?" Jace knew he was shouting, but he couldn't help it. "I just found out about her *special wish*. Wishing on a falling star for a fuckin' threesome. That's not the Kaya I know."

"They told you?" Kaya blushed. She'd wanted to tell him. Show him. "Bailey . . . I mean, *I* didn't wish for that out loud. Bailey did." Her voice lowered and she ducked her head in embarrassment. "But I thought it."

"You have nothing to be ashamed of, honey." Nick glowered at Jace. "You're passionate, kind and loving, Kaya. There is nothing wrong with passion."

He turned Kaya around to face him, speaking loud enough that Jace wouldn't miss his point. "Isn't that why we came here? Why I haven't taken you the way I'm dying to? Because we were waiting for Jace?" He kissed her forehead. "You wished, huh? We know how powerful that can be. Were you thinking of anyone in particular when you made the wish?"

"I didn't want to admit it, but yes. I was thinking of this. Of you and Jace."

Shit. Jace saw her shoulders trembling and wanted to kick his own ass. Why did he suddenly feel like an idiot? A jealous, fucking idiot.

He was no prude, but what he felt for Kaya, what he'd always felt for Kaya had taken him out of his comfort zone. Out of his "in it for good times" lifestyle and in to thinking about forever.

He could have forever. He could have it and not hurt his best friend as well as his woman—if he was as brave as she'd been. If he tried.

Jace started unbuttoning his shirt. "Listen closely, because I rarely say this and I'm not going to say it again. I've never done this before. So where do we start?"

Kaya looked up at the smiling Nick in shock. Jace had said yes?

When he'd come in and gotten angry, she'd thought the chance she'd taken had destroyed everything. That her desires were too greedy, that there was something wrong with her.

She felt like the part of her she'd kept tamped down for so long had taken over the last few days. It wanted to be free to explore. To be outrageous like Bailey. To be loving like Dani. To live.

Maybe that was why she hadn't run when she'd realized that Nick was the wolf. Instead, she'd been fascinated. And even more attracted to him than before.

She'd gone crazy. *This* was crazy. There were no halfway measures in this. She shouldn't want who she wanted. A Navajo and a skinwalker. Neither of them were people she'd ever imagined wanting. Yet she did. She wanted Jace, his dark good looks, the quips that hid his gentleness. She wanted Nick who, like Stax, was special. Who called to her spirit in a way she couldn't define but couldn't question.

She wasn't going to back down. They *were* her wish. It was her chance and she was going to take it. No matter what the consequences.

Nick turned her around and she was snared in Jace's heated stare as he stripped off his clothes.

Drop your towel, honey. Show him what he wants.

Nick was pushing at her again, sending her his commands. And

Kaya wanted to comply. She loosened her grip on the towel and let it fall to the floor.

The expression on Jace's face was more than satisfying. "Kaya."

Just her name. Fraught with yearning and appreciation. And so much more.

Nick had no problem filling the silence. "She's beautiful, isn't she?"

He stepped back and walked around her. She could feel his desire washing over her as he studied her full breasts, her long, dark nipples. "Tell her how beautiful she is, Jace. How much you want to be inside her again."

Jace couldn't tear his eyes from the curve of her belly, the shadow of her sex. "You are. And I haven't been able to think about anything else."

Nick nodded his approval. "It's you, Kaya. Only you who could get the both of us so fucking knotted up that we can't see straight. Only you that keeps us up at night, makes us willing to kneel at your feet just for the chance to taste you."

Kaya sensed the vulnerability in his words. Both men were so raw, so afraid to trust in this. There was no way she could doubt the strength of their desire for her. It filled the air with every breath she took.

She wanted to show them that she was in this too. Completely. No regrets. No holding back.

She wasn't sure where all her courage was coming from, but somewhere inside her she knew exactly what to do.

Kaya took Nick's hand and he let her lead him closer to Jace. She studied them both side by side. So different. One lean and golden—a young warrior in his prime. One large and scarred—the beast with the tender heart. Both wanting her. Needing *her.* "You make me feel special. Desired. You keep *me* up at night, and make me dream of kneeling at your feet to taste you."

She placed her hand on Jace's chest and reached up on tiptoe to kiss Nick's lips softly, tenderly. He groaned.

Then she slid her hand up Nick's arm as she turned her head to press her lips against Jace's. He opened his mouth and slid his tongue along the seam of her closed lips, making her shiver.

Kaya stepped back, making sure they were watching her as she knelt at their feet. A feeling of wonder at the reverence of this moment, at the sacredness of it, bloomed inside her, and she could sense that they felt it, too.

This was right.

She looked up at them through her lashes and smiled. No shyness. No hesitation. Only seduction. She let her gaze travel down their bodies to the two beautiful erections straining for her attention.

Both hard and dark with need—one golden brown, the skin around it smooth and hairless, and the other paler, flushed with desire and framed by dark mahogany curls. Both of them were thicker than her fingers could possibly span, and so large her mouth watered.

She couldn't wait any longer. She leaned forward and opened her mouth over the head of Jace's erection, closing her eyes at the salty, earthy flavors hitting her tongue. She remembered how he'd taken her last night. How deeply, how intensely, he'd claimed her.

Her hand reached up to circle as much of Nick's shaft as she could, loving the silken velvet-over-steel texture and imagining how good it would be when he was finally inside her.

She felt one hand brush her hair to the side, so they could watch her lick and suck Jace in as deeply as she could. Two heartfelt male groans made her smile against his flesh.

When she replaced her mouth with her hand to taste Nick, she felt them both jerk in surprise. Jace covered her hand with his, forcing her to tighten her grip.

Nick slid his hand into her hair, not directing, but gripping it in a way that made her want to slip her hands between her own thighs to relieve the need building inside her.

He moaned. "God, that is the sexiest thing I've ever seen. Her mouth is so . . ."

Jace's response was raspy with desire. "I know. I've never felt anything like it. Kaya, baby, that is one sexy as hell tattoo."

Kaya swallowed, wanting to consume more of Nick's addictive taste. When she felt him hit the back of her throat he shouted, tugging her hair until she lifted her mouth.

She looked up in dazed surprise and Nick shook his head. "We're not coming like this, honey. Not this time. I have to be—*we* have to be inside you."

Jace picked her up and carried her toward his bed. "You took the words right out of my mouth."

Kaya couldn't help but smile. For being new to this they certainly seemed to know what they were doing. But she wasn't complaining. She was so turned on right now she could hardly think straight. She wanted to be taken, and she needed them to be the ones to do it.

They climbed onto the bed, on either side of her, and took over.

In silent agreement, two heads bent to her breasts, a mouth enveloping each hard nipple. Desire shimmered through her, arrowed deep, doubled as they both began to suck.

Two masculine hands slid down her sides, over her thighs, spreading them apart gently.

She felt the cool air of the room skim her sex and then two fingers slipping inside her, both men working as one to bring her pleasure.

Nothing had ever made her feel so complete. So loved.

Nick growled and she opened her eyes. He'd stilled, his teeth capturing her nipple, his eyes on Jace.

She felt the confusion in him. A wolf didn't usually share. Kaya's hand slipped into his hair. "For me. For Jace."

The growling stopped and Nick lifted his mouth, a worried expression clouding his need. "Maybe I should—"

"Get some supplies? In the top drawer, buddy. Including the good stuff." Jace's jaunty tone didn't hide the sincerity in his gaze as he stared at Nick.

She sensed what passed between them. The bond of friendship, the closer-than-brothers connection, that neither would allow to be broken.

Nick chuckled roughly. "That impatient, huh?"

Jace looked down at Kaya. "Aren't you?"

"Yes."

Kaya allowed herself to be lifted onto her knees as Jace kissed her deeply, lovingly.

Lovingly.

She could feel it. She hoped she wasn't wrong.

He reached around her to grab the condom Nick handed him and rolled it quickly down his shaft. She could feel every movement against her stomach, including the fine tremor that had started in his hands.

Nick rubbed her back soothingly, sending her his feelings. Honor. Lust. Love.

Love you, honey. Have from the moment I saw you.

Was that her wishful thinking? Feeling more than desire from both of them? Feeling love?

"Take Jace, honey. Take him and then you'll take me." Nick nipped at her neck with his teeth, making her shudder. "He's right. This is very sexy." His tongue traced a line of the spider's web that covered her shoulder. "You've got us in your web, honey. Well and truly trapped."

Jace lifted her to straddle his hips, restraint and tension vibrating off him. She could sense that he was so aroused, he wasn't sure how long he'd last, but she knew he wanted to. He wanted to find out what happened next, sensed his curiosity, his sense of awe at what was happening. She shared it with him.

Kaya whimpered as he lowered her onto his cock, remembering the feel of him. Loving it. So deep. And in this position she could feel even more.

She gripped his shoulders and pushed down, taking everything. Taking control.

"Damn, Kaya."

"She's a goddess."

Kaya bit her lip. She was no goddess. Just a woman. Only human and dying to feel everything. "Nick?"

She felt the heat of him along her back and he kissed her temple. "I'm right here, honey. Are you ready?"

She nodded, her body pulsing with the need for them both "Please."

Jace closed his eyes and trembled, burying his face in her neck.

Nick smiled against her skin, his breath making her shiver. "I think we're all ready to beg."

His fingers, coated with lubricant, slid between the cheeks of her ass once more, reminding her of how oddly wonderful it had been to have his fingers filling her there, where no one else had. Only Nick.

His voice was gruff. "I'll go slow. Just relax. Lean against Jace, honey."

Jace held her tighter, pulling her closer and kissing her neck, the tops of her breasts. "Don't take it too slow, Nick. I'm dying."

Kaya laughed breathlessly. "*You* are?"

Nick didn't respond. She could feel his focus. His need. And the power it took to rein in his wolf now, with all it wanted so close.

He spread her cheeks and she felt the tip of his erection against her. The pressure made her hold her breath. It was almost pain.

Relax, Kaya. Breathe. You can take me.

She inhaled deeply, forcing her muscles to go lax. He grunted in approval and they both gasped at that first small thrust. He was there, inside her, tightening her sex around Jace with every stretching inch. She'd never felt anything so good in her life, that first sensation of pleasure doubled.

"Oh hell." Jace was shaking against her. He could feel it, too.

He could feel Nick, too. Was it weird that he didn't mind? That this was turning him on? Kaya felt so hot, so good. Anything to please her. Love her. Damn, this felt amazing.

Kaya smiled through the fullness as she sensed his thoughts. Through a pleasure so overwhelming, so consuming that she thought she might pass out. But she didn't want to. She didn't want to miss a moment.

Both of them. Inside her. Three hearts beating as one.

A rhythm slowly began. Nick eased forward, pushing her down onto Jace's cock. Then he dragged his hips backward slowly, pulling her hips back with him. She ached with need, with desire met and fulfilled. With the two pairs of male hands holding her, hot fingers splayed on her skin. Two cocks pushing into her, pushing pleasure deep.

She rocked between them, lost to sensation. Hers. Theirs. It didn't matter anymore. They were all reaching for the same thing. All straining together to find it.

Lips, hands, touching, caressing. Kaya could feel the energy rising inside her once more, so much stronger than before, scaring her with its power.

Faster and deeper, Kaya was claimed by it.

More. More. Yes, so close. Right. Belong inside her. Never want to stop . . . Have to come . . .

Nick or Jace? It didn't matter, Kaya was right there with them. It was too much. Too much energy. Too full. Too—

She cried out for both of them as she let go. Joining their shouts of completion. Black spots and stars filled her vision as she crashed into one wave of pleasure after another.

Was it greedy to want this forever? Because she had a sinking feeling as they laid her down between them that she would never be satisfied with anything less.

Kaya sat on the porch, wrapped only in a blanket as she watched the dawn arrive. Both her men were passed out in the bedroom. She smiled. She'd exhausted them.

Kaya bit into a piece of buttered flatbread sprinkled with cinnamon and let her mind wander.

They'd made love several times last night, each time just as amazing as the first. They'd also showered her, fed her, and made her feel like a princess. It was a wonderful feeling. She was alive. Warm. No more cool Kaya. Not after this.

Nick had told her about the prayer stick Stax had been helping him translate. The one that spoke of the same people who'd made the petroglyph in the cave. The tiny symbols had spoken of appeasing the gods, of finding a way to return to what they had been before. But he couldn't find anyone who could read it except for Stax. And now he was gone.

"Are you thinking about me? You have that, I-just-had-sex-with-two-other-men-but-I'm-still-thinking-about-my-favorite-coyote look about you."

Kaya nearly fell off the wooden rocking chair. "Istaqa!"

Should she bow? How did one react to a messenger? She held out her flatbread. "Would you like a bite?"

He smirked. "Ah. Respect. I appreciate the effort." He took the bread and sunk his teeth in, humming at the taste. "Lovely. Thank you. And may I say you look especially . . . colorful today?"

She touched her hair self-consciously. "Nick was hoping you'd come back."

Stax sat at her feet and chewed. "I know. But he wasn't ready to hear my answer, so I decided to wait. I am Istaqa, as you've pointed out. I can do that."

Kaya nodded. "And now?"

"Now I'm hoping the gift of you will convince him."

Gift of her? "Convince him of what, exactly?"

Stax held out his arms. "That this is his destiny. That there is no curse. The spirits knew he was born to embrace the wolf. Born to be with you, to be a part of this land and protect it. I'm not the only one, you know. There's too much to do."

She wasn't sure Nick would like that answer. "What do I have to do with it?"

Stax shook his head. "You're special, Kaya. Didn't that grand-father of yours tell you? The men who love you and guard you should be special as well."

She heard the screen door open and turned to find Jace and Nick joining them on the porch, both looking as though they'd just thrown on jeans and come rushing out at the sound of another male voice. They watched Stax with wary expressions.

Jace's smile was self-mocking. "Sure, we're special. Nick can turn into a wolf and I make a mean omelet."

Stax licked his lips. "I love omelets. And don't be obtuse, Jace. Never underestimate the importance of balance. And love." He stood up, studying Nick. "Understand now?"

Kaya watched Nick, feeling the conflict inside him. Conflict and . . . acceptance. "I think I do."

"Then I'll be back."

Nick squared his shoulders. "I'll be here."

Stax winked at Kaya. "When you're done with breakfast, I think your grandfather wants to see you. You and all the wishers. You know the spot."

Her grandfather? Did Stax know her grandfather? Kaya stood up from her chair so swiftly she nearly fell. Nick steadied her, but when she looked up, Istaqa was gone.

"What the hell just happened?"

Nick shook his head at Jace. "What always happens with that slippery coyote. Riddles and prose followed by a swift getaway." He noticed Kaya's expression. "Honey, are you okay?"

Kaya turned to them with wide, worried eyes. "I need to get to my grandfather."

She had another feeling. One she could hardly fathom, but she had to follow her instincts. "Call Liam."

Six

She saw him leaning against a tree across from their special spot. She'd run ahead of the others. Bailey and Cameron, Dani and Liam, Jace and Nick.

Kaya needed to talk to her grandfather alone. She got closer and opened her mind in a way she'd never dared around him since she was a child, out of respect, or perhaps fear, of what she might find.

But she had to know.

Almost immediately she felt it. Impossible. Unmistakable. He didn't try to hide his secret from her. What he was now. She couldn't stop her tears, or the momentary disbelief, despite all the wonders she'd witnessed these last few months.

All of it starting with those falling stars. With him.

"Why didn't you tell me?"

He smiled a little sadly, his beautifully weathered face so familiar to her. So beloved. But no longer here. Not in the flesh anyway.

"And miss the fun I've had? Not for all the world."

"Is this why you were avoiding me?"

Her grandfather nodded. "I knew you'd think the worst, that I was judging you, and for that I am sorry. But it couldn't be helped. You are special, Kaya. You have a gift. Once you knew about what I'd done for your *Bahana* friends, you would wonder. And then you'd know. I wasn't ready to leave just yet."

She blushed. "So you made their wishes come true?"

His full, white eyebrows rose to his hairline. "They did it on their own." He laughed, caressing the feathered *paho* in his hand. "Occasionally I helped them along on their paths. Along with Istaqa and Spider Grandmother of course. Your friends are good spirits, Elder Sister. Surprised they aren't Hopi."

And hers? Had he helped her find hers? There were so many things she wanted to talk to him about. So many questions. But one shouted above the rest. "Are you ashamed of me? Because I left like my mother?"

Why did you ask that? a voice inside her whispered. *You don't want to know the answer.*

The old man looked shocked. He reached his hand out to touch her, then dropped it at his side. "No, Kaya. Never. I'm ashamed of myself sometimes. I let you feel all that responsibility, let you try to make up for your mother's absence when I knew it wasn't your fault." He looked at the small group coming closer in the distance. "You took care of everyone for so long. Followed your path the only way you could. The only way that was left to you. It was my turn to make it up to you."

She tried to smile. Tried to wipe the tears away so she could see him. "So why didn't I see any of the signs? The spider? A kachina?"

Stax appeared behind the tree her grandfather leaned against. His expression compassionate. Patient. "Spider Grandmother is always with you, Kaya. She whispers in your ear. You are Hopi, after all." He gestured toward her grandfather. "He is a respected Elder who lived a long life holding true to the Hopi way. He chose to spend his spirit walk helping others, helping loved ones onto their own paths. He's going to dwell on the mountain for a while with the other revered ancestors."

Stax patted her grandfather's back kindly and spoke with admiration. "*He* is your kachina."

Kaya covered her heart with both hands, feeling so full of love, so full of yearning, she thought it might burst. "Thank you, Grandfather."

"Live with one heart, Elder Sister. Always. Know that we are all connected, and love is never wrong." He shook his head. "I wish I'd learned that lesson sooner, Kaya. Don't forget it." She nodded, tears running down her cheeks. "And tell that young man of yours that the spirits in his kitchen should stop pestering him now." He shrugged. "But they'll be watching."

He turned and began to walk through the trees with Istaqa. "I'm really going to miss those *Bahanas*. I had no idea they could be so entertaining."

Stax laughed. "I could tell you stories . . ."

"Kaya? Kaya what's happening?" Dani ran up, Bailey following close behind her. "Is that Stax with Will? Where are they going?"

She stood in silence with her friends, the family of her heart, unable to find words. She watched the two men walk slowly toward the mountain peaks, until a shaft of sunlight pierced the treetops, enveloping them in light.

And they were gone.

"Home."

They were right back where they started. Three women sitting around the patio table, hearing the men speaking in hushed tones on the other side of the glass.

Just like before. So different.

"He wasn't a ghost, right? I mean, he couldn't have been. He was solid. I watched him eat and carve the kachina . . ." Dani blew a stray curl off her forehead, a confused expression on her glowing cheeks. "It just doesn't seem possible, does it?"

After all they'd seen? Kaya sighed and looked up at a sky full of stars. She'd hardly been able to wrap her mind around it herself after she'd realized what had happened.

She'd gone to see her aunt and discovered the reason for her lack of communication. The older woman pursed her lips, but Kaya knew it was so she wouldn't show the emotion she was feeling. "He came to me and the children, too. In our dreams. We all had the same one. He told us to wait until you came to tell you."

Her grandfather had died the night she'd wished on the blue falling stars. He'd gone for a walk in the desert and he hadn't returned.

Only he had. For her.

"Nothing seems impossible. Not anymore."

Dani and Bailey nodded beside her. Kaya could feel their sorrow for her loss. They didn't understand. She couldn't remember the last time she'd felt so much peace. Her grandfather was watching over her, and he'd given her the greatest gift he could have. His acceptance. His love.

She wasn't living under the shadow of her mother anymore. And that knowledge had helped her make a few decisions.

She would stop working at the bookstore. Nick had mentioned needing help with his research. That sounded wonderful. Yoki and Len were fine, and she'd make sure she continued to take care of them, but she would do it because she loved them. Not to prove her aunt wrong.

She would live. And enjoy life. Enjoy her friends. She glanced at Dani. Joyous in her new relationship with Liam. Incandescent in her pregnancy. Her confidence was a blessing that Kaya would always be thankful for.

And Bailey? She hadn't changed, exactly, she would always be unique. But she had become so strong in Cam's love, such a savvy businesswoman . . . Kaya was just waiting for her to run for president and turn the White House pink with zebra stripes.

She was a part of all that. Her grandfather, too.

And she had her own wishes come true, as well. A love that she was feeling even now, separated by wall and glass from Jace and Nick. She promised every day that she would love them in return. No regrets. No holding back.

Kaya smiled at Bailey. "I forgot to tell you something."

"What?"

"Ewan McGregor is at the resort."

Bailey's cheeks turned as pink as the tips of her short, spiky hair. "Bull."

"No bull. And that's not all."

Dani was starting to laugh as Bailey hyperventilated. "How can there be more?"

"He came with his stunt double."

Kaya watched as Dani's chair nearly tipped over she was laughing so hard. "Careful, the baby!"

"Oh my God. *Twins*, Bailey. Ewan McGregor twins! Wasn't that your wish?"

Kaya smiled serenely and passed Bailey a glass of water. "Do you want to tell Cam to hit the road, or should I?"

Liam poked his head out with a questioning smile. "You ladies okay?"

Dani couldn't breathe and her face was turning red, which made Liam rush to her side. "Shortbread? What is it?"

"Wishes." She wheezed. "I think we need to make another one. Hurry up, think up something impossible. We can do it." She glanced at Bailey and started laughing again. "Twins."

Liam turned to Kaya and she shrugged innocently. "Hormones?"

She looked back at the door to find the two, strong warriors who'd won her heart. What else could she wish for that she didn't already have?

Dani snorted behind her hands. *"Twins!"*

No one noticed the blue star fall from the heavens but the coyote. His howl was victorious.

Keep reading for a preview of
the next title by R. G. Alexander

Tempt Me

Available November 2011 from Heat Books.

"Care for another, angel?"

Gabriel nodded at the bartender, ignoring the blatant invitation in her eyes.

Angel. His smile was rich with self-mockery. If he'd ever been one, he'd fallen long ago.

The sexy blonde turned to refill his glass with amber ale, and the sight of his own reflection in the beveled mirrors made him wince. It had been a while since he'd seen himself. Too long, apparently. The first description that sprang to mind when he did was *pathetic drunk*.

Was this who he really was, then? Gabriel Toussaint Giodarno—just another lost soul?

Whoever it was he was glaring at needed a shave. Rough shadows framed a sharp jaw, accentuating cheeks that had hollowed out in the past year. A diet of beer, scotch and shame would do that to a man.

His dark hair curled around his ears and along the nape of his neck—the first time he'd let it grow out since he was sent to Catholic school at the tender age of nine. His heavy-lidded green eyes were bleary with exhaustion, and—his gaze narrowed—the skin around his left eye was still tinged with yellow and blue from his encounter with that angry biker in a Tupelo bar last week.

Nearly all traces of his old reflection were gone. *He* was gone.

"You look like hell, Gabe. As usual."

Shit. He knew he was drunk, but he hadn't realized he'd had enough to start hallucinating again. He pushed his beer away and tapped on the glossy wooden counter. "Any coffee in this place?" Or even better, some holy water?

The man beside him sighed. "I was hoping you'd head to Mambo Toussaint's or Michelle's instead of the nearest tavern. Why you keep gravitating to these shadow-filled places, I'll never know."

"Look, guy, I told you—those shadows aren't real," Gabriel muttered, keeping his eyes straight ahead and his voice down so the bartender wouldn't think he'd gone off the deep end. "*You* aren't real. Not a man. Not a ghost. Remember? *I* don't do that particular parlor trick. All the woo-woo genes went to my sister. You're just a figment of my imagination."

He lowered his head tiredly and shoved his hands through his hair. "Shit, why didn't my broken brain concoct a hot, breathy blonde to follow me around instead of a chatty, grungy man-child like you?" He sent said man-child a sideways glance. "I did what you wanted.

I'm in New Orleans. Nothing has changed. Now run along, shut the hell up and leave me in peace."

He looked up and noticed the bartender was watching him and no longer smiling suggestively. She slid a cup of coffee in his direction, the suspicious look in her eyes clearly retracting any invitation they might have issued earlier. Then she hurried toward the other end of the bar and the safety of her regular customers.

Gabriel smirked. He'd run, too, if he could. Hell, he'd tried. But he couldn't escape the guilt that had kept him up nights, had become a demon that stalked him. He'd even started seeing shadows where there should be none. Watching those shadows notice him. Follow him. Press on his heavy heart and twist his thoughts until there were only three avenues of escape: fighting, fucking or getting blackout drunk. Sometimes it took all three for him to feel human again. To regain control.

Four months ago the game had changed, and his mind brought out the big guns. His new buddy here. His walking, talking, invisible conscience. There could be no doubt now that he had truly gone around the bend.

Gabriel grimaced at the first rich taste of chicory, and glanced at his imaginary friend. He had no idea where he'd dreamed the guy up. A man in his mid-twenties, with black hair that fell to his shoulders and blue eyes that were startling, framed by dark brows and a swarthy complexion. He wore a long, dark trench coat, dirty khaki pants and torn-up boots, looking like one of those disaffected adolescents Gabriel had silently scorned back when he'd been a globe-trotting, self-important businessman.

Had it only been a year ago that employees of his father's investment firm had cowered in fear before him? That Gabriel had taken pride in being known as the Dark Messenger, the smiling bearer of bad news and pink slips? What an evil jackass he'd been.

Maybe he was finally getting what he deserved.

"I can practically feel that self-pity you're wrapping yourself up in, Gabe. You're more stubborn than your sister, and that's saying something. Honestly, I have no idea why I got stuck with you."

He'd gotten stuck? Ha. "I apologize for inconveniencing you. Even my hallucinations can't stand me. There's a certain poetry to that, don't you think?"

"I'm not a hallucination, idiot. I'm real, with a name and everything. But you haven't asked my name, have you? You haven't asked about me, about the shadows—nothing. You need to stop fucking around, Gabe." The young man pounded on the bar in frustration. "I never swore before I met you. You came back here for a reason. You need to find out what you are. You need to see your family. Tell your mother what's been happening to you."

Not *who* he was. *What* he was. Gabriel already knew what he wasn't. He was no angel. No *bon ange*, like his twin sister who could see spirits. The one who had risked her soul for him, despite what he'd done to her. He was no loving son or loyal friend. And even though it felt like it right now, he was no ghost.

He wasn't sure about anything anymore, not even why he'd come back to New Orleans again. Other than to quiet his imaginary stalker. The one no one else saw. The one who could so conveniently appear and disappear at will.

If only Gabriel could disappear that easily, along with the memory of what he'd done—what he'd almost done—to Mimi. Michelle. His sister.

Djab. That was the name his mother had called the thing that had taken over his body last year. A dark entity, sometimes controlled by voodoo sorcerers she named *bokors. Djab* were wild spirits that, when left to their own devices, could wreak havoc on weaker humans.

Weak. That wasn't a word Gabriel had ever associated with himself until it happened. How easily it had taken him over. He'd been angry at the awkward reunion with his mother, and when Michelle had shown up, injured and so distant, he'd blamed her. In his anger, he'd wished *she'd* been the one the priests had beaten, the one who'd been ripped from their mother and told everything she knew, everything she loved, was no longer hers. His need for vengeance had made him the perfect target.

Gabriel took a deep drink, the hot coffee scalding his tongue, his knuckles white around the porcelain mug. As if it were yesterday, he could recall the feeling of being trapped in his own mind, of screaming and shouting in disbelief as something else took over his body.

His hands tying up his sister. *His* mouth speaking words so offensive to his soul that he wished he could claw them out with his bare hands.

How could she ever forgive him for that? How could he forgive himself? He shook his head, coming back to the conversation. "I know what I am. And they are all better off without me. You can add delusional to the list of reasons why."

"That does it."

Gabriel nearly slid off his stool when the bartender appeared across from him once more and purred appreciatively, "Didn't see *you* come in, lover. What can I get for you?"

He blinked. "What? Are you talking to me?"

She rolled her eyes. "Of course not, silly, you've been here for hours. And I'm really glad you decided to have that coffee, by the way." Then she looked over Gabriel's shoulder and batted her eyelashes. "I'm talking to your cute young friend."

He followed her gaze, then turned back to the bartender. "Who do you see behind me?" When she hesitated Gabriel leaned closer. "It's important. Describe him."

She tilted her head, her blonde ponytail swinging softly behind her. "O-kay. I see a sexy slice of cheesecake with dark hair and stunning blue eyes." Her own eyes widened. "And he blushes? Oh, baby, what's your name, what's your sign and where have you been all my life?"

Black spots and stars blurred Gabriel's view as he glanced back at the blushing figment behind him. The figment someone else had just described. She *saw* him?

He heard the bartender's worried voice as if she were speaking through static. "Oh, damn. Listen, lover, if your friend is about to throw up or something, get him outta here. I'm the only one on tonight and I refuse to clean that up."

Gabriel felt hands hoist him up as if he were weightless and drag him toward the back door that led to a narrow alley.

He pushed away and fell to his knees, retching. He leaned his head against the rough wall, a rasping laugh escaping his raw throat. "So this is what rock bottom looks like. I always wondered."

"Congratulations, Gabe. As usual, you set a goal and you reached it. Your father would be so proud."

Gabriel pulled himself up once more and turned, rage suddenly welling up inside him. "You don't know shit about my father. But I just set another goal. If other people can see you, that means you're real. And if you're real, I can kick your ass."

The tall man's lips quirked. "You can try. The shape you're in? I think I can take you." He crossed his arms and shook his head. "You used to be a believer, Gabe. Even when you couldn't see me, when Mimi was the only one who could, you believed I was there. I never thought you'd turn out like this."

He believed . . . even when *Mimi* could see him? "Who the fuck *are* you?"

His illusion's hands rose up to the sky, as if in prayer. "Hallelujah. I think he's finally waking up." Unearthly blue eyes pierced him with their solemn expression. "The name is Emmanuel."

Gabriel scoffed, but he felt the name like a kick in the chest, making it hard to breathe. "Emmanuel was a child. A *ghost* child. I told you. My sister has that gift. Not me."

Emmanuel nodded. "You're right. That isn't your gift." He shrugged. "But all the same, I *am* Emmanuel. How else would I know you cracked your tooth when you fell chasing after Ben and your sister in the back of my old house? The same day you told your father you were playing with spirits for the first time."

Gabriel remembered. How could he forget? That was the day everything had started going to shit.

"If you're Emmanuel, and I can't see ghosts, then how can I see you?"

The younger man was suddenly right beside him, his expression tinged with pain and regret. They were emotions Gabriel knew well.

"You can see me, Gabriel, because I am not a ghost. I'm no longer anything I was. And neither are you. But I've faced a few of *my* monsters. It's time for you to face yours. You need to understand what's happening to you, before you lose yourself completely to the darkness."

This was some sort of twisted joke. Gabriel closed his eyes and saw a flash of a memory. Father Leon, the priest who had taken special delight in punishing him, tormenting him with images of his sister and mother burning in Lucifer's inferno for eternity. Warning him that he would join them if he didn't purge himself of his family's evil. Warning him that he would be taken by the darkness.

Even then, there was a small part of young Gabriel who would have taken that punishment, would have burned, if only he could be with his family again. His mother. If only he could have been like his twin, Mimi. Special.

He felt like he was going to be sick again. This couldn't be happening. He needed to get out of this cursed city. "Fuck the coffee. I need another drink. Maybe two."

Gabriel took a step toward the bar's back door, but Emmanuel was there before he could reach for the knob.

He shook his head. "Stubborn ass. This is for your own good."

Gabriel saw Emmanuel pull back his fist and swore when it connected with his flesh. For a ghost he had a powerful right hook.

He was falling to the ground again, hearing Emmanuel before he hit the dirty floor.

"You'll thank me for this, Gabe. Eventually."

Gratitude wasn't on his mind as the hard ground jarred his bones. As his ears rang with the power of the physical blow he'd just received from his imaginary pest. No, it wasn't gratitude causing the red haze of anger and pain to blind his vision.

It was the need for revenge.

As soon as he could get up again, Emmanuel would learn what everyone who'd ever gotten on the wrong side of Gabriel knew. Clichéd but true . . .

Payback was a bitch.

They were talking about *him*.

Angelique Rousseau grabbed a candied pecan but paused before slipping it into her mouth. She'd been planning on announcing her presence, but she didn't want to miss the hushed discussion between her sister-in-law Allegra and Michelle Toussaint. Not when they were whispering about her current obsession, Michelle's elusive brother Gabriel.

Michelle's sigh drifted into the kitchen from the formal dining room as Angelique hopped onto the marble island. "Mama said she heard a knock on her door at three in the morning. Apparently he was bloodied up and falling-down drunk, with no idea how he'd gotten to her house."

"He's been here a week and he hasn't told anyone why he came back? Has he said *anything*?" Allegra sounded worried and more than a little tired. Angelique wondered if her unborn niece or nephew might have something to do with that.

The little troublemaker. Not even born and it was already driving its mother up the hormonal wall, not to mention putting a cramp in Auntie Angelique's social life.

She hadn't had *any* time to herself from the moment she got home. Instead she'd been mobbed at every turn by Toussaints and Adairs. Tasked with taking her mother to one gathering after another, all so Theresa Rousseau could get to know her new extended family better before the baby came.

It was a strange clan they'd created. The three families had known each other forever, but then her brother Celestin had married Michelle's roommate Allegra, and Michelle in turn had married Celestin's best friend Ben Adair. Then Michelle's former neighbor Bethany had come to town and married BD, and suddenly the six of them were living in each other's hip pockets. In light of what had happened, she supposed it was natural for them all to grow closer. Blood wasn't any thicker than the ties they obviously shared.

They were certainly just as pushy with each other as family, and just as protective. And they'd all been closing ranks around Michelle since her twin brother Gabriel had come home.

Angelique was dying to find out why.

Michelle spoke again, answering Allegra's question. "He's barely said a word. Though a couple of days ago he did ask me some unusual questions. It was . . . an odd conversation, and I'm not sure he was actually listening. He just kept glaring over my shoulder. Other than that, every time I've stopped by the house he's been in his bedroom. Honestly, I'll be surprised if he comes tonight, but Mama did say he promised."

Was that why Angelique had decided to show up for dinner tonight—because Gabriel Toussaint had promised to be here? Why she'd changed her mind and accepted Allegra's transparently half-hearted invitation, even though her mother wasn't invited? Even though she'd had a chance for one night's reprieve, free of family, free to enjoy herself and get away from all this loving togetherness?

She knew the answer was yes. Gabriel's presence had changed everything. Since she'd seen him a few days ago, when she and her mother had stopped by the Toussaint family home, he was all she could think about.

He'd stalked into the room, seemingly unaware that he wasn't alone. His shirt had been unbuttoned to reveal a line of golden skin and muscle that set her mouth watering. His hair was mussed, his jaw set, and to Angelique he'd looked like one hot, delicious mess. Ruffled, brooding and sexy. Everything about him screamed bad boy. It was a quality the rebellious part of her couldn't help but find attractive.

But it was more than that. The moment he turned his head and snared her gaze, she experienced a raw wave of need unlike any she'd ever known, heat washing over her body and nearly buckling her knees.

She'd held her breath as he studied her. Her fertile imagination took over, making her breathless as she wondered if he felt the same intense desire that she did.

But then he seemed to notice the other women in the room. She'd hoped he would look her way again, but he'd just scowled, nodded tersely to acknowledge his mother, then turned and walked out without a word.

Mambo Toussaint had made hurried apologies, but Angelique barely heard them. It took every ounce of her restraint not to follow him back down the hallway. To take him to task for his manners . . . or to rub herself against him like a cat, she wasn't sure which.

She'd gone home that night, irrationally angry with the rude man who'd turned on some switch in her body that couldn't be shut off. She'd touched herself, rubbing her clit and slipping her fingers deep inside her sex, fantasizing about him, coming again and again without true relief.

Feeling the need well up inside her even now, she squirmed on the countertop. Just thinking about seeing him tonight was making her crazy.

That *was* why she'd come. It was too tempting to resist. She hadn't been able to stop thinking about him and she wanted to know more. To find out why everyone was so worried about his homecoming.

Hell, she just wanted to see him again.

"You are now officially my favorite Rousseau, *cher.* Your brother would never dream of being this sneaky. Trust me, I know. However, you lose some points by eating all my pecans."

Angelique nearly fell off her perch at the rich male voice behind her. "BD, I didn't see you there."

Speaking of impossibly gorgeous bad boys. She silently corrected herself: reformed bad boy. Reformed, reborn and happily married.

Angelique blushed while she studied him. Each time she saw him it struck her that he was like living art. If she weren't so oddly enamored with Gabriel, he would definitely be her favorite fantasy.

He'd literally walked out of history, and he was nearly too beautiful to be real. Amber eyes with long, dark lashes. Skin like honey and full lips that always looked freshly kissed.

Too pretty, his wife Bethany always teased him. And it was true.

But Angelique wasn't just fascinated with his looks. It was what he was, or what he'd been, that entranced her.

Bone Daddy. A sexual Loa. A voodoo spirit. Sort of. He'd been around a few hundred years, showing up for voodoo practitioners who needed aid in love and lust spells, making those he "rode" irresistible. Until he'd fallen in love himself and gotten a second chance.

He was also the reason her brother had changed so much after their father's death eight years ago. Why Celestin had gone from her playful, charming older brother to a distant, melancholy womanizer. It had been because of Bone Daddy, and the deal her brother had made with the spirit to protect his family. To protect her.

And now, though she still wasn't sure how, the Loa was human. And before she could work up a good mad on her brother's behalf, Celestin had made it clear to his mother and sisters that BD was a friend. More than that. One of the family. That decree, combined with BD's undeniable warmth and charm, made it impossible to do anything other than love him.

An ex-Loa in her growing family. It was the most exciting thing that had happened in her life so far. Well, maybe the second most exciting thing.

"You didn't see me? I wonder why?" BD smiled delightedly, dazzling her into silence. "Could it be you were too focused on the gossip du jour? The return of the eternally grumpy twin?"

Angelique felt her lips tilt even as her blush deepened. "My family has a lot of secrets. Maybe this is the only way I can find anything out. Or maybe I was just trying to swipe all the good snacks."

"Bah. I know your type. Hell, I *am* your type, *cher*. A trouble magnet." He shook his head, understanding bright in his beautiful eyes. "And I can see you are looking for trouble tonight. Don't deny it. Your brother would be sad to think he wasn't the reason you decided to join us this evening. Although I'm not sure Gabriel is ready for a wildcat like you."

How did he know? How could he possibly know? "I'm not sure what you're talking about, but whatever it is, I'm innocent."

BD made a face when Angelique batted her eyelashes. "I applaud your acting, *cher*, as well as your stealth, but it's wasted on me. Desire was my job long before you were born. Now before you get us both in trouble, you should get down. Your brother is on his way inside as we speak."

The thought of her big brother catching her in the act of eavesdropping had her hopping off the kitchen island swiftly and she gave BD a quick, impulsive hug. "Thanks for the heads-up."

He chuckled, squeezing her shoulders gently before pulling back to look down at her. "Anytime, *cher*." His golden gaze fell to her neck and his expression changed suddenly. "Do me a favor in return, yes? Don't take that necklace off."

Angelique's brow furrowed as she reached up to fiddle with the thin, golden cross her mother had given her at her baptism. "Why?"

"Little one, I'm glad you came." Celestin Rousseau beamed at her happily, his arms filled with food from Allegra's favorite corner restaurant. "I brought dinner. A little bit of everything, so I hope you're hungry."

His relaxed, easygoing expression was so different from the brother she'd known most of her adult life that it still jarred her. She knew it was his wife and unborn child, as well as his freedom from the curse their father had forced on him, that had changed him. She couldn't be happier for him, but it was a big adjustment.

"I'm starving. And of course I came. An evening without Mom trying to get me to move into the new house her son bought for her? Asking me when I was going to give her grandchildren like her daughter-in-law? I couldn't pass that up."

Her brother snorted, setting several bags down on the counter where she'd been sitting moments before. "Can you blame her? Her nest is empty. All her children growing up and flying away. Patricia moved to North Carolina with her husband this year, you came home from school and decided to stay in that old, musty apartment rather than the new room she decorated with you in mind . . ." He trailed off, making a face as BD guffawed.

"Not even a father yet and you already do guilt so well, *mon ami.*"

Angelique nodded emphatically. "He's a natural, all right. I'm a grown woman with a college degree and a normal sex drive. I love you both, but I do *not* want to move back in with my mommy."

Celestin held up his hands in surrender. "And the last thing I want to hear about is my baby sister's sex drive, adult or not. You win. I won't mention it again."

"Thank you."

BD's laughter stopped the conversation in the other room and Angelique sighed. She'd wanted to find out more about Gabriel before he came.

Allegra raised her voice from the other room. "BD? Is my husband with you? I'd get up but his child has turned me into a giant water buffalo."

Celestin's smile grew even more incandescent. "Duty calls.

Coming, *bebe*." He ruffled Angelique's curls and handed her the last small bag he carried in his hand. "Could you put her ice cream in the freezer before it melts and start setting the table, little one?" Then he was gone.

BD was chuckling again. "That boy is going to be a great daddy."

Angelique rolled her eyes, closing the freezer and opening drawers in search of utensils. "If *great* is another word for *bossy*, then sure. Tell me, do ex–sex spirits know where they keep the silverware around here?"

He came up beside her and pointed to a drawer while he opened the cabinet over her head where the plates were kept. "I know a lot of things. My wife is determined I become a truly modern man. I can even do laundry now."

He winked at her and she laughed, charmed. Too bad he was taken. There was just something about him . . .

"Am I interrupting anything?"

The voice sent the pile of forks in her hand clattering to the counter. Her heart started to pound, her body reacting the way it did every time he came to mind. And all thoughts of the captivating BD disappeared.

Gabriel had arrived.